"Would you like to go out for coffee with me?"

Gayle wanted to say yes. To sit with this man, to have his attention focused on her would be wonderful...but only if she was prepared to face the consequences if she let something slip.

She stalled for time, trying to decide if she should take the risk. "When?"

"Whenever our schedules allow. What about Sunday?"

After today's fishing trip, and Adam's obvious improvement, Nate might not be around much longer. Yet she was just a little sad at the thought of not seeing him. The good news was that without Nate around, her secret would be safe.

"Okay, next Sunday it is," she said, trying to sound casual while her pulse danced against her throat.

She watched him leave and felt the loneliest she'd felt since arriving in Eden Harbor. And she knew with certainty that this feeling came from the awareness that she could never have more than coffee with him.

What would it be like to have a romantic relationship with someone like Nate? Someone whose presence sent fissions of awareness and light-headedness spiraling through her?

She couldn't let herself think about the impossible. To have a real relationship based on trust and caring, she'd have to reveal her past.

And to admit to her past was to admit to lying...

Dear Reader,

Learning to trust someone can be a very difficult thing. To trust is to allow another person the opportunity to enrich our lives, but sometimes it can lead to pain and hurt. In order to trust someone, we must first trust ourselves and trust in our ability to know who really cares about us.

Welcome to the second book in the Life in Eden Harbor series. Eden Harbor is a small town on the coast of Maine where most people have known each other for years, and where keeping a secret is very difficult. When Gayle Sawyer moves to Eden Harbor, she is a woman haunted by her past, yet determined to protect her son from her mistakes. When her son gets into trouble, she is forced to share her past with Nate Garrison, a man with his own trust issues.

Like Gayle, I have had issues with learning to trust, with reaching out to others for help. Having nursed my husband while ALS claimed his body, I had no choice but to trust people and to share my agony. Had I not reached out to our friends and shared what was happening during those last months, Garry's passing would have been much more difficult.

If you have had issues around trust and you'd like to share your experience with me, I can be reached at stella@stellamaclean.com. Or you can visit my website at stellamaclean.com. For those of you who enjoy social media, I can be found at facebook.com/stella.maclean.3, or on Twitter, @Stella__MacLean

Sincerely,

Stella MacLean

STELLA MACLEAN

—

To Protect Her Son

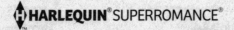
HARLEQUIN® SUPERROMANCE®

Recycling programs
for this product may
not exist in your area.

ISBN-13: 978-0-373-60899-7

To Protect Her Son

Printed in U.S.A.

Stella MacLean loves to write stories about romance and happy endings. A member of Romance Writers of America for twenty years, a past RWA board member and a Golden Heart® Award finalist, Stella is committed to the art and the business of writing stories about people overcoming their differences and finding happiness with each other. Every writer needs a muse, and Stella has found two. Jethro and Sully, two new kittens, maintain a raucous vigil while she escapes into the world of two people about to come face-to-face in their search for love.

Books by Stella MacLean

HARLEQUIN SUPERROMANCE

Heart of My Heart
Baby in Her Arms
A Child Changes Everything
The Christmas Inn
The Doctor Returns

Visit the Author Profile page
at Harlequin.com for more titles

This book is dedicated to my husband, Garry, the love of my life, my champion and my dearest friend, who succumbed to Amyotrophic Lateral Sclerosis (ALS) on July 6, 2013.

You are forever in my heart.

Acknowledgments

In appreciation to my editor and friend Paula Eykelhof, who encouraged me and stood by me while my life descended into chaos brought on by my husband's illness and its inevitable outcome. Without her support and caring I would not have been able to finish *The Doctor Returns*, and I would not have been able to write *To Protect Her Son*.

CHAPTER ONE

IF GAYLE SAWYER could have foreseen the day ahead she would never have gotten out of bed. She and Adam, her thirteen-year-old son, had argued last night and again this morning, leaving her drained and frightened.

Her eyes gritty from lack of sleep, she stared across the raised counter at her friend Sherri Lawson, nurse in charge of today's clinic at Eagle Mountain Medical Center. Neill Brandon would be there any minute, and Gayle had pulled the clinic charts for his patients, who sat with their families in the waiting area just a few feet from the desk.

Everything was ready. Gayle glanced one more time at her watch as worry gnawed at her mind. She should have handled the argument with Adam differently last night. After all, she was the adult and should be able to reason with her son.

"Just one more." Sherri passed Gayle another chart, a square-cut diamond gleaming on her finger.

Gayle couldn't take her eyes off the ring. "Some people are born lucky," she teased her best friend.

Sherri touched her diamond. "Can you believe it? After everything that has happened, Neill and I have our dream back. We've waited a long time for our happiness." A smile lit her face; her eyes shone as she leaned on the counter.

Gayle had stopped dreaming about being happy fourteen years ago in Anaheim, California, when the judge had sentenced her husband, Harry Young, for armed robbery and shooting a police officer.

Pregnant and alone, she'd vowed never to let her dreams mask reality. She'd worked so hard to make her son's childhood a happy one, and to find a respectable life for herself. Nothing could be allowed to take all that she'd earned by dint of hard work and determination away from her.

"Dreams can be wonderful," she offered, unwilling to share the details of her past with anyone here in Eden Harbor. Her aunt Susan had died a year ago and left her a quaint Victorian house on a tree-lined street in this quiet, stately town. Gayle had moved, partly for the chance at a new life, and partly to get her son away from a group of teenagers that were having far too much influence in his life. She was happy to leave Anaheim. She never intended to return to the place that had caused her so much sorrow.

"I've never been this happy," Sherri said, a look of wonderment on her face.

Gayle had never seen anyone as much in love as her best friend. "Your wedding plans are coming together so well. I still can't believe we found those bridesmaid dresses in the first wedding boutique we went into in Boston."

The doors connecting the clinics to the rest of the hospital banged open. Her son, Adam, his dark hair smudging his forehead, his eyes angry, approached the desk where Gayle sat. The scent of shampoo and of the boy he still was swirled around her as he leaned over the desk. "Mom. You left this morning without giving me any money. I need money."

Embarrassed that Adam's loud voice had attracted the glances of the people in the waiting room, she came around the desk, her eyes pleading with him to quiet down.

"What do you need it for?" she asked, even though she knew. Adam had started playing video games, and he was always after her to pay for yet another game. They'd argued about it this morning, and now he had come into her workplace.

"I promised to buy a game from a friend.

He's waiting for me to pay up. You know all this, Mom."

She'd encouraged him to play video games, but not because she approved of them. In her mind they were the lesser of two evils—video games or surfing the internet. She had a very powerful reason for not wanting him online—his father. "We talked about this last night. I don't have the money. And besides, you just got a new one…"

"Where's your purse?" Adam glanced behind the desk. "There, right there." He pointed to Gayle's purse, which was still sitting under her desk. She hadn't put it in her locker yet because she needed to pay her share for a staff shower gift for Sherri. One of the patients had knit a beautiful pale green throw for Sherri and Neill. "I don't have any money…"

"Yes, you do. I saw it last night."

"Adam! What were you doing going through my purse? You know better than that."

"I didn't have a choice, did I?" Adam snorted. "You can go to the bank. I need cash now." Adam came around the desk, reached down, grabbed her purse, yanked it open and pulled out her wallet.

"Adam! Don't!"

"I need it, Mom." He opened the section where the bills were. "You promised."

"No, I didn't. Put that money back," she said, mortified that everyone in the room could hear her son's demands.

Adam counted the bills. "There's more than enough here."

Suddenly Sherri was standing next to Gayle. "Adam, why are you embarrassing your mother this way? She said she doesn't have the money right now."

Gayle reached for her wallet, pulled it gently from Adam's fingers and placed it back in her purse, speaking softly as she did so. "Please go, Adam. I promise we'll talk about this again tonight before dinner."

"Not good enough," Adam muttered, his eyes glistening, his expression one of anger and disappointment. "I want that game. I promised to buy it from my friend."

"You should have talked to me first."

"I did—last night."

"And what did I say?"

"The same old thing—I should mow lawns and pay for my own games."

She wanted the world for her son, but she also wanted him to know how important it was to make his own way in life. "And my answer hasn't changed."

Adam shifted his weight from one foot to the

other, his eyes focused on some spot behind her. "Why do you have to be so mean?"

Out of the corner of her eye, Gayle saw Dr. Brandon come through the doors. "Adam, the clinic is about to start. You have to go."

"You don't even care about me," Adam said, his voice rising as he glanced around the room.

"I love you," she whispered emphatically.

Gayle knew only too well how easily Adam could escalate an argument from a raised voice to yelling—so like his father. She took his arm, gently leading him toward the door. Once out in the hall, she turned to him. "Adam, those people in there are important to me, to us. This is my job and I can't afford to lose it."

She wanted to hold her son in her arms the way she used to do when he was upset. She settled for touching his hand. "I know you're going through a difficult time right now, and I want to help you. But you won't be able to come back here if you act like this."

Adam could not continue this way, and she could not move again. Recognizing that what she was about to say would anger her son, she chose her words carefully. "If you keep this up, I'm going to have to get professional help for you."

"Mom, I… Why don't you understand? All I need is a few dollars." He was quieter now, his head down, the fingers of his right hand viciously attacking a hangnail.

Gayle knew this wasn't just about money. Her son felt angry and frustrated most of the time. Yet when he wasn't angry, he was the Adam she'd loved and cared for these past thirteen years—a kind, bright, wonderful young man. She softened her tone, seeking to let her son know that she loved him more than anything in this world. "Go back to the house, and I'll be there right after my shift. We'll work this out, I promise."

He jutted his lower jaw, the resentment in his eyes fading to acquiescence. He gave a long, exaggerated sigh as he turned and went down the hall.

Sherri came up behind her, standing beside her as she anxiously watched her son leave. "Gayle, I'm so sorry. You've told me a little bit about the change in Adam's behavior, but this is the first time I've seen it for myself."

"Not as sorry as I am." She sighed, the old feelings of inadequacy engulfing her.

"I'm not trying to interfere here, but I've got a suggestion that might help."

"I'm running out of ideas, so all suggestions gratefully accepted."

Except for talking to Sherri, she'd kept her concerns about Adam to herself, hoping that it was just part of being a teenager. But she couldn't have him showing up at her workplace behaving the way he had today. She wanted to confide the whole story to someone, and Sherri was a good listener.

When she'd come to Eden Harbor and the house her aunt Susan had left her, she worried about how Adam would react. It quickly became apparent her concerns were unfounded. He'd been great. He'd gotten a part-time job cutting grass in the neighborhood for his spending money. He had become more helpful around the house, much to Gayle's relief. But in the past couple of weeks, Adam had had to be cajoled into mowing lawns. When he was around the house, he seemed distant, quicker to anger, resentful at times and harder to talk to. In fact, the old rapport they'd shared had almost disappeared. Until this moment, Gayle had let it pass.

"Would it help if he had someone to talk to?" Sherri asked. "Someone who related well to teenage boys?"

Gayle's biggest fear was that her son would get involved with the wrong crowd and turn out like his father. Harry probably had been a normal teenager who'd got in with a bad crowd, and now spent every day inside prison walls. She couldn't let that happen to Adam. "It might make a difference. I honestly don't know."

"There is a mentoring program in Eden Harbor for troubled teens. Would you consider something like that?"

That could be good, but not if it meant there would be questions about Adam's father. No one here knew anything about Harry, and she didn't want that to change. The world they lived in now—a pleasant world with so much potential—was far removed from their life in Anaheim. If Sherri could help her find someone to offer a positive male influence in Adam's life…

"I'd have to think about it, maybe learn a little more before I decide."

"We need someone we can trust to be firm with Adam, right?"

Gayle loved the fact that her best friend had used *we*. She'd never had a confidante like Sherri Lawson, soon to be Sherri Brandon in a wedding everyone was looking forward to. The bright spot in Gayle's life these days was that she would be part of the bridal party.

Gayle gave a wry smile as the two of them headed back to the clinic desk.

"What he needs is a father figure in his life, the one thing I can't provide unless the mailman suddenly turns into my Prince Charming. He's the only male I see on a regular basis."

Sherri stopped, a look of satisfaction on her face. "I've got the perfect solution to your problem. My cousin, Nate Garrison, would be a great mentor for Adam. I don't believe you've met him. He was at Peggy Anderson's birthday party down at Rigby's Bar on the waterfront a few weeks ago. I remember you were intent on getting to know the new guy from respiratory therapy."

"Only to discover that he already had a girl-friend. I should have stayed with you at the bar and gotten a chance to meet your cousin. But as I remember it, you weren't there very long."

"Yeah, Neill and I had an argument and I left." Sherri touched her engagement ring again. "So glad that's all over…" Another smile slid across her face. Her friend was always smiling these days, and Gayle couldn't help but wish she could be as happy.

"You haven't met Nate because he's been re-ally busy since he started working as a commu-nity liaison officer, part of community policing. His specialty is working with troubled teenagers, and he'd be the perfect person to help Adam."

Could it be that something positive was about to come out of one of the most embarrassing mo-ments of her life? "I didn't want to bother you with my problems where Adam is concerned. But now…" She shrugged.

"Why don't you let me see what I can do?" Sherri offered, warmth and caring evident in her voice. "I know this sounds like bragging, but Nate is a wonderful man, a little overprotective at times, but no wonder. He was on duty in Boston and got shot in the leg while investigating a robbery."

The officer was shot in the thigh and bone fragments nicked the femoral artery. The emergency response team who rushed to the scene was responsible for saving Officer Perry's life.

Gayle would never forget those words screaming across the front page of the *Orange County Register*, or the naked fear she'd survived for weeks as she'd waited, expecting to be arrested any moment. Her anxiety as she watched the apartment door that day for Harry to return, praying that it hadn't been him. That he couldn't have shot an officer of the law. But he had, even bragged about it, and threatened to beat her and kick her out if she told anyone.

Harry needn't have worried. What he'd done that day, and what she'd done in the months following, would forever be her secret. "Are you sure about this?" she asked Sherri.

"Why not? You said yourself that you're worried about Adam. Let me help you. Nate's a professional and knows what he's doing. He's helped lots of kids over the past six years since he returned from Boston."

Boston or Anaheim. It didn't matter. Gayle

would never be able to erase the memories of those months after the shooting, the fear and self-loathing. She hadn't been honest when the police officers had come in search of information. She'd been too afraid of what Harry would do if he found out she'd been talking to the police.

All she'd ever wanted from the day she'd escaped her parents' world of drugs and arguments was a place where she could feel safe. A defiant teenager, she'd run off with Harry Young, a dangerous con man who'd promised to look after her. Now, fourteen years later, she still wanted to be safe. Only now she also wanted to be free from the fear that someday she would have to face her ex-husband.

Gayle closed her eyes, a second's respite from the cold reality of her past. "It might work."

"Well, while you're thinking about it, why don't you come over to the house for a barbecue? The weather's lovely. Neill has done a fantastic job putting a new deck on the back of the house, and we can talk wedding talk." She smiled in encouragement. "Remember how much help you were to me when I was going through that awful time with Neill? Let me return the favor. You need to forget your worries for a while. And we need to pick out the flowers for the ceremony.

I'll talk to Nate when I get the chance, and we'll find a way to make it happen. You can trust me."

Gayle wasn't good at trusting anyone. Not even her best friend. Yet an evening out would help her gain perspective, and allow her to share in Sherri's happiness. "That sounds like a wonderful idea."

"Then leave it with me. I'll talk to Neill and get back to you."

LATER THAT WEEK, as the sun's light began to create long silhouettes along the tree line, broken only by the roof of the old barn at the back of Neill's house, Gayle found herself sitting with Sherri and her fiancé on the new deck.

She had to agree with Sherri that the deck Neill had built on the back of the old house made a wonderful space for relaxing after a long day at work.

"Neill and I love this property, and plan to live here for a very long time," Sherri said. A salt-tinged breeze moved through the pines behind the barn, creating a sighing sound that enhanced the gentle quiet of the evening.

Gayle looked at her two friends, and couldn't stop the envy rising through her. All her life she'd wanted to be married to a man who truly loved her, and to live in a lovely old home looking out on the water. But what Gayle wanted had never been anyone's priority, not even her own. It was a stroke of luck and fate that had given her the charming Victorian house she now owned in downtown Eden Harbor. Simply a case of her being the last remaining relative of someone she'd never even met.

All of that aside, she was delighted to be having dinner at Dr. Brandon's home, and even more thrilled that Sherri had chosen her over all her other friends to be her maid of honor. Gayle felt blessed to see what her life had become. The only down note was Adam's recent change in behavior.

"Would anyone like more wine?" Neill asked, holding up the bottle of chardonnay.

Gayle's head was already feeling light. "No, thank you. Not me," she said, placing her hand gently over the top of her glass. She wasn't much of a drinker and had never taken drugs after growing up in the chaos of her mother and stepfather's house.

Sherri shook her head. "One glass does it for me. I need to check my blood sugar now that I've eaten to be sure it's okay."

Gayle remembered the day Sherri had ended up in Emergency after going into diabetic shock, and how afraid everyone had been. In the end it had proved to be what Sherri and Neill needed to get their priorities straight and realize how much they loved each other. It was the first time Gayle had ever seen the powerful impact love could have someone's life. She was sure that other people understood that power, but she didn't.

"Why don't I carry some things into the house for you?" Gayle asked.

Neill pushed back his chair. "That sounds great. While you ladies do your thing in the kitchen, I'll put the barbecue away. Later, we can all sit here and enjoy the evening light… and talk."

Gayle followed Sherri into the kitchen, placing the dishes on the counter while Sherri loaded the dishwasher. When Sherri reached for her meter to check her blood sugar, Gayle glanced around the huge kitchen. She had only been inside the house once before when she had come to pick Sherri up to go to a movie. She was completely in awe of the kitchen's beautiful wood cabinets, and panoramic view of the back gardens.

"Did you get a new table and chairs?" she asked, realizing she hadn't seen the wooden table surrounded by four wooden chairs with navy-blue-and-white cushions before.

"It's new. The set Neill brought from Boston when he moved back home was all glass and wrought iron, not really a good match for the interior of this house. But he'd wanted his daughter, Morgan, to have as many things from her old life as possible, even though he'd disliked the modern set virtually from the day his ex bought it."

"Did you and Neill choose this together?"

"We did. Our first purchase for our home." Sherri smiled, her eyes alight with enthusiasm. "I have never been so excited in my life. After everything we've been through, all those years of misunderstanding and being apart from each other, marrying the wrong people, will finally be behind us in less than two months."

Gayle hugged her friend. "You will be so gorgeous in that antique lace wedding dress. Being with you when you picked it out was a really special moment for me." She wanted to tell her friend that she'd never been a part of anybody's wedding before, but divulging any details of her past would lead to questions she couldn't risk answering.

"And you and Morgan in your green dresses… Morgan is so pleased to be part of the wedding party. She's talked about it for hours on end. Her favorite thing is that she got to pick out the color. And I'm so glad Neill's best friend from medical school, Mark Leighton, can be a groomsman along with Nate."

"Are we going to go over the flower choices tonight? And what about the reception? Have you chosen flowers for the tables yet?" Gayle pointed to the florist's three-ring binder on the counter next to the phone.

Sherri sighed, her gaze turning anxious. "Let's sit down. I need to talk to you about something first."

Gayle tried to block her anxiety. Had Sherri been pressured into making someone else her maid of honor, someone who had a longer history of friendship with her than Gayle? "Sure. Go ahead," she said, forcing her tone to be upbeat.

"Please don't feel I'm prying into your life, but I need to ask you if anything has changed where Adam is concerned since he came into the clinic the other morning."

Gayle forced her shoulders into a shrug and smiled gamely. "He's been home the past two nights well before his curfew. We came to an agreement over the game he wants to buy. I loaned him the money, and he'll pay me back when he mows lawns this weekend."

"How's he doing in school?"

Gayle had spent hours convincing Adam to do his homework this week. She'd made two trips back to the school to get materials he needed to complete his assignments, two of which she'd discovered were overdue. "Adam isn't much of a student at the best of times."

"What else is going on with him? Does he tell you where he's been when he's late?"

Gayle didn't want to talk about Adam and spoil her only social outing in weeks. "Adam seems to be doing a little better."

Sherri sighed. "I'm glad to hear that. What about the next time he stays out too late, or makes a scene at your work?"

Obviously her friend wasn't going to let this go. "I know you think he needs help, but I need a little time to convince Adam to go along with seeing a counselor," she said. That wasn't the complete truth. She hadn't broached the subject with her son yet. How she wished she could tell Sherri about her sordid past, about Harry, about her lies. But she was afraid of what her friend would think.

If she told anyone about her past, her present life would be over. Her son didn't know the truth about his father, and couldn't be told under any circumstances. And now that Gayle had all the things she needed so desperately in her life, she had to keep her past to herself.

Moving to Eden Harbor on the coast of Maine, a continent away, had provided her with enough distance to restart her life. After her divorce, she'd changed back to her maiden name, and she'd left her past behind. She would not let anything stop her now.

One thing she was certain of—telling Sherri about her past would end their friendship. Sherri had shared so much with Gayle. She'd told her the full story of her past with Neill, and all the heartache she'd survived because of him, her miscarriage, her ill-fated marriage to another man, her return to Eden Harbor, all of it. Close friends shared their lives with one another. Should Sherri learn that Gayle's fictional life back in California wasn't true, she would be hurt, and the trust between them destroyed.

"Why don't you give Nate a chance to help Adam? He is so good with teenagers. He'd be perfect."

"How can you be so sure? Besides, he must have a full case load already."

Sherri gave her a smug grin. "Doesn't matter. Nate won't say no to me. So what do you say?"

"Tell me more about him," Gayle asked, realizing too late that she didn't want to hear about the shooting of another police officer. She didn't want to learn firsthand how a family as nice as Sherri's had lived through Nate's injuries. It would only serve to remind her of another family that had been devastated by the shots fired from Harry's weapon.

Sherri grinned with pride. "Nate is the white knight in the family, always riding to the rescue whenever any of his cousins are in trouble.

He's been a rock that we've all leaned on at one time or another. Right now he's helping out his sister, Anna Barker. She's a single mom with two boys."

Gayle knew Anna from the single-parents group she'd joined when she first moved to Eden Harbor. She really liked her, looked forward to the meetings. She considered Anna her closest friend after Sherri. "Anna's a member of my single-parents group. We always try to sit together at the meetings. I had no idea…"

"Yeah, she's Nate's current project, now that he doesn't have to look out for me. Anna told me the other day he's beginning to hover. She was only teasing, of course. We're all so lucky to have him." Sherri chuckled. "I don't know what Anna would do without him. I'm surprised she never mentioned him to you."

"We mostly talk about our kids at the meeting. The couple of times we've gone out to coffee it's been to discuss work and that sort of thing."

"Well, ask her the next time you see her, and she'll tell you what it's like when Nate takes an interest in your welfare." Sherri led the way to the kitchen table, cups of coffee in hand, and they slid into chairs opposite each other. "So what about it?"

"About what?" Gayle asked, stalling for time. She didn't want to turn down her friend's offer of support. She didn't want anything to jeopardize her relationship with Sherri. She was looking forward to the wedding, to being part of her friend's happiness. She'd never been to a wedding in her entire life, let alone a member of the wedding party. She loved the green dress with the tight bodice and scooped neckline, the full-length skirt that hugged her body past her knees before flaring out at the bottom. She felt so sexy in it.

Uncertainty filled her heart and mind. How was she going to turn down Sherri's offer to have her cousin help Adam without Sherri feeling hurt? On one hand, she was well aware that Adam could benefit from the help of a professional. On the other, she didn't want that help coming from someone so closely linked to Sherri and Anna. "I'm... Are you sure Nate would be willing to help? Have you asked him already?"

"No, of course not. I wanted to talk to you first." Sherri glanced at her anxiously. "Gayle, are you all right?"

"I'm...fine." She rubbed her sweaty palms together, and glanced at her watch. "But I really should get home. I promised Adam we'd watch a movie together tonight, part of my plan to get to the bottom of what's going on with him."

"That sounds good. We can talk about the wedding flowers another time."

"Oh! Sorry! I forgot we were doing that this evening. I'll call Adam and let him know I won't be home for a while."

Sherri's smile was reassuring. "No. Don't do that. The flowers will be really easy to decide. I've pretty well made up my mind about what kind I want. All I need you to do is help me pick out the actual arrangements from the florist's book."

Gayle said her goodbyes and headed to her car. She had to stop worrying about something that would never happen. She'd spent too much time worrying about the past. Getting help for Adam was all that mattered.

CHAPTER TWO

A WEEK LATER, Gayle was putting the last load of clothes in the washer and looking forward to watching The Comedy Network on television. She'd been ironing all evening, a tedious chore but one she insisted upon doing every week. Ironing her sheets, pressing the edges of her towels, ironing her jeans, gave her a sense of order. She'd always done the ironing, even as a child living in the midst of her parents' disorganized existence. Tonight it was helping her remain calm.

Adam had gone out with a friend four hours earlier with the firm promise that he would keep his curfew of ten o'clock. It was nearly eleven, and he still hadn't returned. She only knew the name of one of the other boys—Derrick Little. She'd called his mother to be told that Derrick had been home for over an hour, and she didn't know where Adam could be.

She had just unplugged the iron, leaving it on the board to cool, when the doorbell rang. Relief mingled with anxiety, making her bump her wrist against the hot surface of the iron. "Ouch!" she muttered as she headed to the front door, holding her stinging wrist across her chest.

When she peeked through the sidelights of the wide wooden door she saw the clear outline of a police officer standing next to her son. Her heart sagged. Her mind stilled at the fear of what this could mean. Sucking in her breath, she lowered her injured wrist and opened the door.

"Gayle Sawyer?"

She nodded, her gaze fixed on Adam. His face was bruised, his eyes angry. There was a small cut on his forehead. "What happened?" She reached for her son, who immediately stepped back, out of her grasp.

She clutched the door frame for support. "Adam, are you all right?"

"I'm Officer Edwards. May I come in? Your son's been in a fight with a group of teens. We need to talk to you."

"A fight. My son doesn't do that. We've talked about it many times. About how fighting is not the way to solve disagreements and how important it is to respect others…"

She forced herself to stop talking. If she didn't she'd cry. She would not cry in front of a police officer. She would remain calm.

"Please come in. Can I get you a cup of coffee?" she asked, not knowing what to do once the tall young officer was standing in her living room. She couldn't look at Adam, and let him see the worry in her eyes. As much as he was being difficult at the moment, he was a good kid. She would not prejudge him, certainly not with a police officer as a witness.

"Thank you, but no. May we sit here?" the officer asked, nodding toward the sofa and chair in front of the angel stone fireplace.

"Certainly." Still unable to look at Adam, she led the way into the room and sat on the arm-chair next to the fireplace, leaving Adam and the officer to sit together on the sofa.

Adam slouched in one corner, his eyes fixed on the fireplace mantel. Was he not going to look at her, or volunteer even one word of explanation? "What's this all about?" she asked the officer, but her gaze remained fixed on her son.

"There was a fight among a group of boys down along the waterfront this evening. Several of those involved were taken to the police station. I thought it more appropriate to bring your son home while we talked a bit."

"What did Adam do?" Gayle's heart crushed against her ribs as memories of another evening flashed across her mind. The police had shown up at the apartment where she and Harry lived, looking to talk to Harry. When they'd realized she was alone, they'd left. Before they did they told her that Harry was wanted in the shooting of a police officer. If she was withholding any information she could face serious charges. While she'd been waiting to tell Harry that he would be a father in a few months, over a nice dinner she'd made for the two of them, he'd been out shooting a cop.

"Is Adam charged with anything?"

"No. We believe Adam was caught up in something not of his own making. To my knowledge Adam hasn't been involved in an incident like this before." The police officer leaned forward, resting his forearms on his thighs, his eyes searching her face. "The point is, we don't want this to happen again. We usually recommend a mentoring program in these situations. If you agree, we have several skilled officers who work with teens. We'd be willing to set up a meeting between Adam and one of them. The other option is to seek private counseling."

Gayle thought about Nate Garrison. But what was the likelihood of Nate being available, even with Sherri's intervention? Nate might be too busy to help out.

Yet she couldn't risk having Nate take Adam's case. She had to choose the private option. "I don't have the money…" She placed her trembling hands out of sight of the officer, whose watchful eyes held a hint of kindness.

"What if I can get you into the community center program? They're pretty busy, but I'll see if I can get him bumped up the queue."

"You'd do that for Adam?"

"Yes." He glanced over at Adam, who had slumped even farther into the sofa. "I believe your son didn't mean to be part of that fight. He was simply in the wrong place at the wrong time." He turned back to her. "Does Adam have a curfew?"

"He does, but he didn't keep it tonight."

"Well, let's see if we can get him back on track." He reached into his uniform pocket and retrieved a card. "Here's the contact information for the community center program."

She grasped it eagerly, her relief palpable. Maybe she'd found an ally in her efforts to get Adam to straighten out. "Thank you for bringing my son home, and for everything you've done for him."

The officer turned his gaze to Adam again. "I promise that you will have all the help you need to stay out of trouble. In return you have to promise me that you will keep the appointments set up for you. Deal?"

Adam sat up straight, resting his hands in his lap. "Sure. Why not?" There was no cockiness in his voice, but rather a look bordering on hope.

Had Adam wanted this to happen? Was he so

desperate for someone's help and understanding that he'd done this intentionally?

"Okay. That's it." Officer Edwards rose. "I'll be in touch. In the meantime, call that number if you need to contact me," he said, pointing to the card he'd just given her.

Gayle thanked him, walked with him to the door, locking it behind him before turning back to her son. They needed to talk. She couldn't believe that Adam would get into trouble this way. She returned to the living room but he wasn't there. She searched the kitchen and the rest of the main floor, bumping her burned wrist against the door frame of the tiny den. It hurt so bad she nearly cried out. She wanted to sit down and sob until there were no tears left. Instead, she gritted her teeth and climbed the stairs to his bedroom.

She knocked. No answer, only a rustling sound. "Adam, can we talk?"

"Not tonight, Mom. I'm tired." His voice was subdued.

"Do you need a bandage for that cut on your forehead?" she asked, remembering all the times in the past when she'd bandaged an arm or knee after a spill from a bike. Memories that reminded her how much her relationship with her son had changed during the past couple of years, despite her efforts to build a new life. Was he unhappy here in Eden Harbor? Had the move from Anaheim been a mistake? She'd brought him here because of the kids he was hanging out with, but maybe it wasn't those kids but Adam himself who was the problem.

She hated herself for thinking that way.

"No, Mom. I'm good," Adam said.

She could tell by his voice that he was just inside the door. She reached up, placing her hand on the door at the spot where she guessed his head would be resting. She yearned for those days not so long ago when Adam had shared his concerns. For so many years, whenever he had a problem he sought the refuge of his room, where he would be waiting when she came up the stairs. And so it was tonight: only tonight was different. Tonight Adam didn't ease the door open and sit on the end of his bed, waiting to share his problem with her.

She was tempted to open the door, but didn't, fearful that he might be angered by her action. She could handle anything but his sudden outbursts of anger. The first had happened only a few weeks ago. It had not only surprised her, but left her deeply saddened and afraid. Her fear over his behavior had made her avoid confronting him about it, creating a distance between them she hadn't been able to bridge.

It was so difficult to witness what was hap-

pening with Adam. When he was angry, he
seemed so much his father's son. After the ini-
tial excitement of her marriage to Harry, she'd
experienced firsthand what life was like with a
man whose angry outbursts had become a part
of their daily lives. Harry used anger to get what
he wanted from her or from anyone who got in
his way.

ADAM STOOD JUST inside the door, his stomach aching, tears hovering beneath his lids. He
wanted to open the door so bad. He didn't want
to disappoint his mom. He was so confused by
what happened earlier in the evening.

He hadn't meant to cause his mom so much
grief. Really he hadn't. He'd been on his way
home with Derrick when one of his classmates
had caught up with him. Eddie Walsh had
wanted him to join his other buddies at the old
pool hall near the waterfront.

They'd gone over there and shot a couple of
rounds of pool, during which Adam had lost
badly. Thankfully he hadn't bet any money on
the games, despite pressure from Eddie. He
didn't have any cash on him, and until he paid
his mom back he wouldn't have any. He figured
Eddie and his friends would drop him, but they
hadn't. They'd let him play and they'd cheered
him on. He'd felt accepted by them.

It wasn't until they'd decided to go back to the waterfront, and he'd seen the town clock, that he'd realized he had broken his curfew. He'd been trying to decide what to do when the fight had broken out. They'd just been walking along, fooling around, when suddenly someone had walked up behind Eddie and punched him.

When someone took a swing at him, Adam had no choice but to defend himself.

He hadn't meant to get in a fight. He hadn't meant to be late. He hadn't meant to do any of it. But now it was too late to say that. He was old enough to stand up for himself. Eddie had said as much. And there was no explanation for his behavior that his mom would understand.

Moving here had been his mom's decision. He'd gone along with it because for the first time that he could remember his mom was happy. He'd never seen her smile as much as she had at the news she'd inherited this house. And he wanted his mom to be happy. He didn't understand why she was so sad, but he was pretty sure it had to do with his dad dying in a trawler accident off the coast of Alaska.

She had settled right in here, and had made friends. The neighbors loved his mom, and were always asking about her when he mowed their lawns. He couldn't seem to find a friend among the kids at school. The only person who had been kind to him was Morgan Brandon, mostly because she was a new kid, as well.

He liked her. But she was a girl. It wasn't the same.

Wishing things were different, but knowing he couldn't change what he'd done, he waited to see if his mom would insist on coming into his room. For a few minutes he considered opening the door...talking like they used to do. Yet in the end he didn't feel like talking. The fight had frightened him. He'd never hit anyone in his life and regretted what he'd done.

The kid he'd hit was in his class, and now the word would be out that he was trouble. Way to go, he thought to himself as he listened for his mom on the other side of the door. As the minutes ticked away, he felt sadder and sadder.

STILL NO SOUND from inside Adam's room. Gayle had never felt so lonely, so lost, in all her life. Tonight had scared her. And yet she couldn't bear to lose faith in her son, to have him become more distant and difficult. She didn't have a clue how to stop what was happening, and that frightened her so much she could hardly breathe. Adam was her life. She loved him with her whole heart, and wished she had the nerve to open his door.

She waited, trying to decide what to do. In

the end she felt she had no choice but to wait for
Adam to come to her and explain his behavior.
When he did she would listen and try to understand what was going on with him. "See you in
the morning, then," she said, quietly lifting her
hand from the door before going down the hall
to her own room.

She got ready for bed while listening for the
sound of his door opening, disappointed that
there would be no chance for them to talk this
evening. Yet the normal peacefulness of her
bedroom didn't stop her from turning over the
events of the past weeks in her mind, wrestling
with her fear that she'd made some irrevocable
mistake. She fell into a restless sleep, awaking
the next morning feeling exhausted. In the early-
morning light, her thoughts were much clearer.
Regardless of how she felt about seeking help
for Adam, she had to take steps to stop him from
getting into further trouble.

Three days later Gayle approached the office
of community services with trepidation. Adam
had refused to go with her, and had willingly
gone to school instead. The receptionist ticked
her name off an appointment list before leading
her into the office of Ted Marston, the head of
community services. Despite her unease, she
noted that the man was young, his office neat
and orderly. The brightly colored pots filled with

strawberry geraniums cascading over the windowsills of the large bay window behind him created the only touch of disorder in the entire space.

"Please have a seat," he said, his voice instilling confidence. "I've got the report from Officer Edwards about your son's behavior a couple of nights ago."

"Yes. I wanted Adam to come with me, but he refused," she said, concerned that Adam's no-show could jeopardize the whole plan.

"It's okay. I would have liked to meet your son, but this is strictly an organizational meeting. Adam's absence tells me he's not that keen on doing this. How do you feel about it?"

"I'm worried that if Adam doesn't get help now he'll get into worse problems. We moved here..." No! She couldn't mention Anaheim without explaining that this wasn't the first time she'd been worried about Adam's choice of friends. She couldn't betray her son to this stranger. Better to save any discussion of the past for his mentor once he was assigned one.

"How long ago was that?"

"About a year."

"May I ask why?"

"I inherited the Cooper house. Susan Cooper was my mother's sister."

"I've often admired that house, especially

the gingerbread woodwork, and it's got a great veranda. Are you the one who replanted the front flower beds?"

She felt her face relax into a smile for the first time since she'd entered the room. "I did. I like to work with my hands, and gardening is such a pleasant pastime."

"My wife would agree with you," he said, glancing over his shoulder at the mass of red blossoms and green foliage dangling from the windowsill. Returning to the paperwork in front of him, he said, "When I got your son's referral and was told it was urgent, I had no choice but to look for a mentor outside those here in this office. With more people unemployed due to the downturn in the fishing industry, our counselors and mentors are busier than they've ever been. But your son is about to have one of the best in Eden Harbor take his case—Nate Garrison."

Sherri must have convinced her cousin to step in. Despite her worries Gayle was thankful for the help. If it was the best option for Adam, and since Nate had such a good recommendation, maybe she should simply accept the inevitable. "Nate Garrison is my best friend's cousin, but I don't know very much about him."

"You're very lucky to have him take your son on as a client."

NATE GARRISON SHIFTED his weight to ease the ache in his thigh as he sat in a very uncomfortable chair outside Ted Marston's office. He'd arrived a little early, and had welcomed a few moments to relax. The client he'd just seen was a sixteen-year-old boy whose mother would not take any responsibility for what was going on in her son's life. She blamed the father, her ex-husband, for her son's problems, and refused to consider that she might have to change her approach in how she raised her son.

It had been a difficult case for him, but it became intolerable when the woman made it clear she wanted to go out with him. She'd mistaken the interviews about her son over coffee as personal attention from him. He'd let her down as gently as possible. Then he'd spent the past hour getting his notes written up to pass the file to one of the other mentors.

He was here as a favor to his cousin after a teenage boy had been picked up by the police for fighting. The boy's mother, Sherri's friend, was a widow raising her son alone. In Nate's experience single parents, especially widows, had difficulty setting boundaries for their teenagers. This was almost certainly because the mother, who had already suffered a serious loss, didn't want to lose her daughter or son, as well.

But according to his cousin, Gayle Sawyer's

husband had died years ago. He sighed at the thought of facing another difficult situation after the morning he'd had. Not because he didn't want to help, but he wasn't feeling very sympathetic at the moment. This case was too close to the one he'd just signed off on.

Still and all, he couldn't resist Sherri's plea on behalf of her friend.

And this was the life he'd chosen, one that had its successes along with difficult moments.

After he'd been shot in Boston, he'd been angry at the world and had gone looking for someone to blame. That was until he'd met the teenager who had shot him. A boy of fifteen who had grown up in one foster home after another, the child of parents who had abdicated their responsibilities long before the shooting.

Eventually he'd come to realize that he would not be going back out on the streets as a cop. He would need to rethink his life and his career. He had always wanted to help teenagers and young adults before entering the police force, and now he had an opportunity to do that. He wasn't being noble or particularly altruistic, not at all. There was only one thing driving him. If he could keep one kid from picking up a firearm and killing someone, he would feel he had used his time and his abilities for the greater good.

In his experience the parent was often more

problematic than the teenager. He sincerely hoped this wasn't the case here. And after this morning, he didn't need another woman with her own issues messing up his work life. But Sherri had championed Gayle Sawyer's cause, saying that she wasn't a needy woman—in fact, just the opposite.

"The things I do for my cousin," he muttered to no one in particular as he approached the door to Ted's office.

GAYLE TURNED AS a light tap sounded on the office door. Ted Marston got up. "Hello, Nate. So glad you could come on such short notice. And by the way, thank you for helping out here," he added as they shook hands. Turning to Gayle, he said, "I'd like you to meet Gayle Sawyer. Her son, Adam, will be your client."

Nate Garrison walked farther into the room. The charcoal-gray shirt under his worn black leather jacket matched the gray of his eyes. Despite the cane he used, his whole demeanor spoke of a natural authority. Black hair streaked with gray sobered his appearance, and there were lines around his eyes and mouth. She could only imagine what he'd been through—physical pain, rehab and the loss of his rating for active duty.

He walked toward her, his eyes assessing. She

shook hands with him, noting his gentle touch, the look of concern evident in his clear gaze. Guilt engulfed her. What sort of injuries had the police officer Harry had shot in Anaheim sustained? He'd been hit in the leg and the hip, but she had never gone to see him to apologize for what her husband had done. She realized in an instant of mindfulness that she'd been carrying this guilt with her all these years.

"It's good to finally meet you. My cousin Sherri has been on my case for days. When Ted approached me to take your son as a client, she wouldn't let me say no. You know what Sherri is like when she's on a mission." A smile crinkled the corners of his eyes, and it was if the whole room shifted ever so gently. "And you're going to be her maid of honor."

She swallowed over the lump of surprise lodged in her throat. How much had Sherri said about her? What conclusions had he come to? And how much did he know about Adam's issues? "Yes, I am."

"Then we'll be seeing more of each other."

"I'm really looking forward to the wedding. It should be a lot of fun," she said. As she gazed up into his steel-gray eyes, her body tingled, a sensation so unusual for her she gave a little gasp.

"You realize we'll have to dance at the reception," he said, making her pulse jump.

Gayle hadn't danced with a man in so long she couldn't remember—high school, maybe.

Suddenly aware that he was still holding her hand, she pulled away. "I…I'm not much of a dancer. This is my first time being part of a wedding party."

"Seriously? I thought that was some sort of rite of passage for women."

His words reminded her of how socially barren her life had been. And this man had pointed out her shortcoming as easily as if he were talking about the weather. Determined not to let him see the hurt in her eyes, she turned her attention to Ted Marston.

Yet Nate was so gorgeous she couldn't help but surreptitiously glance his way. Someone should have warned her. Even his cane looked sexy. If only he wasn't related to Sherri and Anna, two people she liked and admired. There was probably some rule about Nate dating the mother of one of his clients, but that didn't stop her from wanting him to see her as a desirable woman, not just the mother of a troubled teen.

A desirable woman who hadn't had a date in years. How sad was that?

She listened while Ted and Nate discussed Adam's case, answering their questions as thoroughly as possible without giving away any information about their past.

She had to be careful this handsome man didn't find out about her lies. And even if he decided to check on her story, Harry was in prison under a different name than hers.

"We're pretty well finished here, I believe," Ted said at last. "You do understand that mentoring a troubled teen requires a clear understanding of the family background and the issues that may have contributed to the teen needing help?"

Family background? That would mean Nate would be asking questions she'd have to answer. Would she be able to keep her lies straight given how this man made her feel? And if he was as good at his job as Sherri said, acquiring information on the family he was working with would be easy for him. "I...I guess so."

"Great. Now, all we need is to determine a date and time for Nate to meet Adam."

Gayle forced a smile to her lips. Regardless of how solid her story was about her past, she was suddenly afraid to take a chance on this man who made her feel vulnerable, sexy and out of her depth. "Mr. Marston, could I speak to you alone for a minute before we do that?"

"Is there a problem?" Ted asked.

"There might be," Gayle said, mentally running through the lie she had to offer as the truth.

As the door closed behind Nate, Ted Marston turned to her.

She cleared her throat, and ran her tongue over her dry lips. "I don't think Mr. Garrison will work out well with my son. I should have mentioned it sooner, before you went over Adam's case, but I feel I have to say something."

"What is your objection to Nate Garrison? As I explained to you earlier, he's one of the best, and he is very good with teenagers in your son's situation."

"My son broke curfew and was in a fight. I realize it was wrong, and he and I have talked about it. He's sorry. He's really making an effort to change his behavior. I'm working hard as well, to see that he doesn't make the same mistake again." She caught his inquiring glance. "What I'm trying to say is that there are boys out there in more desperate circumstances than Adam. We'd be willing to wait for someone else in your agency."

"Do you realize who the other teenagers were that were involved in that fight?"

"I assumed they were kids from Adam's school."

"They're among the roughest kids in the area. Two of them have already served time for armed robbery. I'm not trying to scare you here. But do you see how important it is for Adam to get help as soon as possible?"

She did, and she felt really guilty for putting

up barriers. "Could we possibly find someone younger?" she asked, grabbing for the first
thought that popped into her head.

"What difference would that make?" Ted said,
exasperation resonating in his tone.

"He might relate better to someone closer to
his age."

*What a flimsy argument! Is that the best you
can do?*

"Ms. Sawyer, I'm not sure you realize what is
involved in getting the right help for your son.
As I mentioned before, we're very busy. Each
of my counselors has a waiting list, but because
of Officer Edwards's request, I went ahead and
found someone who was willing to see your son
right away. Nate Garrison will make the difference between Adam getting back on track, or
joining up with the boys involved in that fight.
I hope I'm making myself clear. This is the best
chance Adam will ever have." He dropped his
pen on the desk. "But you can always choose
not to take my advice." The expression on the
man's face held a cool finality to it.

Having it put to her that way, what choice did
she have? "No. Of course I'll take your advice.
I was just a little anxious. I've never been involved in something like this before."

"Then let me explain it to you a little more.
Nate will want to meet your son, spend time

with you as well as Adam. He will get to know you and your son, and in the process he'll be able to identify problems that need to be worked on."

Gayle's stomach began to ache. "Why does he have to work with me?"

"Because you're Adam's mother, and your influence on his life is important in getting to the root of his problems. Also, the role his father played in his life, and your family ties, will be significant, as well. Adam has no siblings, but there might be a cousin he trusts or looks up to, a positive influence in his life." He looked at her questioningly.

"No." Gayle directed her gaze to her hands resting in her lap, feeling once again inadequate, alone and completely responsible for everything in her life. She didn't want Adam to live as she did—alone and fearful of what lay ahead. She wanted him to be a happy, well-adjusted teenager, and eventually a young adult with a good life waiting for him when he completed his education. She wanted him to have everything she'd never had.

"So what will it be? Can I call Nate back into the room, and we'll begin the process of getting help for Adam?"

"Yes, please," she murmured, dread filling her mind at the prospect of someone picking around her past. If he discovered anything, would he tell her first? What if he encouraged Adam to go on the internet to find information about his family, especially his father? Thankfully, Adam hadn't shown any real interest in researching family connections. That would certainly change if Nate started asking questions about Harry and her life in Anaheim.

She intended to do whatever it took to help Adam, but she would do everything in her power to keep her past out of it. Harry must never be brought into the conversation.

She should have kept her concerns about Nate to herself. He had to be wondering why she had requested time alone with the head of the center, already putting her at a disadvantage.

She knew it was selfish of her, but she couldn't risk her friends finding out about her past and the shame she would feel when she was exposed as a liar. She didn't want to be the subject of gossip in this town she'd come to love. She felt welcome here, accepted for who she was, who she wanted people to believe she was. And all that could come tumbling down if anyone learned of her lie about Adam's father.

But worst of all, if she wasn't careful, her past could affect her son's future. Adam deserved

CHAPTER THREE

NATE PARKED HIS car in front of Gayle Sawyer's house and started up the walk toward the
bright blue door, his cane supporting his dam-
aged hip as always. He'd been with Sherri at
Anna's house for dinner the other night, and was
impressed with his cousin's continued praise
for Gayle. He'd liked the woman despite the
fact that he'd been sent packing from Ted Marston's office without an explanation. She certainly hadn't behaved the way he'd expected,
throwing him off guard. And the hand holding
thing. He'd never, ever had to be reminded to let
go of someone's fingers. When he was asked to
rejoin the conversation it was clear from Gayle's
body language that she was uncomfortable with
him being there.

She was beautiful and sexy, yet her eyes were
guarded, wary. He'd caught her staring at him,
and couldn't help but wonder if she was decid-
ing whether or not his use of a cane would affect
his ability to help her son. Was Gayle Sawyer

the kind of person that saw his disability first, and made a judgment based on that?

Whatever his feelings, whatever judgment she had made about him, none of it mattered, because behind this brightly painted door lived a teenager who was on the edge of serious trouble. Officer Andrew Edwards was a caring young man who was doing night classes in Bangor in order to get his degree in psychology. From what he'd described of the fight that night, there was a great deal of pressure for Adam to join this gang of high school dropouts.

A tap of the brass knocker on the solid wood door resulted in the door swinging open immediately. Gayle stood there, her mass of black curls swaying around her shoulders.

She'd been waiting for him. The thought pleased him more than he was willing to admit to anyone but himself.

"Please come in," she said just as her son appeared. Adam Sawyer was tall for his age with a smattering of acne on his cheeks. His dark hair was cut short, and his green eyes radiated distrust. They both stared at Nate as if he were bringing bad news.

Once inside, they moved to the living room, where Adam sank onto the sofa, leaving Gayle and him facing each other in chairs near the fireplace. Nate placed his cane discreetly by the

fireplace, but not before he became aware of the
sympathy in Gayle's expression. He'd become
accustomed to the concerned glances of those
he met, the sympathy that followed, and even
the pity he'd seen in others. Such behavior was
now part of his life, nothing more.

To give everyone time to settle in, he checked
out the room's interior. It was small and cozy
with pastel blues and yellows accenting the dark
woodwork typical of many homes in Eden Harbor.

Gayle's hands smoothed the fabric of her well-
worn jeans as she sized him up. "I made the
curtains and the slipcovers. I love decorating,
and this house offers plenty of opportunity." Her
smile was genuine as she spoke, a smile that
Nate found very attractive.

"We'll start off today talking a little bit about
the two of you, and I can answer any questions
you might have."

"That sounds okay…" Her anxious glance
swerved to Adam and back to Nate. "What do
you need me to do?"

"Just be here for your son. Although the focus
is on him, there will be times when you and
I will talk about how you feel, your concerns
as his mother, what your family life was like.
Things like that. Occasionally the three of us
will talk about how things are going." He looked

at Adam. "But mostly Adam and I will be getting to know each other."

"So what's next?" She twisted her fingers in her lap as she eyed him from under thick lashes.

Anxiety was usual in these situations, but Gayle Sawyer seemed a little too anxious. Clearly she was worried about her son. But was that all? Single parents often lived with myriad concerns that were heightened during a crisis: the result of having to make all the adult decisions alone.

"How this works is that Adam and I will get together once a week to shoot pool, go to a sporting event, maybe a basketball game, talk about things that are bothering him. It won't be about the fight he was involved in necessarily, but we'll cover what's going on in his life."

"You don't have to talk as if I'm not here," Adam said in a sullen tone.

"Adam! Mr. Garrison is trying to help!"

Nate watched the troubled teen as he slouched farther into the sofa. Did he feel unnoticed, maybe unwelcome, in his new home? He'd lived here about a year, and making friends was sometimes difficult.

Nate smiled encouragingly as he directed all his attention to the teenager. "You're absolutely right. And I guess I should tell you a little bit about myself. I was eleven when my father died.

I missed him every day of my life. Then I met up with a police officer in circumstances similar to yours. Luckily I had family and friends who were willing to vouch for me, and I got my life turned around. I know what it's like to feel so alone you want to lash out at people, especially as you get older and realize how important it is to have a dad's influence in your life. And of course your move here probably wasn't easy."

Adam pressed his fists into the cushions of the sofa but said nothing.

"I suspect that you came here knowing no one, and had to start over finding friends. You felt like you didn't fit in anywhere."

Adam began picking at his nails. "I should have made the basketball team. I was on the team back in Anaheim. The school I went to there was awesome."

"Why didn't you make the team here?"

Adam shook his head, burying his chin in his chest. "Dunno."

Nate made a note to call Coach Cassidy and see what he had to say about Adam.

"What's your favorite subject in school?" Nate asked.

Adam lifted his head. "Computer science. I want to work in computers when I…when I get out of this place."

"Adam, I didn't know you were so unhappy

in Eden Harbor," Gayle said, her voice tight with worry.

"That's because you work all the time at the hospital, and we don't talk anymore like we used to when…" He rubbed his hands through his short hair, looking at neither of them.

Clearly there was a lot going on emotionally with Adam. Nate changed the subject. "Adam, do you like living in this house?"

"Yeah, it's nicer than the apartment we had in Anaheim. Mom likes working in the garden. I never had fresh vegetables until we moved into this place."

"I like this house, too," Nate said. "I had a summer job mowing lawns, and one of them was across the street. I would watch Mrs. Cooper working in her flower beds and wish I had her talent with plants."

Gayle's face brightened. "Susan was my aunt. She left this house to me in her will."

Adam sat up straighter and leaned forward, resting his forearms on his thighs, his eyes bright with interest. "You cut grass, too? How many lawns did you do?"

"I had five. Two during the week, and three on the weekend."

GAYLE LISTENED AS Adam talked to Nate about his lawn work and began to feel the tension ease

from her shoulders. Nate had found something
he and Adam had in common. She could have
hugged the man on the spot. She had no idea
how a mentor worked, but if Nate's behavior so
far was any indication, this could prove to be
so much easier than she'd expected. Quietly she
slipped from the room and went to the kitchen,
putting the kettle on for tea. She took morning-
glory cookies she'd made earlier from the jar
and placed them on a plate.

When the tea was ready, she put everything
on a tray, including a glass of milk for Adam
and headed back to the living room. Adam was
laughing out loud, a sound she had rarely heard
in the past few weeks. Clearly her son was very
happy with the attention Nate was giving him.
Delighted to be part of this new development,
she put the tray on the coffee table in front of
Adam.

"I thought we could enjoy a cup of tea and
Adam's favorite cookies while we talk," Gayle
said, being careful not to spill anything as she
poured tea for Nate and herself. She was proud
to see that Adam had waited until she'd served
Nate before taking his usual four cookies and
the glass of milk.

Nate and Adam continued their discussion
of which mowers worked best, how Adam had
managed to fix his machine the last time it broke

down. Gayle was pleased to see a look of accomplishment on her son's face, and hoped this was the beginning of a return to sharing their daily lives.

When the plate of cookies was empty, Adam finished the last of his milk and stood up. "If no one minds, I'm meeting a friend to go skateboarding."

Forcing her shoulders down, Gayle drew in a deep breath to ease her instant anxiety. "When will you be back?"

"A bunch of us are heading over to the skateboard park. I'll be back for dinner."

Gayle followed him out to the back door. Once out of earshot of Nate, she asked, "What did you think of Mr. Garrison?"

"He's okay, Mom." He patted her shoulder the way he often did. "Stop worrying. You heard him. He said we'd hang out once a week, and that's fine." Scooping his skateboard off the bench, he skipped down the steps, following the cobbled path to the front of the house before disappearing from sight.

Gayle went back into the house, expecting to find Nate where she'd left him in the living room. Instead, he was standing in the kitchen, the tray on the marble counter. "Was the move from Anaheim relatively easy?"

"Yes. I was ready for a change. When I

learned that my aunt had left this house to me, I couldn't wait to move here. I'd never been to the East Coast before. It's been a wonderful experience. I've made friends with several people at work, and I love my job." Hoping that would end his questions, she started to put the dishes in the dishwasher.

"Most people don't pick up and move that easily. Leaving friends and relatives behind is usually difficult. Why didn't you sell this house and just stay in Anaheim?"

Gayle glanced around the sunny kitchen with its cream walls and blue/green accents, all of which she'd done herself. "Because I had never owned a home before, and I loved the photos my aunt's executor sent me."

"What was your life in Anaheim like? Did you work in a medical clinic there?"

Was this how it worked? He would gain background information on her before he began working with Adam? "I did. It was okay, but not nearly as friendly as the Eagle Mountain Medical Center."

"That's good to hear." He paused. They exchanged half smiles. "You and Sherri have become close friends."

"She's the best friend I've ever had." She'd never admit to him that Sherri was her first real friend. Growing up, she couldn't take anyone to the shabby home she shared with her parents for fear of what state they'd be in, which had left her feeling isolated from her classmates.

She wanted Adam to have friends, and a place he was proud to bring them to. He had done that until about a month ago. She probably should tell Nate about that, but it might be better to wait and see how he made out with Adam before volunteering any information.

"Do you miss your friends in Anaheim?"

"With a child to raise, and very little money, I didn't have many friends."

"Had you moved there from somewhere else?"

"I lived in Riverside for a short time, but Anaheim mostly."

A frown line formed between his eyes. "I can understand that you'd be busy with a child and a career, but why was it easier to make friends here in Eden Harbor than in Anaheim?"

He was asking questions she couldn't answer without exposing the truth she'd vowed to keep to herself. She'd moved out of the neighborhood she'd been living in with Harry as soon as she could. With the grudging help of her parents, she'd taken a medical receptionist course, after which she'd moved to another part of town. There she'd intentionally avoided making friends who might connect her to the sensational coverage of Harry's trial. Having Adam in her life was everything she'd ever wanted, and the one good thing to come out of her past. "I...I'm not sure."

"What about Adam's father?"

Gayle nearly dropped the plate she was placing in the dishwasher. "His father died in a fishing trawler accident off Alaska just a few months after Adam was born."

"I'm sorry. It must have made your life very difficult. Did you have family to support you while you raised Adam?"

"My parents passed away a few years ago." In Anaheim, her mother and father hadn't bothered to stay in touch with her, and she didn't mind because they were always expecting her to do things for them—from housework to grocery shopping. She guessed that making demands on her was their version of being involved in her life.

She finished cleaning up the kitchen while Nate watched, as if assessing her. She was exhausted from the past hour, and needed to get this man to leave before he asked any more questions. He would do what he could to help get Adam's life back on track, of that much she was certain. Once that was done, and it would be, she'd concentrate on the future, her work and her friends.

The man standing just a few feet from her

would not play any role in her life after that for a couple of very good reasons. She couldn't trust herself not to be drawn to him, or worse, to end up wanting him. If she allowed him into her life beyond his involvement with Adam, he would certainly learn things about her he wouldn't like, thus putting an end to any further relationship.

She wanted Nate to leave, but from the way he'd positioned himself along the edge of her counter, he didn't intend to do that any time soon. To stop his deluge of questions, she decided to learn what she could about his relationship with Anna. She and Gayle had had coffee several times, but Anna had never really talked about her brother.

NATE FOUND IT hard to take his eyes off this woman, while she seemed to be totally unaware of him. Gayle Sawyer was gorgeous, worried and hiding something.

All Nate's police training told him, beyond a shadow of a doubt, that the woman before him was protecting a secret so big that she would do anything to keep it from him. Given that his sole purpose in being here was to mentor her son, that secret almost certainly involved Adam. As he stood there watching her, he wondered what would make a mother hide the truth if her son's happiness stood to suffer.

Furthermore, if he was completely honest himself, he wanted to know more about this woman out of a personal interest. He'd liked her from the first moment they'd exchanged glances.

Not that he wanted to date her. He didn't. She wasn't his type. He'd made it a practice to choose women who wouldn't make any emotional demands on him, who were out to enjoy life. Such relationships suited his lifestyle.

He'd once had a different outlook, and was drawn to a different type of woman... Until that disastrous day after he'd been shot when he'd learned that the woman he'd planned to spend the rest of his life with wasn't into a man with a disability.

That moment of truth had nearly been his undoing. Never again would he kid himself into thinking that a woman would want him just as he was, disability and all. Maybe in the short-term, but not the long. Because of that, he would never again allow a woman to get close enough to hurt him.

From what he could tell by being around her, Gayle Sawyer was the kind of woman who took life seriously. Something he wasn't into. He couldn't be.

"Gayle, I understand how you must be feeling right now. Having someone walk into your life under such difficult circumstances and then start asking personal questions would cause any-one anxiety."

She didn't flinch, nor did she offer up any information, as so many people did when they were offered a sympathetic response. This lady had the kind of focused determination he usually experienced with his law enforcement friends and colleagues. Not a woman who was worried about her son.

He hadn't expected her to be so self-contained, so in control. She wasn't the typical mother of a son on the verge of trouble with the law.

There was something going on here...

Or was he simply feeling the effects of her total lack of interest in him as a man?

GAYLE GRUDGINGLY ADMITTED she liked this man, despite his questions. After all, he was only doing his job, and she had to believe that he would help her son, that his questions would lead to a better life for Adam. "I'm not sure if you're aware of this, but I know your sister, Anna. We belong to the same single-parents support group."

"No, I didn't. She's been busy and so have I." He crossed his arms over his chest as he met her questioning gaze.

"She's really great. So brave to be raising her

boys alone after losing her husband in Afghanistan. She's amazing."

"She is. When Kevin was killed we were afraid that she might not be able to cope. Sherri was really supportive, and her mother, Colleen, moved Anna and her family into her house for those awful first weeks after we'd learned about Kevin's death."

"Were you living here at the time?"

"No. I was still in Boston recovering from my injuries."

She couldn't look at his leg or the cane leaning against the counter without wondering about the officer Harry had shot. "I'm sorry you were shot. It must have been really awful." She desperately wished she could change the subject without appearing heartless.

"It was, and there are days when it still is. But life goes on. The one good thing that came out of it was that I made the decision to move back here where I have family and friends."

He didn't say anything for a few minutes, leaving Gayle to wonder if the memories of the shooting still haunted him. Yet she didn't want to know more about that day. She didn't want to know his story. That would only heighten her guilt about what Harry had done fourteen years ago. "Yes, friends and family can be so supportive," she said to comfort him and to keep the conversation moving away from her.

Many times she wished that she'd gone to see Officer Perry and apologized for what Harry had done. But back then she was too afraid that she would be seen as an accomplice. She had been almost eighteen at the time and had lived in fear that somehow she would be implicated. Her ignorance of the law had held her back from acting on her need to somehow make it right with the officer, and then time passed until it was too late for her to say anything.

"How easily a single event can change everything for so many people," she said, feeling an odd attachment to this man—and an even more unusual curiosity about him. "Was it difficult to pick up and move home, leaving your life in Boston?"

His eyes were kind as he spoke. "I had been thinking about making a change. After my injury I wasn't really happy sitting at a desk all day. When Kevin died I was needed here. Anna's two boys had lost their father, and that was something I felt I could help them deal with. When I suggested it to Anna, she tried to dissuade me, but I convinced her that it was what I wanted."

This man cared deeply about his family, a trait she admired very much. A caring family was something she'd never experienced. She envied the family life Nate, Sherri and Anna shared. She longed for the same thing for herself and Adam. How different their life might have been if they'd had a supportive family.

But there was no going back, no wishing for what could never be. This was her new life, and this man had come here to provide support to Adam. With his professional experience and family history, he might make a big difference in her son's life.

GAYLE SAWYER SEEMED so understanding. Yet it was more than that. She seemed to genuinely care about people, and that included Anna. He'd seen the look in her eyes as he talked about his sister. Gayle was a friend Anna could count on, and it made him feel…pleased. Yeah, that was it. He was pleased that his sister had found a friend she could rely on—not that Anna didn't have friends in Eden Harbor. After all, she'd lived here her entire life. But something made him realize Gayle would be special.

And that realization increased his desire to do everything he could for Adam. Not that he hadn't been committed to this case when he'd come here. But Gayle was a friend of both his sister and his cousin. That gave him a whole other reason for wanting to see Adam a happy, well-adjusted teenager.

Although he was fascinated by this woman, that was as far as it could go. His life was just fine the way it was. He wouldn't allow himself to see Gayle as anything other than a client and a friend of the family.

Returning his focus to the present and what he needed to do, he glanced at his watch. How had he lost track of the time? That never happened to him. "I have to get out of here if I'm going to make my next appointment. Thanks for the tea and cookies."

"Of course." She walked with him to the door, her expression warmed by the sudden smile on her face. "Have a nice day," she said as she opened the door.

He could have sworn she was about to say, "Have a nice life."

Was Gayle hoping she wouldn't have to see him again? Did she find his presence in her life an unwelcome necessity? He hadn't considered the possibility until this moment. Yet she had to have serious reservations about the whole process they were involved in. Could her private chat with Ted Marston have been about him? He smiled to himself. Necessity had forced her to accept him into her life. Professional responsibility had guaranteed that he would act in her son's best interests. In other words, the relationship between them was all business.

He had started out expecting that to be the case—counting on it, actually. Yet now as his eyes met hers, he was struck by an idea. She welcomed his leaving. She wanted her space back, free of his interference. The thought made him feel off balance, shaken and for some reason more than a little disappointed.

CHAPTER FOUR

AT THE CLINIC on Monday morning Gayle tucked the phone against her shoulder as she listened to Mrs. Lockhart explain why she couldn't keep her appointment on Wednesday and needed to reschedule. It had been a busy morning, and as a result Gayle hadn't gotten the lab results filed from last week's Thursday and Friday clinics. The normal procedure was that a copy went to the patient's doctor's office and one to the clinic where the specialist or surgeon saw the patient.

Distracted by the mound of paper on her desk while she searched the computerized schedule for an opening, she almost put Emily Lockhart into the wrong clinic. She corrected her error and assigned Emily a new appointment. "There. That's done. See you on the seventeenth, Mrs. Lockhart."

"Thank you so much. You know sometimes it's hard to get a drive into town when everyone is working. Some of my family members work two jobs just to make ends meet."

"I understand," Gayle said, sympathetic and once again thankful that she had stable employment.

When she got off the phone, she turned to the test results that needed to be filed without delay. She had about an hour before the afternoon clinic, and if she ate her lunch quickly in the staff room, she should be able to get the paperwork cleared up before the busy afternoon began.

It was once again Neill Brandon's clinic day, and Sherri, as one of the nurses in the clinics, would be back here any minute to ensure that everything was ready. Meanwhile Gayle dug a health bar out of her bag under the desk and took a quick bite before starting to sort the reports in alphabetical order. They would all have to be filed in the cabinets along the back wall of the reception area. She was halfway through the pile when she came to the results of a referral for Anna Barker from Dr. Ningh, a neurologist who held clinics here every two weeks.

Why would Anna be seeing a neurologist? Gayle scanned the report. "…further study is needed to rule out Parkinson's disease…"

Gayle's hand trembled. It couldn't be. Anna was a single mom who worked as administrative assistant to the mayor of Eden Harbor, Larry Green. Not only did she depend on the money it paid, but Anna loved her job because it allowed her to leave the house when the boys went to school, and to be home within an hour of when they returned. Larry was a good boss whom Anna liked. He was very understanding when she needed time off to care for her boys.

But what would happen to all of them if Anna had Parkinson's?

"Earth calling Gayle," Sherri said in an overly loud voice, making Gayle jump and send the report fluttering to the floor. "Whatever you're reading must be important."

"Just a report," Gayle said, her heart pounding with worry.

"I'll get it," Sherri volunteered.

No one could know about this, not only for reasons of patient confidentiality, but also because she didn't want Sherri to worry until there was good reason. It was the least she could do for her friend. Besides, there was no need to alarm anyone until Anna had her appointment with Dr. Ningh.

"No. I'll get it." Gayle ducked down quickly and scooped up the paper, greeted by a quizzical glance from Sherri. "I was just about to file this, but it can wait," she said, tucking the paper into the pile on her desk.

Sherri took her usual spot on the other side

of the raised counter. "You haven't told me how your first visit with Nate went."

"Fine. He and Adam seemed to hit it off, although Adam left before Nate did."

"Oh, really?" Sherri said, a hint of smugness to her tone.

"It wasn't like that. Adam had a skateboarding date with his friends, and the interview went a little longer than I expected. Nate left shortly after."

"Nate tells me that he enjoyed meeting you. How about you?"

"Nate is your cousin, and I hope one day that he and I will be friends," she said, thankful that there were no questions about the report on her desk. Fending off Sherri's curiosity about Nate and her was easy. Nate hadn't shown any real interest in her. As for herself, she remembered the frisson of excitement she'd felt when he'd come to the door, and wished that she dared to talk about her reaction. But it was out of the question, especially when she would never act on her feelings. "Other than that, there's nothing to report."

"Did Adam like him?" Sherri said, her tone gentle now.

Gayle glanced up at her friend, noted the concern in her eyes and was once again so thankful that someone like Sherri cared so much about her and Adam. "We talked a little when he returned from his skateboarding, and in Adam's words, he's 'cool.' Nate asked him a lot about his job."

"Nate mowed lawns until he went to work in grade nine at Peterson's Pharmacy stocking shelves," Sherri said. "The girls used to go into the store just to catch a glimpse of him, but he only had eyes for Natasha Burnham."

"Did he go with her very long?" Gayle asked, unable to stop herself from wanting to know more about Nate.

"He did. When he joined the police academy and moved to Boston, she went with him. They had planned to be married the summer he was injured, a big wedding here in Eden Harbor. Then one morning Natasha told him she wanted out. That she couldn't imagine being married to a man who would always walk with a cane."

"What a cruel thing to do! Why did she accept his proposal? She couldn't have loved him very much," Gayle said, at once angry at this woman she'd never met and sad for Nate and what he must have faced in the weeks and months after Natasha left him.

"She grew up spoiled, always got what she wanted. And she'd wanted Nate from the time they were in high school. Only not the Nate he became after the shooting."

"What do you mean?" Gayle asked, becoming more aware of how much damage Nate's shooter had done aside from the physical injuries.

"Nate had to focus all his efforts on getting well. Gone were the days of partying and staying up half the night, along with skiing or dancing or playing tennis. It was all gone. At the time we had no idea why they'd split up. Nate wasn't talking and Natasha moved to New Orleans."

"That must have been really hard on him," Gayle said. "No one deserves to be dumped in such a heartless way."

"No kidding! He managed to get to his treatments and appointments in Boston on his own, even though the whole family wanted to help. He fended off all offers, claiming that he had a circle of friends who were there for him, and he needed to devote his time to getting healthy again."

"Maybe he just couldn't face everyone's sympathy over what Natasha had done to him. It must have been really painful to realize that the woman you loved didn't love you."

"Natasha expected that Nate would always be there for her, trying to please her, but the accident meant that she had a new role to play helping him. Obviously she couldn't or wouldn't do that. It's too bad Nate had to learn something that heartbreaking the hard way."

Gayle felt a connection to this man that went well beyond their meeting the other day. He'd had his share of suffering and pain at the hands of someone he'd loved, just as she had. "Natasha's abandonment had to have changed him."

"It did. Nate was a different man when he returned to Eden Harbor. He hasn't hooked up with any of his old gang from school, and the women he dates are all much younger. He only introduced me to a couple of them and they seemed...frivolous. Not the kind of women I would have imagined him being interested in. Maybe he's just a poor judge of women."

"Or keeps meeting the wrong kind."

"Could be. He doesn't bring any of them home, or so his mother says. She wishes he'd find someone, but..." She shrugged. "Nate won't talk about it."

Gayle wanted to know more about Nate. He'd survived injury and rejection and still managed to keep going. To have survived what had happened to him took courage and determination, both admirable qualities in her mind.

"Are you sure there's nothing going on between you two?" Sherri asked.

"No. Nothing. What made you say that?"

"This whole conversation has been about Nate, so don't tell me you're not interested in him."

Wouldn't it be nice to share with her friend how she'd felt the other day when Nate was at the house? How being near him made her feel... better about life. But hearing Sherri's description of the type of women he dated, she began to wonder if maybe Sherri believed her cousin needed a different kind of woman. One that would offer him stability and support.

If Sherri was trying to get her and Nate together to solve what she saw as her cousin's problem with women, Gayle wasn't interested. She had enough issues to work out in her own life. "Sorry to disappoint, but there's nothing to report on the romance front."

Sherri's face was one big smile as Neill entered the clinic space. "We'll talk about Nate later," she said as she crossed the reception area to greet her fiancé.

NATE STOOD OUTSIDE Coach Cassidy's office while he waited for him to get off the phone. Nate had had several appointments with teachers of some of the teenagers he was working with and had decided to drop by and see the coach before he finished his day. In Nate's experience Coach Cassidy was a very perceptive man, a quality somewhat at odds with his size and his aggressive coaching skills. "A man's man" was how the principal of the school described him.

Yet many times Bill Cassidy had known almost instinctively which teenagers were in trouble and how that trouble was affecting them. After watching Adam interact with his mother and detecting his poorly disguised hostility at feeling invisible, Nate suspected that the boy was very lonely and it was affecting his relationships with fellow students and teachers. That was to be expected under the circumstances, but also something to cause concern, should it continue or get worse. Feelings of loneliness could easily lead to feelings of alienation, and he didn't want to see that happen to Adam. He hoped the coach could explain a little bit about Adam and how he behaved around his peer group off and on the basketball court, but more important, why he hadn't made the team.

"Well, hello," Bill Cassidy said as he opened the door to his office and beckoned Nate in. "What can I do for you? Or is this a social call? I'm nearly done for the day. Want to go for a beer?"

"Yeah, that would be great," Nate said, watching the other man grab his jacket, flip his keys out of his pocket and lock his office door all in one smooth movement.

"So how's life treating you these days? Still busy as ever, I assume," the older man said as they took the stairs to the back entrance of the school. Nate noticed that Bill didn't rush down the stairs, giving Nate a chance to keep pace with him.

"Too busy, really, but that's the way it is, I guess."

They walked in unison along the cobbled walkway toward the downtown, stopping at the entrance to Missy's Bar and Grill. "And of course you're getting ready to be a groomsman at Neill's wedding. That's going to be quite a party."

"I'm looking forward to it. It's about time those two got married, if you ask me."

Bill shook his head slowly as they climbed onto bar stools and ordered two locally brewed draft beers. They talked sports, weather and the state of the fishing industry, and all during their conversation Neill sensed that Bill was working up to something.

Bill toyed with the napkin placed in front of him by the waiter. "Mind if I ask you a question?"

His tentative tone aroused Nate's curiosity. "Sure."

"How far would you go to find love?"

"What?"

Bill hunched forward. "What I mean is this. Look at Neill and Sherri. They were so in love and planned to be married when they were in high school. Then suddenly it was all over.

And if Neill hadn't come back here they would never have known how much they still loved each other."

"I guess I haven't really thought about it." Nate was feeling a little embarrassed at the turn the conversation had taken. He'd never have expected Bill Cassidy to bring up such a topic. But he had to admit he didn't really know Bill except on a professional level.

"Take you, for instance. You must have loved someone in high school—Natasha Burnham, if I remember. Would you want to have a second chance at love like Neill and Sherri? What would you do if you got the chance?"

The subject of his ex-fiancée was nobody's business, and he was becoming very uncomfortable with the direction this conversation seemed to be going. "Unfortunately, it's not something I've given much thought to recently. I guess you could say I had my chance."

"You think we only get one chance at love?"

What was Bill getting at? The man had to be close to retirement, but he had been a fantastic basketball player, valedictorian of the first class to graduate from the newly built high school on the edge of town thirty years ago. He'd dated Ellen Donnelly in high school. He could have played pro basketball, but had refused the opportunity, choosing instead to go to the Univer-

STELLA MacLEAN   83

sity of Maine. When he had come back to Eden
Harbor with a degree in physical education, the
town had welcomed him back.

Nate had no idea where Ellen had ended up,
and she'd never been back to Eden Harbor. Some
people believed Bill had a long-standing relationship with a professor of psychology who va-
cationed in Eden Harbor each summer.

He had also heard that Bill was coaching a
volleyball team made up of women who worked
in the town. And he was quite certain Sherri had
mentioned that Peggy Anderson, the phlebotomist at the medical center, was on the team. In
fact, she was the only one among Sherri's friends
who made the team, which had sparked rumors
about her and the coach. But Nate knew only too
well how easily rumors could get started with
little or no basis in fact.

Regardless, Nate was pretty sure that Bill was
talking about his love life. Maybe he was involved with Peggy but worried about the age
difference. But Nate would never ask Bill something that personal. He wanted people to respect
his privacy, and that meant he respected theirs.

"Can I ask you something?" Bill wiped the
dew off the full glass sitting in front of him.

What now? "Sure."

"If someone was looking for a good private
investigator, who would you recommend?"

Surprised by yet another sudden change in topic, Nate studied the older man, seeking a clue as to what was going on. Bill's gaze was fixed on the glass in front of him.

Nate took a long swallow of his beer as he considered his answer. "Is this about one of your students?"

"No. Nothing of the kind. I have a friend who's in need of a little help locating someone, that's all."

Nate sighed. "I have no idea. But I'll ask around and see what I can find out. It may mean that the private detective will come from Portland or farther south. Would that be a problem?"

"You're wondering what I'm up to, aren't you?" Bill asked.

"No." Yet in truth he was. The cop in him couldn't help digging for details. "It's none of my business. I'll ask around and see what I can come up with."

Bill's gaze was steady as he assessed Nate. "Thanks for helping me. I appreciate it. Being asked for advice about a private investigator can't be an everyday occurrence for you."

Nate shook his head.

Bill leaned forward, resting his elbows on the bar. "But you aren't here having a beer because I need something. If I remember correctly, it was you who came to my office." He raised his eyebrows in question.

Relieved to focus on something other than Bill's odd behavior, Nate pushed his glass aside and turned to him. "I'm mentoring Adam Sawyer, and he tells me he didn't make the basketball team this year. I'm wondering if you could tell me why?"

Bill took a long drink of his beer, wiping his lips with the napkin before putting the glass back on the shiny bar. "Adam is a good player, but not a team player. Despite my coaching him to do so, he seldom shared the ball, making the most routine plays pretty well impossible. I talked to him about it, and he promised to do better. But the minute he got his hands on the ball, he'd bolt for the end of the court. He cost us a lot of fouls in practice, not to mention loss of a concerted team play or a good offensive strategy. In the end, he wouldn't listen to me or make the changes I needed. I already had too many boys trying out for the team." He shrugged. "I'm sorry, because I really like him. I have to admit that when he got that ball in his hands, there were few players on the team that could stop him."

"I'm sorry he didn't work out." Nate stared at the mirror behind the bar in silence for a few minutes. He'd hoped to be able to help Adam, to make him feel more a part of the community by getting Bill to reconsider. "Is there any chance you'd change your mind?"

"No, unfortunately. Not a chance. I had to cut two other players who were more seasoned than Adam. That doesn't mean that with a change in approach he won't make the team next year. Why are you so concerned?"

"He's been in a bit of trouble, picked up by the police, being rude to his mother, not keeping curfew, that sort of thing. I'd like to intervene and get him away from a group of older teenagers who are already on the road to trouble."

"I see what you're getting at. Does his homeroom teacher know about your concerns?"

"Not yet."

"Does he have good support at home? His dad died, trawler accident, I believe. What about his mom?"

"She's very concerned, and she seems willing to do whatever it takes to keep her son out of trouble."

"Are there days you wish you had an easier job?" Bill asked sympathetically.

Nate nodded, thankful to have someone who understood how difficult it could be working with vulnerable kids.

They finished their beer in companionable silence.

"Would you like another?" the bartender asked.

"Not for me," Bill said, grinning at the bartender. "I need to get home. I'm coaching the women's volleyball team tonight." He slapped Nate on the back. "If there's anything I can do to help, you've only got to ask."

"Thanks." Nate watched him leave and wished that he had something to look forward to tonight, or someone. When he'd decided to stick to short-term relationships, he'd forgotten how lonely life could be without someone who was interested in his day and what went on in his life.

He smiled to himself. Who was he kidding? He'd chosen his love life, and with few exceptions he liked it the way it was. No one knew better than Nate that the future was tomorrow. One day away and no longer. He'd known that the day Natasha Burnham had walked out on him.

"I'll have another," he said.

FOR THE PAST ten days Adam had not missed his curfew, had done all his chores, mowed his lawns and worked on his home assignments. Gayle couldn't help but note that in the past week several of the calls she'd answered for him had been female voices, not the usual sullen male tones.

She didn't want to jump to any conclusions just yet about what would happen in the coming weeks, but she felt very hopeful that maybe the worst was over with Adam. Wouldn't that be a relief? Wouldn't it be great if she and Adam were able to look to the future, to Adam doing well in school and having a better chance to make the basketball team next year?

Nate had come over last weekend and taken Adam to a basketball game in Portland, which from Adam's account had been awesome. She tried not to be too obvious in her inquiry about Adam's time with Nate, but from what she could learn the two of them were really hitting it off. Had Nate's visits been all her son needed to get back on track?

She checked her watch. Nate was due here any minute to take Adam fishing, something she'd never had the opportunity to do, and had been pleased that Nate suggested it. From the moment Gayle learned she was pregnant she'd dreamed of a life for Adam that included things like fishing, hiking and all different kinds of sports. Even if someday soon Adam didn't need any more of Nate's counseling, having someone to go fishing with would be wonderful for her son.

She was at the door on the first ring, throwing it open to see Nate's smiling face.

"Were you waiting for me?" he asked, his smile lighting the space between them.

"Yes…yes, I was." She fidgeted with the doorknob, her head whirling from the pleasant feeling rushing through her. She let go of the door and just stood there, knowing she must look a little silly.

"Can I come in?" Nate asked.

She glanced up at his face, her eyes moving to his. What would it feel like to have Nate coming to the door asking for her? About her? Like a real live date? Or maybe as a boyfriend?

He smiled encouragingly, but didn't move.

"Oh! Yes, please come in," she said, her cheeks warm. She bit her lip and tried to think of something intelligent to say, but nothing… "Adam is just finishing his breakfast."

"No. I'm ready," Adam said, coming down the stairs dressed and ready to go. "Do I need to bring anything, Nate?"

Gayle was delighted to hear the upbeat tone in her son's voice. She caught the smiling glance he gave Nate, one filled with a camaraderie she hadn't seen before.

"I have all the gear in the car," Nate said, grinning at Adam. "We'll be fishing for a few hours."

Gayle was so relieved to see how much her son seemed to be looking forward to the day ahead.

As Adam came up and stood beside Nate, Gayle realized that the two of them were nearly the same height. Her son was growing tall and slim, so like Harry. She blocked any more comparisons between her son and her ex. Adam would not be like his father…she hoped.

Nate turned his attention to Gayle with a look so intense it took her breath away. "I packed lunch for the both of us."

For a split second she thought he was referring to her—to her and him—to a day for just the two of them. The thought of someone caring enough to invite her on a picnic made tears sting her eyes, longing crouch near her heart. "That wasn't necessary…but thank you."

"You're welcome. We're going to have a great day."

"I'll bet the fish aren't looking forward to our arrival," Adam said, a grin on his face as he walked past Nate with his backpack slung over his shoulder.

Acutely aware of the handsome man standing so close, Gayle waited uneasily for Nate to turn and leave. He didn't. Instead, he moved a step closer to her, his wide shoulders blocking the light from the front door. "Would you like to have coffee sometime? We need to talk about a few things."

His words startled her. "What? Adam's doing okay, isn't he?"

"I believe so, but I would like to run through a few things with you." His grin was so endearing.

"You and me having coffee?" she asked, feeling exhilarated, until she realized that he probably did this with all the parents of the teenagers he mentored. Yet it didn't stop her from wondering about him, about the women in Nate's life. They were probably supersophisticated, and wouldn't be acting as stunned as she was right now.

She wanted to say yes. To sit in a cozy booth someplace like Bobby's Bistro down on Market Street while they sipped coffee and watched people on the street. To be with this man, to have his full attention focused on her, would be wonderful…only if she was prepared to face the consequences should she let something slip out…some inconsistency in her story that contradicted what she'd already told him. Darn!

She stalled for time, trying to decide if she should take the risk. "When?"

"Whenever our schedules allow. You work all week and so do I. What about tomorrow?"

"That's Sunday."

"Yes, it is." He cocked one eyebrow, his smile charming her.

"I'd...I... Can we do it next Sunday?"

His brows burrowed together. He looked genuinely disappointed. "Sure."

She felt like a jerk for not simply accepting his invitation, but she had little choice. If Adam continued to improve, Nate's part in their lives would quickly come to an end. She was pretty sure that if Adam no longer needed Nate's mentoring skills she wouldn't have to worry about being invited out to coffee.

She could take heart in the idea that this man didn't have the time to mentor a teenager who was clearly doing so much better. And after today's fishing trip, and Adam's obvious improvement, Nate would not be around much longer. Yet she was just a little sad at the thought of Nate not coming here. At least then her secret would be safe.

They stood together, neither saying a word, the only sound the deliberate *tick-tock* of the hall clock. "Okay, next Sunday it is. In the meantime, the fish are waiting," she said, trying to sound casual while her pulse danced against her throat.

She moved with him to the door and out onto the veranda. Adam was in the front seat of Nate's SUV, looking happy and content. She waved to her son and he waved back as Nate climbed into the driver's seat.

She watched them leave, and felt lonelier than she had since arriving in Eden Harbor. Would it have hurt her to accept his invitation for Sunday? Was her concern over what she might say, what secret she might expose, worth the loneliness she was feeling now?

What would it be like to have a romantic relationship with someone like Nate? Someone caring and connected to a real family? Someone whose presence set frissons of awareness and light-headedness spiraling through her?

She pursed her lips in denial. She couldn't let herself think about the impossible. It wasn't fair to her. Even the thought of such a relationship was doomed from the start. To have a real partnership based on trust and caring, she'd have to reveal her past. To admit to her past was to admit to lying.

She returned to the kitchen to clean up the breakfast things, her mind still on Nate. He'd made it clear that the invitation was for her only. She was still mulling it over when the phone rang.

"Hi, Gayle. It's Anna Barker calling. How are you?"

"I'm fine. And you?" *Remember not to mention the lab report.*

"I'm great, really. I called to see if you'd like to come over for dinner this week."

Nate's sister was asking her to dinner. That hadn't happened before. Their friendship was through the single-parents group, the occasional coffee together after the meetings. Yet it would be wonderful to spend a quiet evening with a friend, to feel part of a family unit. "That would be nice."

An awful thought suddenly struck her. Was Anna calling about something going on in school? Her son Jeremy was in the same class as Adam... "Has Adam done something?"

"What? No. Not at all. In fact, I'd invite him along, but I need to speak with you privately... if you don't mind. And I thought having dinner together would be the easiest way. I'm sending the boys over to Mom's house for the evening."

Would Nate be there? she wondered. "So just the two of us."

"Is that a problem?" Anna asked, hesitation weaving itself around her words.

"No. Never. I..." What was she worrying about? She and Anna were friends, and it was about time they had dinner together. The last meeting of the single-parents group, they'd both been concerned about their boys. That was probably what had prompted the invitation. "Of course I'll come to dinner. I'd love it. When would you like to have me?"

"How about tomorrow evening?"

"Sounds great. What can I bring?"

"A salad, if you'd like."

"Absolutely."

As she put the phone down, Gayle remembered the report she'd filed concerning Anna's possible diagnosis. What would she do if Anna wanted to talk about her health issues? And what if Anna wanted her advice on something related to her family?

Nate. That had to be it. Sherri hadn't convinced her to go out with Nate. Now it was Anna's turn. She didn't know which would be worse—trying to offer advice on health issues, or trying to take advice on dating Nate.

Either way, she was about to find out.

CHAPTER FIVE

THE NEXT EVENING Adam stood with his hands on his hips, a scowl on his face. "Mom! I don't need a babysitter," he said, his lips drawn down. "You're going out to dinner and you've gotten someone to babysit me. I don't believe it."

"It's a school night, and I may be at Anna's for a few hours."

"So what? You don't trust me to stay here by myself and do my homework?"

Gayle's friend Peggy Anderson had volunteered to stay at the house while she went to Anna's. Peggy was the clinic phlebotomist, and she was always babysitting for friends, partly for the money, but mostly because she loved children of any size or age.

"I do trust you, Adam. It's the friends you've been hanging out with lately that worry me."

"Mom. What makes you think I'd have someone in while you were out of the house? I never have before." His eyes radiated unhappiness.

He was right. She should have trusted him, especially at this crucial time. To do otherwise might put an end to the good behavior she'd been seeing from him over the past couple of weeks. "You're right. I should have trusted you. I'll call Peggy and tell her I won't need her this evening. I'm really sorry."

Adam patted her shoulder with one hand while he scooped up a handful of cookies cooling on the rack with the other. "It's okay, Mom. You've been worried about me, and you were only doing what you thought was right."

"When did you get so grown up?" she asked in a teasing tone, but she was so proud of him she wanted to hug him.

"You really want to know?" he asked around a mouthful of cookies.

"Yes."

"Nate Garrison is a cool guy. We had a great time fishing, and he's invited me to go out with him again next weekend."

Nate had to have other teenagers to mentor. Why was he giving Adam so much time? Could he be looking forward to their coffee date together as much as she was?

Not likely. Stop fantasizing about the man! "I thought he was going to take you after school."

"He was, but we both love basketball, and there's a game in Bangor we want to go to."

"I see," she said, punching in Peggy's number. Peggy didn't answer her home line, and Gayle didn't have a cell number for her. "She's not answering. Should I go around to her place?"

"Not unless you want to be late. And we both know how much you hate being late," Adam said, his voice sounding so grown up.

"So what am I going to do?"

"When she arrives, I'll tell her I convinced you I didn't need a babysitter. She can call you at Anna's house. You left the number on the fridge. No big deal."

"Clever *and* handsome, is that it?"

His eyes sparkled. "Of course."

"By the way, speaking of handsome, a girl from your school called here the other day. She didn't want to leave her name at first, but I convinced her. Are you and Morgan Brandon friends?"

Bright pink traveled up Adam's neck to his face. "Mom!"

"Is she in your class?"

Adam wouldn't look at her. "I'm not answering any more questions about Morgan."

The idea that her son might have a crush on one of the girls in his class appealed to her very much. She wanted him to experience all the nice, normal things of being a teenager, and having a girlfriend was one of them. "I won't grill you any further, but you will keep me in the loop."

"Can't promise," Adam said, making his escape to the den.

"You'll do your homework, right?" she called as she pulled on her jacket.

"Yep," he said over the blare of a football game.

It was too bad she hadn't been able to reach Peggy before leaving the house, but she'd see her at work in the morning and would apologize then.

ADAM WAITED TO hear his mother's car pull out of the driveway. He'd seen Eddie after school today, and had promised his friend that they'd get together here for a bit while his mom was out. Adam wanted to ask Morgan Brandon to the junior dance the school was having in two weeks, and he didn't know how to do it. He couldn't ask Nate. He was way too old to understand. Nate could fish and he was great to go to games with, but it ended there as far as Adam was concerned.

What he needed was someone who was cool with the girls. Eddie was the coolest guy he knew. He would help him.

He felt really bad that he couldn't tell his mom about Eddie coming here. She would have freaked out if he'd mentioned the name of one of the kids involved in the incident with the police.

But Eddie had been as surprised about the fight as he had. Eddie had stopped him the other day at school, wanting to know what happened when the police took him home. Adam had told him about the mentoring thing, and he'd been cool with it. Eddie was cool about a lot of things.

Still, he was feeling seriously annoyed over his mom's decision to leave him with a babysitter. He didn't need one. No way. What he needed was to talk to Eddie about Morgan. Of course, his mom's friend Peggy was due here shortly. He'd have to make sure she was gone before Eddie arrived.

He watched the game some more, waiting for Peggy. When the doorbell rang he jumped up. Opening the door, he was surprised to see Eddie standing there with a couple of the guys from the pool hall. "What are you doing here?"

"Don't you remember? You invited me over," Eddie said.

"Yeah, sure."

He couldn't tell them his mom had hired someone to stay with him, and that she was due here any minute. They'd make fun of him and never speak to him again. He couldn't risk Peggy finding them in the house, either. She'd be sure to tell his mom, which would mean that he'd be in trouble and Nate would be told what had happened.

"What are you waiting for?" Sam Mason pushed past Eddie and strolled into the hall, his heavy boots grating on the hardwood floors his mom had spent hours polishing.

"Wait!" Adam called out.

"What for? Do you have any beer?" Peter Porter said as he sauntered past Adam.

"No. Nothing like that here," he said, pulling Eddie aside. "Sorry, but your friends can't stay. My mom's friend is coming to the house in a few minutes. If they're still here, she'll tell Mom."

"You're worried what your mom will think?" Eddie asked, his voice filled with surprise. "Be cool. Nothing's going to happen. A couple of the guys arrived as I was leaving the house. We're going to play pool. I just stopped by to see what you wanted. What did you want?"

He couldn't tell Eddie that he needed advice on asking a girl to a dance, not with the other guys listening in. He had made a terrible mistake inviting Eddie here, not realizing that he might bring some of his friends from the pool hall. And he would never live it down if Peggy showed up at the door and announced she was there to babysit him. He'd look like a sissy, a mama's boy in front of the only friends he had in Eden Harbor.

"Let's have some music," someone yelled out.

The house began to throb with sound, and Adam started to panic. How was he going to get them to leave?

THE DRIVE TO Anna's house took only a few minutes. As she got her salad out of the backseat and walked up to the modest bungalow with its array of ceramic pots filled with herbs and nasturtiums, Gayle felt a little anxious. She had to put what she knew about Anna's health situation out of her mind. If Anna brought the subject up herself she'd deal with it then. In the meantime, she wanted to relax and enjoy the evening.

She knocked on the door, which was immediately opened by a teenage boy. "You must be Jeremy," Gayle said, noting that he had his uncle's clear-eyed gaze and easy smile.

"I am. Come in, please," he said, leading the way down the hall to the kitchen where Anna was working at the stove.

If Gayle could choose a new hairstyle, it would be Anna's. Her straight brown hair framed her face in a pageboy cut that enhanced the clear blue of her eyes. "So glad you could make it," she said, looking up from the pot she was stirring. "I don't have a slow cooker, so I'm doing my Moroccan chicken on the stove, and it's about to burn."

"Smells delicious."

"Thanks. The boys don't really like this dish so I made a stir-fry for them. They're going to finish their homework and go with Mom for an hour or so." She raised her eyebrows at her son.

"Right," Jeremy said, ducking his head as he took off toward the other end of the house.

"Have a seat." Anna beckoned with her spoon to the table set for two. "This masterpiece is nearly ready. Kevin and I loved to eat dishes that came from countries around the Mediterranean. Kevin believed the diet there was much healthier, and I enjoy trying out new dishes." She slid into the chair across from Gayle. "I don't have much opportunity anymore without Kevin. Did you find it difficult to cook dishes you and Harry enjoyed after he was gone?"

"I...I'm afraid we ate out mostly. I wasn't a very good cook back then. In fact, I'm still learning," Gayle said. At least the comment about her cooking was true. But how she wished she didn't have to keep her past a secret, that she could share the whole truth about her life the way others did. She'd always felt separate and apart, and had hoped that the feeling might change once she moved here. She hadn't considered that not being able to tell the truth to her new friends when she really wanted to would be more lonely and isolating than when she lived in a city of strangers and casual acquaintances.

"You and I have a lot in common, both losing our husbands when our children were young," Anna said.

Gayle had to get Anna off this subject. There was simply no way she was discussing anything to do with Harry Young. She'd told Anna about Harry back when they first met. She felt obligated to give some explanation as to why Adam didn't have a father. Funnily enough, she'd talked about Harry more times since she'd moved here than she had during her life in Anaheim. Proof that the curiosity of caring friends had its drawbacks. "It was a long time ago, and I've had to move on."

Her expression tense, Anna got up from the table and picked up a basket of rolls from the counter. When the doorbell rang, she called to her sons, who promptly appeared, kissed their mother and left.

Bringing the basket to the table, Anna said, "I doubt they eat rolls in Mediterranean countries, more likely a flatbread, but rolls are all I have."

"That's fine by me."

Searching for a neutral topic, Gayle asked, "What's in the dish you're making?"

Anna smiled in pleasure as she described the ingredients and filled plates for each of them. They talked about work, the upcoming wedding and the parent-teacher meeting being held at the

school the following week. Gayle hadn't spent
a more pleasant evening in a long time. She
reached for a roll, tearing a piece off and dip-
ping it in the sauce. "I'll have to get this recipe
from you," she said, noting that Anna seemed
very much on edge.

Suddenly the front door burst open, and Anna's boys were home. "Gran said she would stop
by tomorrow, Mom, and for you to call her when
you're free," Jeremy said.

"Aren't you guys home early?" Anna asked.

"I left part of my science project back here
at the house, and she drove us home so I could
work on it."

"Okay. Then why don't you both go to your
rooms and finish any homework you have. I'll
be in when Gayle and I are finished having our
dinner. Okay?"

The boys grabbed their books and headed
down the hall toward the bedrooms.

"I don't know what I would have done without them," Anna said, a wistful look on her face.

"I know what you mean. I can't imagine my
life without Adam."

As they continued to eat the stew, Anna said,
"I hear you've met my brother, Nate."

"I... That's right. I haven't seen you since
Adam was assigned Nate as his mentor." She

explained the circumstances of Adam being brought home by the police.

"Do you spend much time with Nate now that he's working with Adam?"

"No, but Adam really likes him. You're lucky to have a brother living so close."

"Yes. And he has been so good to my two boys since Kevin was killed."

There was a long silence as they looked at each other. Gayle knew her friend wanted to talk about Kevin, but she couldn't go there. She had no idea what it would be like to lose someone you loved, and she knew by the grief in Anna's eyes she couldn't fake the kind of feelings this woman had experienced.

The safer subject was Nate. "Your brother is so kind. The agency spoke very highly of him."

"I don't know what I'd do without him where the boys are concerned, and he's always been so supportive of me." She moved the food around her plate. "But that's not what I really wanted to talk about." Anna pushed her plate aside and went to close the door leading to the bedrooms.

Returning to sit across from Gayle, she said, "I haven't been feeling well." She placed her hands out of sight in her lap. "I've been to my doctor, and now I've been referred to a neurologist." Her gaze was steady as she looked at Gayle. "I might have Parkinson's."

Instinctively Gayle reached across the table. "Anna, I'm sorry to hear this." She didn't know what to say next. "Does anyone in your family know?"

Tears shone in Anna's eyes. "No. I haven't mentioned it to them, and I don't want to until I know for sure."

"Anna, I probably shouldn't be telling you this, but I saw the report from your doctor and the referral request to a neurologist. I filed it before anyone else could see it."

Anna let out a long sigh of relief. "Thank you so much. I don't want to worry Nate or Sherri or any of my family. They worry enough about me as it is. Besides, Neill and Sherri's wedding is coming up, and nothing can be allowed to interfere with their happiness."

How Gayle wished she had a family like Anna's. People whose lives were intertwined both by blood and love for one another. She fought the tears forming, tears for her friend and tears for the life she would never experience. "Anna, I'll do anything I can to help you. In the meantime, let's hope that it's a false alarm."

"Wouldn't that be great? I can't imagine how Nate will feel if it isn't. He doesn't need this worry after what he's been through." Anna's shoulders slumped. Her jaw trembled. She lowered her head and held it in her hands, the tears dripping onto the shiny surface of the table.

Gayle awkwardly patted her on the shoulder. "Neither do you." She couldn't say the usual consoling words about how Anna would be fine, and things would work out. She really didn't believe in that sort of blind trust that life would work out for the best.

Anna lifted her head, a smile wedging the corners of her mouth as she blotted the tears with her fingers. "Do you like him?"

Gayle was surprised by the question. "Have you and Sherri been talking?"

"About what?" Anna's expression was the picture of innocence.

"About Nate and me."

"Maybe..."

She decided to meet Anna's questioning gaze head-on. "Your brother has been so nice to me, and I haven't been easy to get along with at times," she admitted as she helped gather the plates. It was clear that neither of them felt like eating for now. "I have to say, your brother can be very appealing when he puts his mind to it," she added, remembering those few moments in the doorway of her house. To take her thoughts away from Nate, she helped Anna get the coffee organized.

Her friend placed an apple crumble and a

pitcher of cream on the table. "Would you go out with him?"

"Oh, no. I mean, he's very busy and so am I. Besides, I can't imagine there isn't someone special in his life already."

"Are you fishing for information?" Anna asked as she brought the coffeepot to the table and filled their mugs.

"No...well, maybe," she said, realizing that she was sharing her feelings with a woman who could so easily go right back to Nate with whatever she said. "But please don't say anything to him. It would be embarrassing for both of us."

"I won't mention a word to anyone about anything we talked about here tonight. But for the record, Nate isn't seeing anyone serious. If there was one thing I would wish for him, it's that he would move on with his life and find someone to love. A woman who would love him through thick and thin." Anna cradled her coffee cup in her hands. "My brother has a lot of love to give to the right person."

NATE DROVE DOWN the narrow street leading to Anna's house, his mind on the young man he'd counseled this afternoon. It hadn't gone well, mostly because the parents proved to be very uncooperative, blaming all the issues their son had on him rather than taking any responsibility. He'd had to intercede several times on behalf of the teenager. The meeting had ended with no resolution to any of the areas of conflict between the young man and his parents. In most circumstances, this case being an exception, he was very sympathetic with parents and the amount of responsibility they had to assume from the moment their child was born. In his opinion, kids needed all the guidance parents and society could offer if they were to grow up into healthy, well-adjusted adults.

A strange restlessness overcame him as he eased around the block toward Anna's house. Maybe he should have headed over to the gym, done the therapy exercises for his injured leg, but he wanted to see Anna and the boys, find a little normalcy in his life.

He was thankful his nephews seemed so well adjusted, having lost their father only two years ago. Everyone had rallied around Anna, family and friends alike, and given her all the support they could. He also knew that his connections with the police would guarantee that he be notified of any incident involving either Jeremy or Silas.

His mind on his nephews, he nearly rammed into the back of a car parked in Anna's driveway. He was so used to pulling into her yard without thinking that he hadn't seen the dark vehicle in the low light from the street. His eyes took in the scene in front of him. For some reason Anna hadn't put on her outside lights, and he couldn't see anyone moving around through the living room window. He didn't recognize the car… Maybe he should have called before he came over. Or maybe…

He parked on the street and went up to the door, knocking gently on the solid wood surface. In a few minutes he heard footsteps down the hall, and the door swung open.

"Nate, what are you doing here?"

It was on the tip of his tongue to admonish his sister for not checking to see who was at the door before opening it. After Kevin's death, he'd gone over all the safety precautions he could think of for a woman living alone. But she wasn't alone… and there were tears on her cheeks. Did Anna have a boyfriend? She'd never mentioned anyone to him.

"Just thought I'd drop by and visit with you for a little while. But if you're busy…" He wasn't going anywhere until he knew who else was in the house. Because someone had made his sister cry. It was his guess that the owner of the car had caused the tears.

"Nate, don't be silly. Besides, I invited Gayle over for dinner tonight—my famous Mediterranean stew and apple crisp. Want some?"

A mixture of relief and pleasure brought a smile to his face. "I've already eaten, but apple crisp…" He put aside his cane and hugged her close, making her laugh, a sound that relieved his worry. Whatever she'd been crying about, Gayle had been there for her. The thought that Gayle had been a support for his sister gave him a pleasant buzz.

GAYLE COULD HEAR Nate's very male voice as he and Anna came down the hall toward the kitchen. She smoothed her hair and wiped her napkin over her lips. She watched the two of them enter the room arm in arm, Nate's expression one of happiness as he walked with the help of his cane.

Watching him, she could only imagine what it must be like to always need a cane to walk comfortably. How must he feel every morning when he woke up, knowing that he had to use a cane to get around? Did Nate's shooter ever learn what he'd done to this man? Or was he like Harry and didn't really care?

"I hear you've been allowed in on a family ritual," Nate said.

"Ritual?" She watched as he came around the table and eased down into the chair next to her.

"The chance to partake of my sister's famous

apple crisp," he said, his eyes on her, the air between them suddenly a warm, inviting space.

"Brother dearest, would you do me a favor before I fix you a huge bowl of crisp and chocolate ice cream?"

"No job is too great for such a reward," he replied, although his focus remained on Gayle. His gaze moved over her face so slowly she held her breath, waiting for his eyes to return to hers. When they did, she felt suspended in space, alone with a man who drew her to him with his magnetic force. Her pulse pounded in her head. A rush of heat rose through her, making speech impossible.

This couldn't be happening to her. Handsome men with soulful eyes were part of her fantasy life, not her real life. She waited for him to break the contact, to make light of it or simply to turn away. He didn't. She couldn't. And so they sat there staring at each other as if neither knew what to do.

Anna finished putting the plates in the dishwasher before coming over to stand behind her brother, her hands on his broad shoulders as she leaned close and kissed his cheek. "Now would be a good time for you to stop making eyes at my friend and go in and make sure that Silas and Jeremy have settled into bed. Put all the video games in my room for the night, would you?"

He blinked, gave Gayle a smile.

"At your service," he said, climbing out of the chair and heading down the hall toward the bedrooms.

When Nate had disappeared, she sat down in the seat he'd vacated. "There is one small favor I'd like to ask of you," Anna said, nervously smoothing the place mat in front of her.

"Name it."

"If I have Parkinson's, it's going to be really hard to tell Nate. My appointment with the neurologist is in a couple of days, and Nate wanted to come to the appointment with me. Will you be there?"

"Your appointment is at the clinic, right? So of course I'll be there."

"No, I mean, with me in the room."

"I don't know if I'd be allowed. I'm not family."

"Then would you stay a little longer tonight while I bring Nate up to speed on what's going on? He doesn't know about the testing or my appointment with the neurologist. I didn't tell him."

"Why? Are you worried he might not be able to cope?" she asked, feeling drawn into the family, yet not sure she'd be able to handle her own emotions if the news from the neurologist wasn't good. No one had exhibited such a level of trust in her before. As much as she craved having a real family, she was also afraid of what it would be like to share in such an intimate relationship.

Anna bit her lip in worry. "It's just that he's done so much for me, and if I could make this all a little easier for him…"

"So you'd like me to be here while you tell him that you have an appointment with a neurologist."

"If you don't mind."

Gayle had never had a friend who had asked for her help in this way. Sure, she'd driven acquaintances to appointments, picked up their car at the garage, that sort of thing. This was different. Whatever she might feel about sharing her past with any member of the Garrison family, she knew one thing for certain. She wanted to be Anna's friend. And she would stay for as long as it took for Anna to talk to Nate.

"I'd be more than willing to be here while you explain to him what's going on."

Anna hugged Gayle so tight she could hardly breathe. "You are such a good friend. This will be so much easier with you here."

"Explain what?" he asked as he came into the room.

"How did you sneak up on me?" Anna asked, her sudden intake of breath audible.

"The floor is carpeted and my cane is quiet

this evening," he said, tapping it against the chair leg as he sat down.

"Did you know my brother named his cane 'Hot Damn'?"

He gave Gayle a sheepish grin. "I used to swear a lot when I was learning to walk with a cane, and being able to say *damn* covered for some of the more profane language I wanted to use."

Anna arrived at his shoulder with a large bowl. "Okay, here you go."

She sat down on the other side of Nate as they watched in disbelief while he motored through the dessert, wiping his lips on a napkin when he finished. "What's next?"

"Next?" Anna said, her glance sliding to Gayle and back to her brother. "Oh, you mean on the food front?"

He looked questioningly at his sister. "I mean whatever…" He put his napkin down. "I know an anxious look when I see one. What are you two up to?"

Anna leaned her elbows on the table and began to explain about her tests and the fact that she was afraid it might be Parkinson's. Or at least that was her family doctor's best guess. She'd been notified by the neurological clinic that she had an appointment.

As Gayle listened, her eyes were drawn to

Nate's face and the raw worry shadowing his handsome features. As Anna continued to confide in Nate, she began to cry. Nate pulled her into his arms, consoling her with gentle words. He glanced at Gayle over Anna's shoulder, the raw agony in his eyes stabbing her.

As his gaze held hers, she felt his pain like a physical force. Her throat went dry, blocking any attempt to speak. She reached for him, then thought better of it. She had never been in a situation like this before where people could love without condition and draw support from one another in a time of crisis. She felt almost ill as the rush of emotion slid through her.

She had no choice but to leave, to escape this world she had no right to be in. "I have to go," she said, getting up and grabbing her purse off the counter, her jacket off the hall rack, before rushing out the door.

THE NEXT MORNING, Gayle headed into work, her thoughts still on Anna and Nate and what she'd witnessed. They must have thought she was crazy to run out like that, but she couldn't have stayed and witnessed the love and caring that was so foreign to her. Feelings she had never experienced in her life, except where Adam was concerned. During those few moments last evening, Gayle knew she had missed out on so much that was important, or been robbed of it by her parents and Harry. She'd been overcome by the pain of that revelation, and had had no choice but to leave. This morning she knew she'd made the right decision.

She didn't deserve to be there with them. She'd been emotionally upset, but it wasn't only about Nate and Anna. It was also about the jealous feelings she couldn't seem to control. Jealousy and loss. She had never felt the kind of love Nate offered his sister.

She'd lain awake most of the night as confusion and fear rolled through her. She kept seeing Nate with Anna, and the kindness he'd shown her. The compassionate way he talked to her, offering her support. Yet he'd had to have been coming apart inside. This was his only sister. He had to be worried and scared for her. Gayle had never known a man like Nate. That someone had nearly ended his life with a bullet was too awful to think about.

If his shooter had succeeded, Anna would have been left to raise her boys without the support of her brother.

She had seen how well Nate and Adam got along, and until now she'd thought of it as simply part of his job, a way to gain the confidence of a teen in danger of getting in serious trouble. After last night she was aware of so much more.

Nate Garrison genuinely cared about people. She understood so much more about this man who was now involved in her life.

As she went in through the main clinic doors just off the emergency entrance, she met Peggy carrying a coffee. Her expression was guarded.

"Oh, Peggy, I'm so sorry about last night. I didn't think that Adam would mind having a babysitter, but I keep forgetting that he's a teenager. Teens hate to be treated like kids. I have to remember that he's desperately trying to figure out how to be an adult." She fell into step beside Peggy as they approached the phlebotomy department. "I didn't have your cell phone number. I tried to call you at home, but there was no answer. I left a message. Did you get it?"

Peggy placed her coffee on the counter of her workstation before turning to face Gayle. "Did you get *my* message? I left it on your home phone about ten o'clock last evening."

"No. I was a little preoccupied when I got home and didn't think to check. Was there something important you wanted to tell me?"

Peggy glanced around. There were no patients waiting to have their blood drawn as the clinic wasn't actually open yet. "There's no easy way to say this, so I'll just come out with it. When I got to your house last night there was a car in the driveway. I didn't recognize who it was, but when I went to the door Adam was there with a couple of teenagers." Peggy rubbed her forehead. "At least, I assume they were teenagers. They could have been older. Anyway, when I got to the door the two standing just inside the door were quite rude with me, asking me who I was and what I wanted."

Gayle's stomach clenched in dread. "Oh, Peggy, I'm so sorry. I had hoped things had settled down where Adam was concerned. He's been so good about chores and his curfew... When I left he was watching a game on TV. He promised me he'd get his homework done when he was finished. I don't understand what could have happened. What were those kids doing there? He didn't mention anyone coming over, and he didn't call me. I had my cell phone on all evening."

"I wanted to know what was going on. I stepped past the two boys and went into the kitchen. Your son was looking pretty anxious. I asked him to tell me why those boys were there. He said that his friends had brought over some schoolwork he needed, and they were just leaving. I had a hunch he wasn't telling me the truth. They didn't seem in a hurry to go, so I stayed until they left. Maybe they returned later." She shrugged. "I did tell Adam that I hadn't expected there to be anyone at the house other than him. He said he knew that."

Worry tightened Gayle's shoulders. Had Adam pretended to be asleep when she'd come home so he wouldn't have to explain anything? "He didn't mention anything about last night when he got up this morning."

"Gayle, I'm really sorry I had to tell you all this, but I felt you needed to know given how concerned you've been about him."

"And only yesterday I thought that the worst was over, that he'd turned a corner."

"And maybe he has. Maybe those boys were school friends who happened to drop by to do just what they said they were doing. I don't have any kids, so I'm not really in a position to say one way or the other. I am certain of one thing— they were not very pleasant and they clearly didn't think they had to leave your house."

Gayle rubbed her forehead in defeat. What else could go wrong in Adam's life? "Thanks, Peggy. I really appreciate you telling me. I'll talk to Adam."

Peggy's relief was evident in her smile. "If there's anything I can do to help, you have only to ask."

"I know, and I appreciate it so much. Everyone here is so good to me."

"That's because we care about you, and about

Adam. Will you come by and go to lunch with me later? It's a nice day. We could eat outside if you like."

"That would be *so* nice."

As Gayle moved along the corridor toward the clinic doors, her heart hurt. Who were these boys and what did they want with Adam? And worse, what would have happened if Peggy hadn't come along? She wished she could go home and check on Adam, but that would be pointless, as he was in school today. Or was he?

As much as she appreciated what Peggy had done, in their one short conversation she'd begun to distrust her son. They had shared everything until the past couple of months when Adam had become so defensive and distant. She'd blamed it on teenage hormones, but whatever it was, she had to know she could trust Adam.

They'd made it this far together. She had to believe that Adam would tell her the truth when she got home.

CHAPTER SIX

As she approached the clinic area and walked through the glass doors, she was relieved to find Sherri alone at the desk.

Her friend took one look at her face and rushed over.

"Gayle, what's the matter?"

Gayle and Sherri faced each other across the counter. The silence in the empty clinic space was a sharp contrast to the anxious pounding of Gayle's heart as she told her friend about Adam's behavior last evening.

"Why don't you ask Nate's advice on all this?" Sherri asked. "He's Adam's mentor and it's his responsibility to do what he can for him. Besides, Adam may find it easier to talk to a man."

"Are you saying I shouldn't talk to Adam, tell him how upset I am that he had friends in without my permission?" Gayle asked in disbelief.

Sherri shrugged. "I'm not a parent, so I can't really say. But maybe you should get Nate to talk to Adam about boundaries."

"You're thinking about the day he arrived here angry and upset?"

Sherri nodded.

"You're probably right. I'll call Nate this afternoon before I leave for home."

"I happen to know he's on his way over here for his yearly checkup and blood work. Why don't you speak to him after that?"

"Do you think he'd mind?"

"No, of course not. It's his job."

"If you say so," Gayle said, feeling really anxious about how Nate would react. When had she become so concerned about Nate's response to her worries about Adam? Up until now, she'd managed on her own. Maybe that was it. She didn't feel nearly so alone now that Nate was in the picture.

She suddenly found herself torn between wanting to hide somewhere and wishing Nate would arrive. Was this how it felt to be attracted to someone? If that was the case, she had to be on her guard around him. She could not risk letting him see how she felt.

The first hour of work was agony as she waited for the call from Peggy, who had been happy to alert her to Nate's arrival. Not physical pain, but a weird feeling that Nate would care how much this was affecting her as well as Adam. She bit her nail as she watched the phone, a habit she'd managed to break when she was fifteen.

When the phone rang, she grabbed it. "He's here with two coffees. Shall I send him in?" Peggy asked.

"No. Tell him I'll be right out." She put down the phone and hurried out of the clinic.

He passed her a coffee as she approached. "One cream, no sugar. Am I right?"

She took the foam cup in her hand. "Someone must have told you. Sherri?"

"You got it."

He looked slightly awkward, balancing his cane in one hand and his coffee in the other.

"Here, let me take that for you," she said, motioning to his hot cup of coffee.

"You don't have to wait on me," he replied, a hint of defensiveness in his tone.

"I'm helping a friend, aren't I?" she asked, looking up into his gray eyes fringed with enough lashes for two people.

"Okay. I'll let you have your way with me," he said, and there was a sweet undertone of sharing their own private moment when he spoke the words so close to her ear.

They headed to the patio outside the entrance, where there were several vacant benches under a large oak tree. The short walk was one of the nicest of her life. She could smell his sexy cologne, the clean scent of his cotton shirt with the sleeves rolled up, displaying curly dark hair. They sat down side by side, and she passed him his coffee.

"Thank you for everything you did last night for my sister," Nate said, his voice filled with warmth.

"Including my sudden disappearance?" she asked, both surprised and pleased at his compliment.

"It was a pretty emotional time for all of us."

She saw the worry in his eyes. "I was glad to be there for her…for you." She wanted to say something more, something that would ease his concern, but realized that words were not going to change the situation.

"Gayle, you're a very special person. I hope you know that."

Only once in her life had anyone ever said that to her—a teacher in her final year of high school just before she quit. She clung to Nate's words of praise, her heart beating so hard in her throat she could barely breathe. To think she'd been afraid of this man only a few weeks ago. "Thank you" was all she could get out.

She longed to tell him the truth about her past, but now with his eyes on her face, his evident willingness to share his feelings with her, she had to face an unalterable fact. The truth could never be revealed. Admitting to this man, who had shown genuine caring for her, that she had been lying about her past would end his belief that she was a special person.

People who were special didn't do what she'd done. Maybe on some bizarre TV reality show, but not in real life.

With his loss of faith in her would go any chance that they might care for each other enough to have a relationship—a love affair. A sob caught in her throat, and she was mortified. Had he heard it?

She glanced at him and was relieved to see that he seemed to be simply enjoying his coffee. But as her gaze moved over his face, she couldn't hide from her feelings. She cared about him. She genuinely cared about this man sitting so close she could smell his aftershave. And she knew instinctively that he would never intentionally hurt her. She let the realization wash over her, the sensation of closeness, praying it would last.

"Are you okay?" he asked.

She pulled her thoughts back to the present and the reality of her problems with Adam. "Nate, I need your advice."

His smile was gentle, his attention focused only on her. "Sure. What's up?"

"It seems that while I was out last night,

Adam had…I think they were classmates of his…in the house."

"You don't know for sure?"

She picked at the plastic lid of her cup. "I haven't asked him yet."

"Why not?"

"Because…" She pushed the mass of curls off her face. "Because we were doing so well, Adam and I. He was behaving the way he used to, and I wanted to believe that everything would go back to normal. I'd asked Peggy to come over while I was out, but when I told Adam he got upset."

Nate was watching her closely, creating a tiny cocoon of reassurance…if only for a few minutes.

"Now I'm afraid that he intentionally refused to have Peggy there because he was planning to have friends in while I was out," she said. "He's not allowed to have anyone on school nights unless he talks to me first."

"How does that make you feel?"

She sighed. "That I can't trust him." She felt her eyes grow damp. "That if I say anything it will only drive him away." That sneaking around had been a way of life with Harry.

No! Had she said the part about Harry out loud?

Nate took her hand in his, his heat warming

her chilled fingers. Once again she wished she didn't have to keep secrets from this man.

"Gayle, you're going to have to talk to him about this. He needs boundaries. Everything in Adam's life is changing at the moment. He's still adjusting to being in a new town, seeking out new friends, trying to get good grades, disappointed at not making the basketball team. And now he's done something he knows is against the rules you've set for him. He needs an opportunity to tell you what went on that evening."

"And how do I do that?"

"When you go home today, give him a chance to talk. Make him understand you want to hear his side of the story."

"And if he doesn't talk? What then?"

"You bring it up in the gentlest way possible, but make sure he understands that you and he have to talk it out. You need to have house rules."

"House rules? But we already do."

"Not necessarily. If the two of you are to live happily together, there has to be rules on both sides. Have you ever talked about rules for you?"

She gave him a surprised look. "For me?"

"Well, I assume you're not allowed to bring dates home for the night, unless it's a serious relationship. You have to tell him where you're going, when you'll be back, right?"

"I suppose."

"In other words, there are rules in your house. Some are yours and some are his, and some you share jointly. He's broken one of the rules. You two need to talk."

"You make it all sound so simple and straight-forward."

He placed his arm on the back of the bench behind her. "It can be, if both of you can talk openly about what's bothering you. Adam has things he wants to talk to you about, and you have things you want to talk to him about. If it helps, both of you could make a list of what you need to discuss with each other, starting with the incident the other night."

"I…I'm not sure."

"Give it a try," he said. "Remember that I'm here, and that I'll be seeing Adam later this week."

Gayle reluctantly went back into work. She really wanted to stay in the warm protectiveness of his arm for the rest of the day. The feeling made her wonder even more about his personal life. According to Sherri, he didn't seem to have had a steady relationship since he'd returned to Eden Harbor, which was strange for a man as sexy and nice as Nate.

When the clinic day finished, she went home to find Adam sprawled in front of the television, asleep. She clicked it off, which didn't wake her son, so she started preparations for dinner. She was about halfway through assembling a stuffed pork loin with root vegetables when he appeared at the kitchen door.

"What are you making, Mom?" he asked, yawning as he sat at the table.

"I'm doing a pork dish with veggies," she said, opening the door to the oven and placing the roasting pan on the rack.

"Mom, I... We need to talk."

She settled into the chair across from him, both thankful that he'd brought the subject up and anxious about how the conversation would turn out. She clasped her hands on the table. "Yes, about the other night. You didn't tell me you were having friends over."

"Peggy Anderson told you, didn't she?" Adam asked, scowling.

"Were you having friends over?"

"Why was Peggy sneaking around here? She had no business coming over."

"I couldn't reach her, so she still thought she was supposed to stay with you." Determined to follow Nate's advice, Gayle took a deep, calming breath. "Please tell me you didn't invite them."

"No. They arrived on their own. They were about to leave when Peggy showed up."

"Then why did you tell Peggy they were bringing schoolwork to you?"

Adam scrunched his face and sighed. "Because I knew she wouldn't believe me if I told her they'd just dropped in."

Gayle wanted to scold him for lying, to admonish him for fabricating a story just to stay out of trouble. But wasn't that what she'd been doing all her life? "Adam, I believe you when you say they just dropped by, but who were they? Were they kids from your class?"

Adam ducked his head. "One of them was. The others were the guys I met...that night."

"The night the police brought you home?"

He nodded.

"Oh, Adam. You can't have anything to do with them. Promise me you won't."

He stared at her for a moment. "They didn't mean to get me in trouble. They said it wouldn't happen again. Mom..."

"No excuses. You cannot have anything more to do with them. The police officer said they were trouble and obviously they are. They came over here without calling first. And why didn't you phone me when they arrived?"

"Mom! How would it look if I called you to tell you they were here? I'd be made fun of by every person in the high school." He crooked his fingers into quotation marks. "'This just in.

Mama's boy reported to his mom that his friends came to the door,'" he said, his voice rising with every word.

She was shocked at the anger in his tone, the harshness. This was not how she wanted this conversation to end. She had hoped to follow Nate's advice and talk to her son about the house rules they needed to live by. But she'd lost her cool when she'd learned that Adam's friends were the same ones who had gotten him into trouble with the police.

She took a deep breath, forcing back the awful feeling that life was repeating itself, only this time her son was the victim of bullies who didn't care what their behavior did to him. Harry had hadn't cared what havoc his behavior had created for her, the lies she'd had to tell the police, just like the lies Adam felt he had to tell the other night. She feared where this might lead, and she was powerless to stop it. If Adam continued to be involved with these boys who were already known to the police as troublemakers… "Adam you have to promise not to see or talk to them again."

Adam got up and left the table. The next thing she heard was the loud blaring of the TV in the den.

CHAPTER SEVEN

GAYLE HADN'T SLEPT for the past three nights, and when she finally did fall into an exhausted sleep she dreamed that Harry was with her, yelling words at her she couldn't understand. She woke up frightened and lonely. She hadn't dreamed of her ex-husband in years. It had to have something to do with the past few days.

Nate had taken Adam out bowling last night, but neither said a word when they returned. Adam was back to being sullen and unresponsive with her, and she blamed herself. She shouldn't have let her own fears destroy the chance for them to talk about what had happened the night those boys had come to the house.

Why didn't being a parent come with a foolproof set of instructions? Why couldn't she simply check the index of some book, or go online and find the answer to the question "How do I discourage or stop my child from hanging out with the kids who are trouble?"

Being a parent was easily the hardest job in the world, in her opinion.

She arrived at the clinic with a headache that none of the usual remedies could ease. And if that wasn't enough, they had a full day ahead with the two neurologists here from Bangor and then an afternoon arthritic clinic.

The phone was ringing when she got to her desk, and she scooped it up mostly to stop the noise. It was the lab telling her that the blood work for the afternoon clinic wouldn't be available until noontime, meaning that she'd have to skip her lunch if she was to get the results on each chart before the doctor arrived.

She had pulled the charts for both clinics with the neurology ones in a neat pile on her desk, ready to go. Anna was one of those patients. It was Sherri's day off, but she was going to the neurologist's appointment with Anna.

The clinic nurse, Carolyn Sinclair, approached the desk. "I'll take the charts and put the first patients in their rooms."

Gayle handed the pile to her. "If you don't mind, I need to go to the cafeteria for something to eat. I won't get a break later and my head is hurting. Must be my empty stomach."

"Sure. I'll listen for the phone. Besides, Sherri ought to be here any minute. In a pinch she can man the phones."

Gayle was about to leave her desk when the door opened. Nate walked in, looking so handsome in his blue cotton shirt open at the neck, his dark hair framing his face. She felt all warm and excited at the sight of him.

"What are you doing here?" she asked, trying to keep the exhilaration from her voice.

"I couldn't stay away. I'm hoping Anna's appointment goes okay." He hesitated. "I rearranged my schedule so I could be here."

She hadn't known he was coming. Yet she wasn't that surprised, given how he'd behaved at Anna's house the other night. His kindness toward his sister was so sweet. What she wouldn't give to have a brother like that. Having a family like Nate's would be everything she could wish for. "That's really nice. I'm on my way to get some coffee to try to cure my headache. Want to join me?"

"Lead the way," he said, pivoting on his feet with the support of his cane.

The cafeteria was only a short distance down the corridor from the clinic. She adjusted her stride ever so slightly to keep pace with him. She caught him looking at her, a hint of a smile on his handsome features. It felt so good to walk beside him.

The cafeteria space was painted in bright orange and yellow with turquoise chairs and tables.

"What would you like?" she asked. "I'm buying this time."

They both got a coffee with cream, and she decided on a cranberry muffin. Joining him at the table, she slid into the chair across from him. Something had changed between them since the night at Anna's house. It wasn't just that they had shared a special moment; it was as if they were now on the same team. No. It felt more as if they had some sort of connection beyond a casual one. Whatever it was, she would enjoy it while she could.

Nate sipped his coffee, watching her in a way that made her wish she could sit here with him forever. Searching for a topic of conversation that would distract his thoughts away from Anna's appointment, she said, "My neighbor needs a lesson in trimming his hedge. He started last evening, and when I glanced over this morning the hedge was two feet shorter, and looked like a green roller coaster."

His smile spurred her on. "He should have gotten someone to help him. His wife didn't look any too pleased when I saw her this morning. Come to think of it, that's the first time I've seen her out and about before seven o'clock since I moved in."

He chuckled. Her heart rose in her chest at the sound. She had managed to ease his worry, and it felt wonderful.

But a minute later the wariness was back in

his eyes. "This won't be an easy appointment for Anna, will it?" she said.

SOMETHING ABOUT THE way she flushed a little as her eyes held his made Nate feel good. Real good. Despite the mass of curls floating around her shoulders, she never once flicked her hair away. He used to believe that when a woman constantly played with her hair she was nervous. But he'd seen so many women do it he'd become suspicious that it was a silly affectation to attract attention.

Your cynical side is showing.

His natural reticence stopped him from commenting on how pretty—no, make that beautiful—Gayle Sawyer was this morning. And her beauty wasn't all that he admired. For just a few moments she'd made him forget about Anna's appointment. "You're right. It will be difficult, but there is still more testing to be done, and that always gives us reason to hope that it's some other neuromuscular disease, one less debilitating…"

Her eyes searched his face, alight with interest. "You and Sherri are so good to Anna. She's always been quick to praise both of you. She also told me how difficult it was when your dad died."

"Yeah. I was eleven at the time, just a kid,

and couldn't understand why he was never coming home. For months after he died I waited for him. I didn't tell my mom or Anna what I was doing. I wouldn't let anyone near my dad's things in the basement. Thankfully my mother understood how important it was to me to have them around. Then one day, probably a year or so after Dad passed away, I went into my parents' bedroom to put on a sweatshirt of Dad's. All his clothes were gone."

His gut still hurt at that memory. He tried to meet her caring gaze but couldn't. He cleared his throat. "Not long after that I started skipping school, and I got away with it for quite a while until my English teacher threatened to tell my mother if I did it again. A day later I skipped the last class, and she reported me to the principal and he called Mom." He shrugged off the memory. "Mom got busy and convinced a cop friend of the family to take me under his wing."

"How did Anna react to your father's death?"

"Better than me, but she had Mom. Anna spent a lot of time at Sherri's house with Aunt Colleen. Somehow it seemed to be easier for her."

"So that's how you got involved helping troubled teens. You understood where they were coming from."

"In most cases yes, but I didn't start out with

teens. I was working the beat when I was shot—by a punk kid who shouldn't have had a gun. The good news is that if he had had any marksmanship training, I wouldn't be sitting here today."

Gayle's eyes were wide, glistening with tears. "I'm *so* sorry."

Her sudden tears took him by surprise. "Hey! It wasn't your fault. You had nothing to do with it." He reached in his pocket for a tissue and offered it to her.

Dabbing the corner of her eyes, she smiled at him. "Thank you."

She took a sip of her coffee and seemed to compose herself. "I was so surprised when the lawyer contacted me about Aunt Susan's will. But since I've moved here, everyone I've met has told me what a wonderful person she was. Did you know Aunt Susan well?"

"She was very kind to me. I remember one Mother's Day I wanted to get my mother a bouquet of flowers but I didn't have quite enough money for the ones I wanted. I was really upset as Mom and I had been going through a rough time, and I wanted to make it up to her somehow."

"What did she do?" Gayle asked, the look on her face so focused on him he felt something stir deep inside him. She was really listening to him, and she genuinely wanted to understand what he'd experienced.

He had the urge to kiss her right here in the cafeteria, but with a huge effort on his part, he refused the invitation of her lips, and the dark curl lying so invitingly on her cheek. "Your aunt rang up the exact amount of money I had, added a beautiful red organza ribbon, wrapped the flowers in florist's paper and sent me on my way. I never forgot that."

"You must have been one of her favorite neighborhood kids." Her smile was warm and inclusive.

He wanted to hold her attention, to bask in her wonderful smile. "After that, I let her know that if she needed any help with groceries or errands done I'd do it for her. She made the best raisin cookies I've ever eaten."

"I don't think I've ever had a raisin cookie," she said, a wistful smile turning up the corners of her lips.

"You haven't lived until you've had one made by the ladies in Eden Harbor. Those cookies are one of the town's greatest delicacies."

She compressed her lips and looked away, leaving him to wonder what he'd said to upset her.

"If you play your cards right, I just might take you on a tasting expedition to the Cream Puff

Bakery. There are several versions of this illustrious cookie," he said, hoping for the reappearance of her lovely smile.

Gayle finished her coffee in silence. "I'm sorry, but I really need to get back to work." She didn't meet his gaze as she got up from the table.

"Oh! Of course. I'll walk with you."

As they moved along the corridor, he chose his moment carefully. Touching her arm he pulled her to a halt. "One of the things I planned to say back there was that you and I have to talk about Adam. He needs help, and you and I should talk about that in private."

Her eyes darkened with worry. "I know we do." She sighed, and for half a second he thought she was going to lean into his arms.

The thought startled him. Deep down he knew that he would have welcomed her. Quelling the impulse to reach out to her, he scrambled to come up with a meeting time. "Why don't we get together after your shift?"

She glanced around. "Where? Adam is supposed to be home studying for a test."

"Could we meet here in the cafeteria?"

"Won't Anna need you?"

"Oh, yeah, maybe."

"Adam usually studies in his room. You'll want to spend time with Anna when her appointment is over. If you like, we could sit out in my backyard. I'll be around all evening, so don't rush."

He wanted to spend time with her very much. Just being around her made him feel…excited about life. The idea unnerved him. As caring and kind as she was, Gayle was not his type of woman—the kind of woman who might want to get close, or worse still, have him wanting her in a real way, not simply as a casual relationship.

"You feel you can't leave Adam alone right now because of those teenagers the other night?"

She lowered her head in defeat.

"I understand. I'll meet you at your place around seven this evening?"

"Yes," she said before turning away from him, and striding down the corridor.

GAYLE DID HER best to concentrate on her clinic duties for the rest of the day, but her worry over Anna, and Nate's presence in the clinic, made it difficult to maintain her outward calm. She had really enjoyed coffee with him. When he'd followed her back into the clinic she'd found herself wondering what it would be like to have dinner with him. A real date. Having a wonderful evening with him during which they focused only on each other would be a life-changing event for her.

She had been out to a real dining room with a

real date only once, and it had ended badly. The man had insisted that, since he'd bought dinner and drinks, she owed him. Regardless of how much she'd like to go out with Nate, his interest in talking about Adam really worried her. She remembered Ted Marston's remark that mentoring included getting to know Adam's family background, which would mean questions about his father. Nate's history as a police officer would suggest that he'd know how to question her, to get answers she didn't want to offer. Because she had to protect her past, she couldn't accept a real date with Nate, even if he asked.

After what Peggy had told her and Adam's recent behavior, she was seriously concerned about her son's willingness to lie to her. Sure, teenagers often hid the truth, but this was more serious, or at least she felt it was. The root cause of her worry came from her fear that Adam might turn out to be like his father.

She glanced around the waiting room as if in a daze. Had Anna already been taken to an exam room? And if so, how had she missed it?

"I just put Anna Barker in exam five," Carolyn Sinclair said as she approached Gayle's desk. "She's the last patient."

The waiting dragged on. Finally the clinic came to an end. Anna, Nate and Sherri hadn't stopped by the desk when they left, leaving

Gayle to worry about what the neurologist had told them.

She finished filing and was getting up to leave when she got a call from Adam. He wanted her to bring home a pizza for dinner. She had planned to cook chicken curry tonight, but pizza was easier, and since Adam had called and asked, she felt it might prove helpful in restarting their conversation. Besides, pleasing Adam somehow made her feel better about everything.

When she reached the house with the pizza, Adam was waiting.

"I've got a science project I'm working on." He brushed his hands through his hair. "I gotta get a decent mark on this."

She was relieved to hear him talk about doing well on the assignment, a positive thing in her mind. "Why don't you take your pizza and soda up to your room and work there? Nate is coming over later this evening to see me." She placed the pizza on the counter, opened the box and took a pizza cutter out of the drawer.

"What does he want?"

She looked up and met Adam's intense gaze. Her first impulse was to make up an excuse for Nate's visit, but she wanted her son to be honest with her, which meant she had to be honest with him. She had to tell him the truth. "He's coming here to talk about you. I have no idea what he wants to tell me, but whatever it is…" She touched his arm, wishing she could hug him close the way she used to do. "I know this whole thing with Nate is going to work out for you. I have faith in him. Don't you?"

Adam pulled away and went to the cupboard for plates. "Yeah, he's cool," he said, but his voice lacked enthusiasm.

She watched helplessly as her son gathered up his supper and went to his room without saying another word. Where had her sweet little boy—the one she'd dedicated her life to all these years—gone? She longed for the days when Adam would come racing home from school, excited about something he was planning with his friends, or a subject the teacher had talked about in class.

She remembered one day when Adam had fallen at the school playground and the teacher had called her. She'd raced to the school, her heart pounding, and the look of relief and love shining from her son's eyes had made that moment unforgettable.

She was still thinking about Adam when the doorbell rang.

Shaken from her reverie, she went to answer it.

"Is that for me?" Adam called from his room.

She glanced through the side panes, immediately aware of a set of broad shoulders.

A man outside her door. A nice man who wanted to help her, not get her into bed.

"No. It's Nate."

"Oh" was all Adam said, but his tone told her he'd hoped that some of his friends were stopping by to see him.

She opened the door.

"You remembered I was coming over tonight, right?" Nate asked, a look of mild surprise on his face.

"Oh! Yes, come in. I was just out in the kitchen."

He followed her. Spotting the open box on the counter, he said, "How much do you want for a slice?"

"You haven't eaten, either." She felt so happy to have him standing across from her with that engaging grin on his face.

"You got that right."

"Why don't we take the pizza and something to drink outside? I'm sure I have a bottle of red wine somewhere around here," she said, glancing at the wine rack built onto the end of the wooden counter.

"I'll get the glasses," he offered, and they gathered up what would be dinner for both of them and headed outside.

The backyard was illuminated by the light from the street behind her house and the neighbors' windows next door. She led him to the table and chairs that sat on a patch of patio she'd built near the back of the lot.

He opened the wine and poured them each a glass. They ate in silence, both hungrier than they'd realized. When they finished, she said, "I have some homemade gingerbread if you'd like a slice."

He leaned back in his chair. "Why don't we enjoy our wine while I tell you about Adam? When we're finished, we can have dessert."

"Okay."

She waited, the night air chilling her arms. He topped up their wine. She reached for her glass before settling as far back in the chair as she possibly could, the feel of the wood a comfort.

NATE NOTED THE anxious lift of her shoulders, the way she pulled her pink turtleneck closer to her chin as she watched him. His eyes followed her hand, the tentative touch of her fingers to her throat. He forced his own hands into his lap in order not to reach for her. In that moment he knew that he would like the chance to get to know her better. But that had to be in the future, once he'd done what he could for her son.

Meanwhile, he had to be careful what he said.

He had to make a convincing argument if he was going to get her to cooperate with his plan for Adam. "Thank you for dinner."

A ghost of a smile flitted across her face. "It was only pizza."

"Dinner for a starving man was what it was," he said gently, waiting for her eyes to meet his. When they didn't, he decided to use the direct approach.

"Adam is a smart young man who wants to do well in school. But that's not easy for him because the friends he has right now think that doing well in school is stupid. He's afraid that if he gets good marks, they'll drop him. Or worse, they'll spread the word that he's a complete nerd, someone to be avoided. At his age, it's really easy to get taken in by other, seemingly more adult, members of the class. No one wants to be seen as inept socially or unable to make friends, especially not a teenager looking for acceptance in a new place."

"I can identify with that," Gayle said, taking another sip of her wine.

He forced his eyes away from her lips as they touched the glass. "He's not comfortable enough in his own skin right now to see that he is capable of finding new friends. And it didn't help that he missed out on making the basketball team."

Gayle put her glass on the table with a thud. "I don't understand why he didn't. He's good. I went to a couple of practices and he seemed to be doing fine. I never played basketball, so I have no idea about his skill level or anything like that. All I know is that he was devastated when he didn't make the team, and so was I. I had hoped that he'd find new friends there."

"I spoke to Coach Cassidy, and he says that Adam is not a team player, that he's a loner."

Her eyes were angry when she looked at him. "But wouldn't you be that way if you were the new kid and all the others had played together before?"

How quickly she'd come to his defense. She clearly had not lost faith in her son. "Yeah, you might be right. Since I grew up and played basketball here, I didn't take into consideration how much of an outsider he must feel like. Basketball is a team sport. Playing and practicing together is what makes a team cohesive and therefore successful on the court."

"And what looked like being a loner, not a team player, might simply be the fact that he hadn't really found his place on the team. He played basketball in Anaheim and did well. It was the whole focus of his life until he got mixed up with one of the kids up the block from us…"

Her voice trailed off, and even in the low light of the yard he could see the anxious expression on her face.

"I had hoped I could help Adam with this. I tried to convince Coach Cassidy to give him another chance, but he said he already had more than enough players. He'd had to turn down several other talented kids, not just Adam. But maybe next year he'll make the cut."

Gayle cupped her wineglass in her hands and took a sip. "Thanks for trying."

"You're welcome," he said, waiting for her to respond in some way. He'd never had to wait for a woman to talk to him in his entire life. Women were always anxious to talk, to flirt or gain his attention in some way.

What he wouldn't give to simply sit here in the quiet of the evening and enjoy this woman's company, to discuss anything other than her son. After what his sister had experienced this afternoon, and what he knew he had to discuss with Gayle, he wanted to forget his responsibilities and just be with her. To spend time with her, watching her smile, inhaling her scent… touching her.

Hey, go careful here.

He sighed. Not tonight. Tonight he had to do his job. "But that's not all I need to talk to you about."

"I'm AWARE OF THAT," she said, feeling the air around her turn cooler. Or was it her fear making her feel chilled? Just a few moments ago she was so sure he wanted to touch her. Or was it her own need to be touched by him that had made her believe that?

"What Adam really needs is to feel connected to people, to family. To feel valued by those he loves and who love him."

"I love Adam. I wasn't aware that I didn't make him feel valued," she said a little defensively.

"He has expressed an interest in connecting to family, and I was wondering if there might be a relative on his father's side that he was close to in Anaheim."

She had to stick to her lie about Adam's father, but at least she could tell the truth about her only remaining family member—if you could call him that. "There was no one. I have a half brother, Alfred McGuire, but we've never been close. I think he's living somewhere in Hawaii."

"That's too bad."

His words were so gentle she wanted to reach for him, feel his arms around her, admit the truth to him.

"Adam never had an opportunity to know him." She waited for Nate to ask her more questions about her brother, prepared to steer the conversation to a safer topic if need be.

"Adam told me about the incident with Peggy Anderson."

A sigh of relief slid past her lips. He must have decided to drop the subject of her family. "He did?"

"You sound surprised."

She rubbed her neck to ease the tense muscles. "What did he tell you?"

"That his friends dropped over unexpectedly. Peggy saw them and told you. When I asked him about those friends, he didn't say much. I'm guessing that they chose him, knowing he was the new kid in school, and he needed to be accepted. Adam is searching for his place in the world, and so getting involved with these boys was almost inevitable."

Her chest tightened. Her pulse slowed. "What can we do? What can *I* do?"

Nate rubbed his palms together slowly, as if in thought. "I'll keep seeing him, and in the meantime, you need to widen your base of friends and contacts here."

Feeling the sting of rebuke, she turned on him. "I work full-time, and I have a teenage son who needs me to be around for him. That doesn't leave a lot of room for socializing." She knew by the surprised look in his eyes that he hadn't expected her sharp response. She softened her tone. "I met Anna at the single-parents group."

"What about coworkers?"

"Sherri and I are friends, but you already know that."

"Do you confide in her?"

She would never confide in anyone, if it meant risking them finding out about her past. "A little, but since she and Neill got back together our conversations have mostly been about her wedding."

"Anyone else?"

"Peggy Anderson, but we don't see each other outside of work. Peggy invited Adam over to see her two horses one day a few weekends ago, but he didn't seem to be that interested. Can't say I am, either. Peggy loves them."

"Do you have any contact with the parents of kids Adam's age?"

"I have Anna. Jeremy is Adam's age."

He nodded his head slowly. "Does Adam have contact with him at school?"

"Yeah, I'm quite sure he does."

"Then I'll bring Jeremy up the next time I'm alone with Adam. It would be a good place to start in developing a circle of friends. Jeremy's a good kid. Anyone else?"

"The night he was picked up by the police, he

was with Derrick Little, a boy from his class. Although I doubt Derrick's mother would want Adam hanging around her son after that incident. He's had a couple of calls from Morgan Brandon."

"That's Neill's daughter. She's a really nice girl and she's also new to Eden Harbor."

"I think he might be interested in her," Gayle said.

"How do you know?"

"Mother's instinct, and the fact that he blushed when I brought up her name."

"That's interesting," Nate said, rubbing his jaw in thought.

Her eyes met his. She yearned to confide in him, to tell him how much she wanted a normal life—the kind of life people in Eden Harbor took for granted. Tears welled up; her throat filled. She swallowed.

His eyes held hers. She couldn't look away from the caring she saw on his face. It was as if time stood still, as if no one existed but them. She had never felt like this ever in her life.

Nate rose from his chair, came around the table and pulled her gently to her feet. "Gayle, this is going to work out, you'll see. You have to trust me, and you must trust Adam. He needs to know that you love and trust him."

She focused on the buttons of his shirtfront, fearing that to look into his eyes would be to lose control. "I came to Eden Harbor so certain that I'd made the right decision for Adam and me. I've worked so hard to build a life here for both of us." She bit her lip to keep from telling Nate how lonely she had been. No man would want a woman whose life had been as sad and lonely as hers. "What seemed like a dream come true back in Anaheim is turning into a frightening mess. I don't know what to do..." She choked back a sob.

"Shh..." His hands on her arms were warm and strong. Slowly he pulled her to him, his face angled to hers, his breath hot on her cheek. She breathed in his scent, lifting her chin to draw closer to him.

His lips were so close to hers she could feel their heat. No man had ever been this gentle and caring with her. Suddenly her heart jumped in her chest. She offered a silent prayer that he wouldn't let go, that he would kiss her and wipe away her loneliness. She eased up on her tiptoes as her hands slid up to the open neck of his shirt.

With an anguished sigh, her lips played over his chin, along the edge of his mouth. Groaning in pleasure, he pulled her into his arms, his mouth on hers, crushing the air from her lungs.

All the pent-up emotion of the past weeks and years clashed with her iron self-control, overwhelming it in a rush of passion that drove her to cling to him, aching for more than just a kiss. So much more.

He pulled away, his breathing jagged, his eyes dark. Before she knew what was happening, he was on the other side of the table, reaching for his cane. He was leaving her. Hurt and disbelief made her knees buckle. She grabbed the chair to steady herself, wiping her lips with the back of her hand. "I'm sorry."

"Sorry for what?" he asked, the gentle tone having abandoned his voice.

She couldn't answer him. She couldn't let him see the tears pooling on her cheeks. He must not be allowed in on her newest secret. That with one kiss he'd seared her heart and her life. In that same instant it dawned on her. Nate would not seriously be attracted to a woman whose only sexual experience had been with a husband who took what he wanted. A husband whose idea of sex was harsh and uncaring.

She fixed her gaze on the rhododendron leaning against the fence at the back of her property while she waited for him to cross the yard toward the house.

"Gayle, look at me." His words hummed in the still night air.

Her eyes sought his. He was standing there looking like someone who had lost something. "Gayle, that kiss was a mistake. I shouldn't have done it."

"What do you mean? Why shouldn't you have done it?" she asked. When he turned from her she wanted to pull him back, make him answer her.

"I'm taking Adam to the movies this week. I will do everything in my power to see that he's okay. I want you to trust me on that."

To trust was to allow someone close enough to influence her life. Trust meant that when people failed you—and they did on a regular basis in Gayle's experience—you were the one left picking up the pieces. "I'm not very good when it comes to trust."

Turning back, he nodded in agreement. A smile softened his features. "All you need to do is risk a little, and see that there are people in your life who will be there for you. You're not alone, Gayle. You're not."

Her heart trembled with the force of the emotion flooding through her. She'd always been alone, always distrustful. It would take more than this man's kindness to change that history. "Sometimes...I wish..."

He leaned on his cane, and still he towered over her, filling her with hope and dread. "I'll be in touch," he said before turning back toward the house.

CHAPTER EIGHT

A COUPLE OF days had passed since she and Nate had been together in her backyard. They proved to be long days for Gayle. The memory of his kiss had been so perfect—until he'd walked out. She hadn't heard from him since that evening, and had been driven a little crazy by how much he'd made her want him. Sherri hadn't mentioned anything, which probably meant that Nate had said nothing to her about that evening.

Face it. Attraction is as rare in your life as sex.

THE PHONE WAS ringing when Gayle arrived home from work. Caller ID identified it as Nate's number. She answered before putting her groceries on the table.

"I'm taking Adam to the movies tonight, and wondered if you might like to meet us for dinner afterward."

After the other night, an invitation out to dinner was the last thing she expected. What had changed? "Yes. Yes, I'd like that," she said, dropping her bag of groceries on the counter to the sound of at least one egg breaking.

"We'll meet you outside Pastelli's around eight o'clock."

"Great. I'll be waiting," she said, trying to sound upbeat, in control and just a little bit sexy. Still reeling from the invitation, she sat down on the chair with a hard thump. Excitement rose through her at the thought that she would be having dinner with Nate Garrison. With Adam there, surely Nate wouldn't ask her questions about her past. She could look forward to something fun and exciting for a change.

Suddenly energized, she cleaned up the mess from the broken eggs and was singing along to Lady Gaga when Adam got home from school.

"Mom, are you all right?" he asked, dropping his backpack onto the sofa and joining her in the kitchen.

"I am. Grab a snack before the show. Nate has invited you and me out to dinner when your movie is over."

"You're kidding! What's he want with *you*?"

"Adam! That's not very nice."

"I didn't mean it that way. But you guys talked for hours the other night. Remember?"

There was no way she'd ever forget that night, and that kiss. "You were supposed to be doing your project."

"I was. But I'm not as completely zoned out as you think I am. I know he didn't leave here until later in the evening, so you must have got all your talking done then."

"We're adults. There are always things to talk about. Besides, is it such a crime for me to join you and Nate for dinner?"

In a dramatic gesture, Adam swept his arms wide. "Is this a date? Will I be in the way?" A grin lit up his face.

"No date. Just dinner. Can you handle that at your tender age?" she asked, happy to be teasing him.

"Watch me." He spun around pretending to peer through a pair of binoculars at his mother. "I'll be keeping an eye on both of you."

He whistled as he went upstairs. She listened to the sound of doors closing, the shower running.

WAY TO GO, Mom, Adam thought as he peeled off his jeans and T-shirt and climbed into the shower. His mom was seriously excited about going to dinner with him and Nate. And the two of them were together the other night. Were his mom and Nate going to start dating? He sure hoped so. Nate was really cool, and he didn't get upset or angry when Adam talked about things that really bothered him. He didn't make light of his worries, either.

So many things were going his way today. His science project had gotten him an A, resulting in Derrick Little coming up to him after class wanting to know if he'd like to hang out, maybe go skateboarding this weekend.

He scrubbed his head in happiness. Going with Derrick wouldn't mean he'd have to lie to his mom. He hated lying to her. He hated it. She'd always been the best mom, but lately he didn't seem to be able to connect with her. But when she got his good news about the science project, she'd be really happy. He wasn't quite prepared to share his other news. He got out of the shower and toweled off. When he returned to his room, he pulled on clean clothes and dialed the number Morgan Brandon had given him.

She answered on the first ring—not cool, but still, it had to mean she was waiting for his call. "Morgan, I… How are you?" he asked, realizing at just that exact second how much of a nerd he sounded like.

"Hi, Adam. I'm fine."

Crap! He couldn't remember what he wanted to talk to her about. What was it? He rubbed his head in thought.

"Adam? Are you there?"

He rolled his eyes in frustration. "Yes."

"What did you want?"

He wanted to ask her to the dance, but suddenly he worried that she might be going with someone else. He recovered enough to say, "Would you like to come over and study here with me tomorrow?"

"Will your mom be there? My dad will want to know," she said, and he could hear her sigh.

"If you want her here, she'll be here," he said, trying to show by his words that he was in control just like Eddie said.

"Okay. Look, I've got to go. I'm not supposed to be talking on the phone when my homework isn't finished."

"Nothing to worry about. See you at school," he said, hanging up. He'd done it. He'd called Morgan and she hadn't laughed at him. She hadn't refused to study with him. She was the coolest girl in his class. His hand shook as he put the phone down. He wouldn't have to worry about his classmates laughing at him, not as long as Morgan Brandon liked him. Every guy in his class thought she was cute. He'd be the envy of them all.

He did a couple of shadow punches for good measure, just the way Eddie did. He couldn't wait for tomorrow and the chance to see if Morgan would go to the dance with him. He needed to talk to Eddie about how to approach this whole thing. He wouldn't admit that he'd chickened out earlier.

Now all he had to do was ask her tomorrow at school. Maybe Nate would help him…or not. He didn't seem like the kind of guy who knew much about women. If he did, he'd be married by now, wouldn't he?

Eddie said that after sex a woman's next job was to keep their man happy in the kitchen, making meals, ironing, that sort of thing. Adam didn't know how a woman would keep a job and do everything around the house. But then again, his mom did most things around their house. So he hadn't argued with Eddie. He didn't have any experience, so for all he knew Eddie was right.

He heard his mom calling from the hall downstairs. Smoothing his mop of hair over his brow, he called out to her, "Hold your horses. I'm coming."

ADAM CAME CLATTERING back down the wooden stairs into the front hall. He'd changed his jeans for a clean pair and put on a shirt she'd bought him, one he'd threatened to put in the recycling bin. Before he went out the door, he gave her a salute, a teasing look in his eyes. "I'll be seeing you at Pastelli's."

He was on the front porch when Nate drove up. As he walked down the sidewalk and climbed into the car, she saw not only her son, but a handsome teenager who was on the brink of adulthood whether she was ready for it or not. She hugged herself in excitement. Adam was the best thing that had ever happened to her, and she was about to spend a very pleasant evening with the only two males on the planet she cared about.

Gayle had tried on half her wardrobe by the time she settled on a pair of navy blue pants and a navy-and-green top. She told herself not to get her hopes up, that this was dinner with her son and a man she genuinely liked—a friend.

Yet as she stared at her image in the mirror, she recognized the truth. She was seriously attracted to Nate, a man who by Sherri's account had women hanging off him at every turn. And yet he had invited her to dinner this evening. So maybe the invitation had more to do with her son than wanting quality time with her, but all the same…

She tucked her shirt into her pants and swung around to get a better look at herself. She worried the pants might be baggy, as she'd lost a few pounds in the past couple of months. She slipped into her sandals and went into the bathroom to check her makeup.

You're going all out tonight, she thought, giving her eyelashes one more coat of mascara.

She stopped with the wand halfway to her right eye. What was the likelihood that he'd be interested in her? After all, one kiss did not make a relationship.

"Besides," she muttered at the mirror, "he hasn't actually asked you out on a date. Stop making more of this than it is—just dinner."

When had she started talking to herself? She sighed. Brushed on a little more lipstick, grabbed her jacket, locked the house and headed out to her car.

She arrived at the restaurant and went in. Nate and Adam were already in a booth near the back. Adam slid over to let her sit down, placing her directly across from Nate, and for a few seconds their legs tangled under the table. *Sorry* was on her lips, but tonight she decided that she would not say that word. She'd said it and thought it far too many times in her life.

They ordered, and when the food arrived they ate and talked together. Gayle spent the entire time trying to keep her eyes off Nate, which was nearly impossible given that he was sitting there, his gaze moving from Adam to her throughout the meal. Adam and Nate talked like old friends, and Gayle was so happy to see her son engaged in real conversation for a change.

What sort of person would her son be now if he'd had a father like Nate all these years?

Would he be talking about going to college? Would he be on the basketball team? Where would they have been living if she'd married a decent man? Would there have been more children? She'd always dreamed of having a house filled with children...

If he'd had a real father, would Adam still be having problems finding friends? She doubted it.

"Gayle, are you okay?" Nate asked.

She forced a bright smile. "Yes. I'm fine. Why do you ask?"

"You looked so sad for a few moments..."

She glanced over at her son, who had a goofy look on his face, and back at Nate, whose expression was one of genuine concern.

Stay in the present moment. Don't let your thoughts ruin this wonderful evening.

Her heart lifted in her chest, and she felt warm all over. "I'm fine, really."

She was more than fine, but she needed a break from Nate's intense scrutiny. "I'm going to the ladies' room." She scooted out of the booth and headed to the restroom, passing the long panel of glass behind the bar without looking up. In the restroom, she spotted the high points of color on her cheeks.

She felt like a schoolgirl—silly, awkward and excited by how the evening was going. It wasn't a date, but it was certainly the first time she'd had dinner with a man and really enjoyed it. Wouldn't it be nice if this happened again?

NATE WATCHED GAYLE leave the table, his mind on the evening and how much he'd enjoyed it so far. When he'd invited her along, it was because he needed to see how Adam and she related to each other in a social setting away from the conflicts arising from day-to-day living. Now he recognized just what a dilemma he had gotten himself into.

He hadn't been prepared for tonight, for the easy way he and Gayle talked, her open attention to him, the things he said only to see her smile.

He had never been with anyone who appealed to him more than Gayle did. When he'd first met her, he'd been attracted to her, found her different from other women. But now he found himself viewing each day in terms of whether or not he'd be seeing her.

Thankfully this evening he'd been able to legitimately say that they were out together to help him better understand his client. But in understanding his client, he'd come to understand a little about Adam's mother and her courage in raising a child alone.

Yet he had to admit there was more to his feelings than simply admiration. Her vulnerability drew him to her, made him want to protect her from whatever had caused the desolation he'd seen in her eyes the other night in her backyard.

As she walked toward him from the ladies' room, her hair swirled around her face as she moved, the curve of her hips making his body tighten. He had to be very careful not to have her misunderstand that helping her son came first. Yet he hadn't been out with a woman who made him feel this good for a very long time.

Gayle slid back into the booth across from him, her legs brushing against his. Their eyes met. He wanted to reach across the table and take her hand in his, simply to touch her. For a few seconds he thought she was about to do the same. She hadn't moved her legs, and he could feel their warmth through the fabric of her pants.

"What about dessert?" Adam asked.

"Sure," Nate said, still focused on Gayle.

"Do they have chocolate cake?" Adam glanced around the restaurant. "Hey, Mom, are you having dessert?"

"I'll ask the waitress for a dessert menu," Nate said, continuing to watch her, the way she pressed her lips together, the hesitant smile that turned up the corners of her luscious mouth.

"Hello, you two," Adam said. "I'm here, wondering if we're going to have dessert."

They both laughed at the same time. With an effort Nate turned his gaze to Adam. "Absolutely."

NATE HAD TO admit that he felt a little let down when it came time to leave. At the same time he was relieved to be able to focus on something other than how he was feeling, and how those feelings were making him want to do something he probably shouldn't do.

He'd followed her back to her place on the pretext of wanting to speak to her for a few minutes. But the cop in him wanted to see for himself that she got home safely. When they arrived in the driveway, he got out and followed Gayle to the door. Adam went in ahead of them while Nate waited with her. As they reached the front step, he couldn't stop himself from breathing in the strawberry scent of her hair. He could feel the warmth of her body so near his, and wished to hell he could run away.

But running away wasn't the answer, any more than kissing her senseless and following her into her house. He settled for searching out the right words to let her down easy and give him an opportunity to escape before he did something he might later regret.

She lifted her hair off her shoulders, exposing the white skin at the nape of her neck. "I'd invite you in, but it's late, and I have to work tomorrow," she said, her hand reaching out to him in farewell.

In that instant he lost all semblance of control and did what he'd wanted to do all evening.

NATE LEANED DOWN and kissed her hard on the mouth, his hand coming around the back of her head and holding her lips against his. His kiss was hot and demanding, sweeping every rational thought from her head. Driven by the pressure of his lips, she wrapped her arms around him, letting her body lean into his, soaking up the warmth. Giving in to her need, she returned his kiss, opening her mouth to his, kissing him, holding him, her hands working over his back, her breathing rapid and erratic.

All the lonely years, the lack of love and attention, were swept away by an overwhelming need to feel his heat, his body pressed to hers. His hands holding her head in a gentle vice, he continued to kiss her lips, moving inexorably toward her throat.

She groaned her pleasure, delighted in his touch.

His body eased away from hers. His hands released her, pulling away as he awkwardly grasped his cane resting against the wrought iron railing. His jaw worked as he stared down into her eyes.

"We can't do this. You're my client. I mean, your son is my client." His eyes were dark, his breathing harsh, his expression tight. "I have to go."

And before she had a chance to speak or to respond in any way, he was gone. The icy pain of abandonment shimmied through her. Her body ached for him while her mind scrambled to understand what had just happened, yet was too numb to make sense of it. She backed into the house, leaning against the door frame for protection from the thoughts flooding her consciousness.

She had never been kissed that way.

She'd never kissed anyone that way in her life until now.

She had never felt this vulnerable in her entire life.

NATE DROVE AS if possessed, vaguely aware that he was speeding, but he didn't care. He could still taste her lips, feel her arms and smell her hair, those lustrous curls that his fingers had been drawn to like magnets.

When he'd kissed her that night in her backyard, it had been a trial run. He'd wanted to know how she would respond to him, and he'd felt certain that she wanted more when he left her place. Hell! He'd taken a certain pride in the idea.

But tonight was a whole different story. He'd wanted her in a way he'd never wanted another woman in his life. He wanted to be around her, to get to know her and what mattered to her. He wanted to make love to her all night, to wake up beside her in the morning and know that she would be there. What the hell had happened to him back there? What had he done?

She was not his type. She would never be his type. He was attracted to her vulnerability. That had been what first attracted him to Natasha. She'd been a woman who'd sought his support for everything in her life from the time they were teenagers. He'd willingly become part of a couple in which he had to be there for her, every moment. They'd shared everything. He'd wanted to marry Natasha Burnham, and had believed they were meant for each other. After she'd broken their engagement, he'd intentionally dated women he didn't really feel a connection to. A casual relationship was so much easier, leaving little opportunity for him to develop feelings for the woman.

Until Gayle.

And now he'd left himself vulnerable to another woman. And he was damn scared that getting involved with Gayle could lead to another painful end.

Besides, he was happy just the way he was, wasn't he? Without thinking he pulled onto the highway leading toward Bangor and drove faster. He *was* happy, dammit!

He had every man's dream life. A good job. Great digs. Great friends. Women who met his needs.

He had it all.

So why was he feeling so mixed-up? What was it about Gayle that made him wish…

He slowed down and pulled over. Resting his arms on the steering wheel, he stared out at the starlit night. He'd always been in control of his life, his career. He prided himself on that, and being a cop was a natural career choice for him. Even when his life had careened out of control that fateful day of the shooting, he'd regained his equilibrium by doing everything he could to get back to his normal self.

He'd even hidden his feelings of disappointment when he'd learned he would not walk without a cane ever again. He never let anyone see how much he despised having to use that cane. He'd hidden his anger behind a show of bravado that fooled everyone. He had always been proud of the way he'd handled himself during those months of hospitalization and treatment.

He was that good at being in control. But having to face rejection from the one woman he believed would accept him no matter what had forced him to abandon control of everything. When Natasha had told him she wanted out of their relationship, he'd felt her pity like a knife blade through his ribs. When she'd returned his engagement ring, he'd been forced to coax her into reconsidering what she was doing. He loved her. He couldn't imagine living without her.

The months after, long months spent regaining his identity, finding out who he was and what he wanted out of life, had shown him that loving someone, being vulnerable to their control over his life, was the wrong move for him.

Back there in the restaurant, he'd wanted to make love to Gayle, and at her door he'd nearly succumbed to his desire. He couldn't hand control of his life over to another woman. He couldn't feel the need he'd been feeling, the ache to be with her, and not in a casual way.

She could hurt him. That was what frightened him most. He would never expose himself to the possibility of being hurt that way again.

He sat for a while longer, forcing his thoughts away from the evening and how close he'd come to letting Gayle Sawyer get under his skin. He rubbed the back of his neck and drew in a deep, cleansing breath.

Being around Gayle was a mistake he couldn't afford to repeat.

THE NEXT WEEK, Gayle was picking up a prescription at the local pharmacy when she spotted Nate in the checkout line two people ahead of her. Keeping her head down to avoid making eye contact, she waited her turn, thankful for the wide shoulders of the man standing directly in front of her.

She gave a small sigh of relief when she saw Nate going through the sliding doors to the street. There was no way she wanted to see him without some plan, some way to escape. After the way he'd kissed her the other night, she had to keep her distance from him. She wanted what his lips had offered. She found herself needing him, missing him, wanting him—all emotions that didn't belong in her life. She'd spent a sleepless night after he left, her heart aching for what he offered, her heart breaking for what he'd denied her when he left so abruptly. When dawn had come, and along with it her feeling of losing out on life once more, she'd had to face the truth. Nate had regretted kissing her. He didn't want any part of what those few moments might have led to.

She paid the cashier and went out the doors to the parking lot, only to find Nate leaning on the post next to the disabled parking spot, his cane cocked against his leg.

"I thought that was you in there. Where's your car?"

"I didn't bring it. I needed a walk and decided to leave the car at home."

"Want me to walk back with you? I'm picking Adam up in an hour to take him for his first swimming lesson at the YMCA. It's part of the program for teenagers, and I thought it might be a chance for him to be involved in a sport... after not making the basketball team."

"That's very kind of you," she said, feeling both grateful and frustrated with him at the same time. How could he kiss her senseless one minute, walk out on her the next and then offer to accompany her home as if nothing happened?

She tried not to look at his cane or let him see that she was concerned that the walk to her house was too far for him. "Sure, I guess. If you'd like to. But what about your car?"

"I'll walk back and pick it up. I could use a little exercise."

She hesitated.

"Look, you let me worry about whether I can make the distance," he said, his tone hard.

Obviously Nate was annoyed, but maybe that

was best for both of them. He made her jittery and on edge, anxious and excited. He'd turned her world on its side all because of a kiss. She'd lain awake well into the middle of the night, remembering the touch of his lips on hers, the heat of his body. All the agony of that night made one fact undeniable. It was easier to forget his kiss if he behaved like an ogre. She turned toward the street. "Fine. Let's go."

They walked in silence for most of the two blocks to her house. She had to admit that Nate's injury didn't seem to slow him down one little bit.

As they turned the corner onto her street, she noticed a motorbike parked along the curb in front of her house. Suddenly very anxious, she sped up. When she reached the house, she went inside to find two older-looking teenagers in her living room and the music blasting from Adam's bedroom directly above.

"Well, what do we have here?" one of the teenagers drawled.

She felt her head pound in anger, her breath come in short gasps. "Who are you? What are you doing in my house?" she asked, looking from one to the other. "And where is Adam?"

"I'm right here, Mom. And these are my friends." Adam came and stood between the two young men.

"Adam, turn down your music, please."

"Mom, stop bossing me around. We're only here for a few minutes and then I'm going out."

"It's a school night."

"So?" Adam said, his tone cocky.

The door closed quietly behind her. She was aware of Nate standing beside her.

"Adam, do as your mother asks. Boys, get out of here before I call the police," Nate said, his tone demonstrating that he would accept nothing less than compliance.

Adam went up the stairs, his boots slamming into the steps, while the two boys left the house. Gayle clasped her hands together to keep them from shaking. "Thank you. I don't know if I could have handled this without you."

Nate remained at the door, his eyes unreadable. "Yes, you could. Adam is your son, and he has to respect you."

She shook her head, swallowed against the lump in her throat and sat down on the sofa. "What am I going to do with Adam? He isn't paying any attention to what I want. This is the second time he's had people in my house without my knowledge or permission." She glanced up at him. "Nate, I'm afraid."

"Let me handle this. I'll take Adam to his lesson and when I bring him back we'll talk."

After Nate and Adam left the house, Gayle

tried to eat something, but couldn't. She settled for a chocolate bar and a long soak in the tub, but nothing seemed to help. She was waiting at the door when they came back, her anxiety constricting her throat. Adam went to his room, mumbling that he had homework to do.

"Would you like a cup of coffee?" She managed to get those few words past her dry lips.

"That would be great. Adam's lesson went well. I think he'll enjoy them, and at least have a chance to meet other kids outside of school."

Nate's voice was devoid of any emotion. He didn't look at her when she brought the coffeepot to the table and placed it on a heat-proof coaster. If only there was a quick and easy answer, but by the look on Nate's face, she knew how futile that hope was. How had things gotten so out of hand?

"I'm losing him, aren't I?"

"Adam is struggling to find his place at the moment. It would be really helpful if he had more family, but since that isn't possible, more structure, more opportunity to interact with people who care about him, would be very good for him."

"I *care* about him. I *love* him," she said, letting her exasperation show.

"You love him, but you need to set boundaries for him."

"I do. No TV until his homework is done. No friends in during the school week. An eleven o'clock curfew on the weekends."

"And does he always follow those rules?" His skeptical expression hurt.

She poured the coffee before she answered, "Not all the time."

"Adam tells me he doesn't really believe he has to do anything. He sees your boundaries as flexible. Tell me, does he have any responsibilities around the house?"

Gayle rubbed her forehead in frustration. "Like what?"

"Does he clean up after the evening meal? Does he do his own laundry?"

"He helps sometimes. But lots of times he has lawn mowing to do."

"And that's good, but maybe you should sit down with him and talk about how you live together here. Why don't the two of you decide what's fair on both sides? You need to be able to trust Adam whether you're here or not. Adam needs to feel valued, to find a place where what he feels and what he thinks are important. That's what these teenagers he's mixed up with offer him. They offer acceptance, and to gain that acceptance he has to abide by certain rules, not our kind of rules, but rules all the same."

"But what if Adam won't…" She brushed

her hair off her face. "Sometimes being a parent sucks."

"Sometimes life sucks, but that doesn't stop us from trying, does it?" He reached across the table and took her hand in his, his touch warm and comforting, and surprising to her. "Gayle, you're going to get through this, but you have to be open to changing the way you approach your son. Listen to him. Seek his opinions on things. Make it clear that he has responsibilities while he's living here with you, just as you have responsibilities to him."

"I wish this was easier," she said, hoping he'd talk a little more with her, help her figure out what to do. But the look in his eyes wasn't encouraging. Sure, Nate was helpful, and his advice was sound, but she needed more than just advice. She needed to feel supported by someone. She needed someone in her life to be there for her, no matter what, someone who would know how to handle Adam's problems.

Her need made her feel vulnerable to everything about Nate—his kindness, his caring and his willingness to help. She met his gaze across the table. "I'll try to do the things you suggest, but I don't want to lose Adam. He's all I've got."

His expression was one of resignation. "I can't make your decisions for you or for Adam. But I'm around if you need me."

With that, he got up and left the house without looking her way.

For a few minutes she sat reeling in shock. Why had he simply gotten up and left? He'd done the same thing the other night after he'd kissed her. What was going on with him?

He'd seemed so supportive and caring, and suddenly he was gone. Just like that. He was supposed to be helping Adam, and yet he'd brought him back to the house and said nothing about what had happened earlier with the two teens. And he'd left her feeling as if she'd done something wrong. That she'd failed some sort of test.

Worst of all, why was it that she felt so lonely? She'd lived with loneliness all her life, but it hadn't felt like this. A feeling that left her wanting to run after him, to convince him to come back and stay by her side, offer her support, anything but leave her alone like this.

She was about to lock up the house and go to bed when Adam came out of his room. "Mom. I can't finish my homework."

"Why?"

"Because I left some of my notes at school. I need to call someone and see if I can borrow their notes."

She thought about what Nate had said. "Adam,

this happens at least once a week. You have to be more responsible."

"Mom! Do you want me to fail? I need those notes," he yelled.

"Don't yell at me. And no, you're not calling anyone tonight. It's late. I'm tired. You'll have to get up early and go into the school and find your notebook."

He turned away. "I can't wait to get out of this house. I'm sick of school, and I'm going to quit. My friends are right. School is for nerds."

"Don't talk like that," she said, anger flooding through her. "You have a good life here. I've sacrificed everything for you! Don't you ever talk to me like that again. Do you hear me?"

Tears oozed down her cheeks. "My whole life I've done what others needed me to do, and I'm tired of it," she said, her voice faltering.

"I'm sorry, Mom. I didn't mean it."

She glanced up the stairs and saw a forlorn young man—her son. And her heart ached to go up and put her arms around him, but exhaustion held her back. Exhaustion and Nate's voice in her head telling her she had to find a better way to deal with her issues around her son.

THE NEXT DAY on her lunch break, Gayle called Nate, relieved to hear his voice after her sleepless night. "Nate, I'm sorry to bother you, but I need to talk to you. You're right about me and about Adam. I set rules for him, and then he breaks them."

There was a long pause on the other end of the line. "He needs real boundaries and a sense of being part of something that matters to him. If he had someone in his life he could relate to, someone who could help him through these critical years…"

"Meaning?"

"I guess I'm repeating myself a little, but he needs someone who could act as a father figure."

He let the words hang in the air as if he knew something. Did he? He was a cop, and they would have access to information sources she could only imagine. But he'd have to first know Harry's last name and that he was in prison… not hard to find given Nate's advantages.

"What was Adam's dad like?"

Gayle squeezed her cell phone so hard it nearly popped out of her hands. "His dad? Why does that matter?"

"Have you ever talked to Adam about his dad? About what he was like? Why you loved him? Have you ever told him about his father?"

Nate did know something. Oh, no… "I told him about his dad," she lied.

"Adam says he doesn't have any of his dad's things. That you didn't save even an old T-shirt."

Guilt swarmed her mind; anguish surrounded her heart. Nate was right. She hadn't saved anything of Harry's, because the last thing she needed was a reminder of the man who ruined her life. And now, fourteen years later, Nate was telling her that those very reminders would have been helpful to her son.

He had to be wrong. If he wasn't, it would mean that she'd made another mistake that, fourteen years after the fact, was still hurting her son. Another mistake that left her feeling guilty and alone. "Nate, I appreciate how much you missed your father's things and its impact on you. I'm grateful that you believe Adam could be helped by having a few things of his father's, but my life with his father and the circumstances were different."

"How?"

"Harry was away a lot…on the boats. He didn't have a lot of interests or hobbies."

The first part was a lie, but the last was true.

"Was he a good father to Adam?"

"Yes, I guess so."

"You guess so? He doesn't seem to remember anything about his father."

"That's because Adam was a baby when his father died." She sighed. "Look, I appreciate all your help, but maybe it would be better if Adam and I moved to another town. I could sell the house and start over somewhere new."

There was a long pause on the end of the line, followed by a long sigh. "Gayle, you know that's not going to be a workable solution. Your problems will only follow you as long as Adam feels the way he does about his life."

Tears formed under her lids. Her throat felt thick and tight. "I want Adam to experience a normal life. I don't want him to be lonely and feel like an outsider like I have most of my life. You think I could have done more to give Adam a sense of family. The plain truth is that Harry didn't have any family that I ever knew of, and my only living relative is a half brother who blamed my mother for ruining his father's life and wanted nothing to do with me."

Oh, God. What had she done?

She waited, holding her breath until her head began to feel light.

"Oh, I didn't realize that. I'm sorry. That must have been a difficult situation for you."

Anxious to change the subject, she asked, "How is Anna doing?"

"She's waiting to hear more from the neurologist."

"I'll call her this weekend."

"Tell me more about Harry."

Her heart jumped. "Harry? There's nothing

to tell. He was my husband until I d…until he died and I became a widow. Why do you ask?" she said, making her voice as firm and demanding as possible.

But she didn't feel either. She felt empty and drained. She'd done everything she could to keep her life separate from Harry's life, to create a story that would protect her son, even registering his birth name as Adam Sawyer, all to hide her connection to him. But what if Nate had discovered the truths she'd so carefully hidden all these years? If Nate had found something, and told her friends and her coworkers, she would be crushed and humiliated. She had managed to become part of the community, largely due to her job at Eagle Mountain Medical Center.

When people found out the truth about her, everything would change. She would once again be an outsider. If Nate had uncovered her lies and was willing to talk about them, she couldn't face living here any longer.

NATE WAS IMMEDIATELY sorry for upsetting her, yet it was clear to him that Gayle wasn't telling the truth about her husband. "I didn't realize that talking about your husband would be so disturbing after all these years."

"Well, it is, especially when you try to make

it sound like I'm not a good parent because Adam's father isn't around."

"I don't seem to be very helpful in your case, and I take full responsibility for that," he said, trying to remain professional when all he wanted to do was go to her and hold her close. To explain to her that he genuinely cared what happened to her and Adam. He couldn't imagine how it would feel to be alone with a child to raise, to take on a new career in order to provide a living. And do all this without family support and help.

He'd looked forward to having children when he and Natasha married. He'd put off a family life to focus on his career, only to have both his career and his marriage plans snatched from him. He'd always assumed that he'd be a good parent, but how would he have managed if he'd found himself in Gayle's circumstances?

"I'm doing the best I can. I'm trying to take your advice on how to help Adam, and all you can do is dream up ways to make me revisit the past. I didn't have the pleasant upbringing you did. I didn't have family and friends I could call upon when things got rough. I had me. That was it."

There was a moment's pause during which he could hear her quiet sobs, and it pained him to realize that he could have been so thoughtless.

This woman had become important to him. He could hear the anxiety and fear in her voice, and one thing became crystal clear. Finding out about Gayle's past wasn't worth the risk of losing her.

The thought startled him. Had he stepped over the line professionally? "I'm sorry, Gayle. I didn't mean to hurt you. I like you, and I admire your resolve to make a good life for your son. You're a very brave woman."

"Then please stop picking at my past and help us get on with our future."

He was doing a lousy job communicating with this woman, even though he really wanted to do what was best for both Adam and Gayle. "Maybe I should arrange for a different mentor for Adam."

"Maybe you should," she said over muffled tears.

The last sound he heard was the click of the phone cutting him off.

Why had he been so damn impulsive? He didn't mean it. He wanted to help her and Adam more than any of his other clients.

Despite his determination to remain professional, he was now personally involved with Gayle and Adam. He stared at the phone as thoughts ricocheted through his mind. Would it help if he went over and apologized? Maybe he could take her out for coffee or lunch, anything to make up for hurting her. He didn't want to hurt her, not Gayle of all people. He liked and admired her. No, it was more than that. A lot more...

What was he doing? If he wasn't careful, he could lose his objectivity where Gayle was concerned. What was even worse, he might end up doing what he'd said to her on the phone—be forced to hand Adam over to someone else.

CHAPTER NINE

AFTER A RESTLESS NIGHT, Gayle arrived at the clinic to learn that Anna had been called in to see the neurologist. She and Sherri exchanged anxious glances as Anna was placed in an exam room.

"Does Nate know about this?"

"I didn't have a chance to call him. I picked Anna up and brought her here. Nate is away at a seminar in Boston. She doesn't want him called until he gets home."

"What can I do?" Gayle asked, regretting that she'd rebuked Nate when he had his sister to worry about. If the news was what they expected, Anna's life would be changed forever.

"Nothing at the moment. I'm going in with her," Sherri whispered, disappearing into the room with Anna.

Gayle tried to remain calm as she checked in other clinic patients and placed their charts on the counter. She answered the phone, afraid each time that Nate had somehow learned that his sister was here. She didn't want to be the one to tell him. Call it cowardice, but she was afraid of how he'd react. Not that he'd be unpleasant, but he would want to be here. His life would change as well, when he learned Anna's future prospects. If the diagnosis turned out to be Parkinson's, the whole family would be affected.

Finally, the neurologist left the exam room and went across the hall to the doctor's dictation room. Unable to stand the suspense any longer, Gayle walked down the hall to find the door ajar. She tapped lightly. Anna and Sherri were hugging each other and crying. She closed the door ever so gently to give them the privacy they needed, and went back to the desk.

When they came out, Sherri's arm around Anna's shoulders, they approached the desk.

"I'll pick up Silas and Jeremy from school and bring them to the house on my lunch break if you want," Gayle said, not knowing what else she could do. If she were diagnosed with Parkinson's, she'd want Adam with her.

Anna's smile was gracious. "Could you? It's a small community, and I don't want the boys hearing anything from anybody but me. It's going to be hard enough as it is."

Even though her heart was breaking for Anna, Gayle did her best to remain upbeat. "Maybe you can tell them the basics and then after that only what they need to know or what they ask about," she offered tentatively.

Anna looked at her, and in an instant they connected in a way that was totally different from before. Gayle felt as if they'd known each other all their lives.

Anna hugged her. "Thank you for that. From the moment the doctor gave me the diagnosis, all I could think about was how to tell my boys. I'm going to take your advice and keep it very simple in the beginning and let them decide when they want to ask questions." Anna hugged Gayle again so hard she nearly knocked her over. "You are the best friend I could ask for. I'm so glad you moved to Eden Harbor."

Gayle felt needed and included as she hugged Anna back. She appreciated those words. Words that made her feel valued and part of Anna's life. She craved the feeling of belonging to a family unit where love and caring was offered freely. As she smiled at her friend, she realized that having an extended family was exactly what Adam needed, as well. She understood what Nate was getting at when he'd asked about her family. He wanted her and Adam to be surrounded by people who loved them. "I'm glad I moved here, too…so glad. I'll pick up the boys and bring them home."

And she did. Yet the entire time she was driving to the school, her thoughts were on Nate and how he'd deal with the news. She wanted to call him, but it wasn't her place to tell him about his sister.

NATE CHECKED HIS phone messages on the way to his car. The seminar had been interesting but he had this gut feeling that something was wrong. He couldn't put his finger on it, but he'd always trusted his instincts. They'd proved especially valuable when he'd been a cop on the beat in Boston years before. Some of his friends from the old days had asked him to stay overnight and go to dinner with them, but he needed to get home.

The traffic was surprisingly light driving out of Boston, and he was on Interstate 95 and nearly to the exit leading to Eden Harbor when his cell phone rang. He glanced at the number and pulled over to the side of the road. Anna wouldn't call him during his workday unless she needed him. He clicked the phone on. "Anna, are you all right?"

"I will be when you get home," she said, her voice shaking.

"What's going on? Are the boys okay?"

"They're here with me. Nate, where are you? Still in Boston?"

"No, I'm about to turn off I-95. I should be home in an hour. Is something wrong?"

"I want you to come to my house when you get home. We need to talk."

"Sure. What's up?" And then he knew. His heart shrank in his chest. His jaw tightened in a desperate bid for control. "You heard from the neurologist."

"This morning at the clinic."

"Sweetie, hang in there. I'll be at your house as soon as I can get there. Is anyone with you?"

"Sherri's here. Gayle picked up the boys from school and brought them home."

"That's good. Look, I'm going to be with you as fast as I can. Have you told Mom?"

"No. I was waiting for you before I talked to her. Nate, this will break Mom's heart." Anna sobbed.

He talked consolingly to his sister, giving her time to regain her equilibrium.

Once he couldn't hear any more tears in her voice, Nate pulled back onto the highway, moving into the left lane as he picked up speed. "Can I speak to Sherri for a minute?"

Sherri's calm voice allowed him a few precious moments of control. "Sherri, how's she doing?"

"You know Anna. She's a strong person. The boys have been told and have gone next door to the neighbors' house for a while. Then the neighbors are taking them out for pizza. I'm going to stay with Anna tonight."

"You don't need to. I'll stay with her."

"Why don't we wait and see how she's doing after the boys go to bed?"

Anna's job at the town hall was often exhausting, depending on how many tourist events were going on. It wasn't a high-paying job, but Anna loved her work. If only Kevin was still with her. Her future would be so much easier to face with her husband by her side. "Sounds good to me. I'll see you when I get there."

"Nate, drive safely please."

"I will," he said, taking the off-ramp a little too fast. He closed his cell phone and concentrated on his driving.

He couldn't believe this was happening. Anna had been so confident that it wasn't anything serious that she'd convinced the rest of the family, as well…or nearly. Nate had gone to see Neill, but he wouldn't discuss Anna's case, saying only that her symptoms needed to be investigated.

Nate drove as fast as he dared along the two-lane highway. He realized he'd convinced himself that Anna was okay. He *needed* her to be okay. Not just for her boys, but for him.

He clutched the wheel tighter in his hands as he tried to find the resolve to be upbeat and ready to face his sister when he got to her house. He couldn't help her if he couldn't manage his own fear and anger at the unfairness of life.

Dusk was gathering when he pulled into her driveway. He jumped out of the car, leaving his cane in the seat beside him, and walked as calmly as he could to her door.

Anna opened it and ran into his arms, sobbing. He held her tight, unnerved by his sister's emotional outburst. She'd always been so calm, so reserved, and for some idiot reason he'd expected her to be like that now in the middle of the second-worst crisis of her life.

"Let's go inside," he said, smoothing her hair from her tearstained face.

Once inside, Nate and Sherri hugged each other—a hug Nate desperately needed at the moment. Sherri put a pot of coffee on, and poured each of them a cup. Without saying much they sat at the kitchen table, nobody touching their coffee.

"We'd better talk about this before the boys come back," Nate said, glancing from his sister to his cousin. "They don't need to hear the news all over again."

They reviewed what the doctor had told Anna, the concern being how Anna would manage to continue in her job at the town hall, and what she and the boys would face in the months ahead as they began to experience the impact of this diagnosis.

"I have to call Neill. He's been in the OR all afternoon, but I'm sure he'll be able to help us," Sherri said.

Anna reached across the table and took Sherri's hand. "Thank you for that."

They were still staring at their coffee cups when the doorbell rang.

"I'll get it," Nate said, already out of his chair and headed for the door.

"It's probably the boys back from their pizza outing," Anna said, wiping the tears from her cheeks.

Nate opened the door. "Gayle." His breath came in a short gasp. "What are you doing here?"

She held a casserole dish out to him. "I was at the clinic today…thought you might need something to eat."

"Yes. Yes." He reached for the casserole carrier. "Thank you."

He stood awkwardly staring down at her, wishing he could think of something to get her to stay. But his thoughts were all tangled up with Anna. "Wait a minute while I put this in the kitchen."

He strode to the kitchen, the casserole in his hands.

"Who sent us this?" Anna asked as he slid the dish onto the granite counter next to the table.

"It's Gayle."

Anna got up quickly from her chair. "Did she leave? I can't imagine that. She was so kind to me today. She brought the boys home from school."

"I know," he said, and without another word he headed back to the front door. In the background he could hear Anna ask Sherri if he was all right, that it wasn't like her brother to leave someone standing at the door.

He was definitely not all right on a variety of fronts, one of them being the woman waiting at the door. "I'm so sorry. You must think I'm a little crazy abandoning you like this."

"You have reason to be a little crazy. And you didn't leave me—I could have walked in behind you. I didn't because I don't want to impose at a time like this."

"You're not imposing, really."

Her worried expression was unmistakable. "You look completely exhausted, and I know Anna's tired."

"Everyone is," he said, a thought rising quickly in his mind. "But I would really like a chance to talk to you."

GAYLE STEPPED BACK OUTSIDE, clutching her purse close as she did so. "Is this about Adam?"

Was he really thinking about her problems with Adam in the middle of Anna's worst nightmare? What was wrong with this man? She looked him over carefully. There were blue bowls of fatigue under his eyes. His hair was unkempt, his clothes wrinkled. "You came straight here from your seminar, didn't you?"

He scrubbed his face with the palms of his hands. "I did."

She couldn't get over how lost he looked, how totally vulnerable... "You haven't been sleeping well, have you?"

He gave her a half smile. "It's that obvious, is it?"

"It's that obvious," she affirmed, nodding. "I have an idea. Would you like to come over to my house later? I'm a good listener, and it might help you adjust to all this."

His surprised glance caught her off guard. "Adam is studying with one of his classmates, and he won't be home for another hour or so. And unless you're needed here, it might be easier for you if you talked to someone who's not a family member."

"Are you serious?"

"Yes. You need a chance to absorb the shock of all this. Anna will need you more in the coming months."

He cocked his hands on his hips. His jaw

worked. He seemed to be making up his mind about something. "I'd like that one hell of a lot. Do you want to come in?"

A part of her would love to be included, to be part of a real family. The other part of her knew that Anna needed her brother right now. Gayle wouldn't impose. She would wait until Anna had had time to get used to the idea that she had Parkinson's, and then she'd invite her to dinner and a chance to talk. "No. But the casserole goes in a three-hundred-and-fifty-degree oven for forty minutes."

"Thanks for that," he said, making her feel good about her gesture.

"Meet me at my house when you're ready," she said, offering him a smile of encouragement.

"I will."

She heard the front door close as she went down the walkway to her car, her feelings a jumbled mass of contradictions. She liked this man very much, but she didn't like how he'd made her feel the other day. He was kind to her in so many ways, and yet he could be stern and difficult.

Welcome to the world of men.

She drove home slowly, wishing that she had gone in for a few minutes, if only to say hello to Anna and Sherri. Yet that old sense of not belonging had made her reject Nate's invitation without thinking. At least she was aware of how she behaved, and with recognition came the chance to change her response...next time, maybe.

She had just pulled into her driveway when she saw Nate's car drive up to the curb. She hadn't expected to see him for at least a couple of hours. Was he as anxious to see her as she was to see him?

Secretly pleased at the thought, she called to him when he got out of the car. "You must know a shortcut to my house."

"Yeah, I do," he said as he walked slowly up her driveway, leaning on his cane more than usual. His eyes were assessing her in a frankly appreciative way.

Wow!

No man had looked at her that way in a very long time. She shouldn't feel so happy when her friend had experienced such a frightening diagnosis, but something in the way he moved toward her made her feel so lighthearted she wanted to sing.

How corny was that?

They went into the house together. She offered coffee, which he refused, and they settled down on the sofa in the living room. She hadn't sat this close to a man she really liked in a long time, and it made her feel so very happy.

He seemed more at ease with her than he had in weeks, and she liked the idea that they might soon be more than friends. In fact, under different circumstances she'd be fantasizing about their next kiss.

"This is just what I need," he said, resting his arm on the back of the sofa, his hand inches from her shoulder. "It's been a long day for all of us."

He seemed almost lost, his expression sad. She wanted to move closer to him, to offer comfort. "Want to talk about it?"

His glance was speculative. "Yeah, I do. I'm not much of a talker when it comes to myself."

"I gathered that," she said wryly.

He gave her that appreciative glance again, making her toes curl in her shoes. "The cop in me, I suppose."

She watched with concern when his hand moved from the back of the sofa to his face. He rubbed his cheek vigorously without saying a word.

"I want to help. What can I do?"

His hand returned to the back of the sofa, his fingers playing with the ribbed binding along the top edge. "Anna and I have always been close. Kevin was the brother I never had. Silas and Jeremy are more like my sons than my nephews. I couldn't love them more than I do right this minute."

The anguish in his eyes had her scrambling for words of consolation. "You're very close."

"That would be an understatement."

She wanted to touch his fingers, his cheek, any part of him that would make the connection to him that she was feeling right now complete. "She'll be okay, won't she? I mean, she will have a lot to deal with in the coming years, but she has family and friends and good medical care."

"I don't know. I just don't know. She's strong. She's always been strong, but everyone has a breaking point. Kevin is gone, and she loved him so much. She has to face raising her boys alone while learning to cope with a serious illness. And God knows how long she'll be able to work. I'm seriously worried about her finances, especially once she needs more expensive care. I went through something similar, but my costs were covered. I'll have to look into her insurance for her and see what she has. Her house will have to be fitted out for wheelchair ramps. She'll need aids to do even the normal things around the house…"

Unable to bear the desperate look in his eyes, she clutched his hand in hers, her fingers automatically rubbing the back. "Don't do that to yourself."

His eyes locked on hers, and it was as if she were looking into his soul. The pain and agony she saw there closed her throat.

He clung to her hand. "You're right. I'm usually much better at controlling my feelings, but this is my sister…"

His look begged her to understand, to help him. She'd never seen a man so vulnerable. It was as if his vulnerability was a precious gift he offered her. As unfamiliar as this was to her, she felt they were both embarking on a new phase of their relationship. She was not just Adam's mother, but a woman who would be his friend and supporter. The bond between them offered a shield from the outside world.

In that split second of connection, she knew without reservation that she cared a great deal for Nate. Was it love? She wasn't sure.

"I understand," she murmured, her hand reaching to touch his cheek. "I understand."

He pulled her into his arms and buried his face in her shoulder.

WITH DERRICK LITTLE'S HELP, Adam had managed to finish his science essay. It had been a tough go, but he was feeling pretty accomplished when he came cruising up his street on his bicycle. He braked hard when he spotted Nate's car in front of his house. Holy crap! Nate didn't like to be kept waiting. Oddly enough, one of the things he liked most about Nate was that he didn't take any guff from him or any of his friends.

But wait a minute. He didn't have an appointment with Nate until tomorrow after school. He walked his bike up the driveway and locked it to the drain spout. He didn't understand what his mom saw in this old house, but probably its biggest attraction was that she hadn't had to pay for it. Neither he nor his mom had ever inherited anything before, and he kind of liked the idea that he was in a house now. Back in Anaheim they'd only lived in apartments, something he'd never questioned until he had his own room and his own bathroom in this rambling old place they now called home.

He lifted his backpack off his shoulders as he went in the back door, wondering what Nate was doing here with his mother. "I'm home," he said, on the really weird chance that the two of them were up to something they wouldn't want him to see. He had never imagined his mother alone with a man. Yet he knew she was lonely. How would he feel if she started dating someone? Probably okay… He remembered the night at the restaurant and the dessert thing. He was pretty sure if he hadn't kept pushing them, he wouldn't have had dessert. He was glad he had, though. The chocolate cake had been awesome.

His mom was going to be part of Nate's cousin's wedding party. Maybe that was why he was at their house. Thinking about the wedding reminded him that he'd get a chance to spend time around Morgan without his other classmates seeing him. They'd gotten together to study after school a few days ago, and she was fun to be around. She'd even laughed at his jokes. But best of all, when he'd asked her about the dance, she'd said her dad was dropping her off, and he could come with her if he wanted to. He'd walk into the dance with her and let his friends think it was a real date. Good enough for him—at least for now.

When he reached the living room he stopped. Nate was looking as though he'd fallen off a skateboard and hit his head. His mom had tears in her eyes.

"What's wrong?" he asked, expecting to be shooed away up to his room while they continued their conversation.

"Adam, come and sit with us," his mother said, pointing to the armchair next to the sofa. "We've got some news."

He sat down on the chair she offered, sitting on the very edge just in case he needed to escape to his room.

"Anna was at the clinic today, and she has Parkinson's," his mother said, her voice shaking a little. The way his mother was acting frightened Adam.

"What does that mean?" He glanced from his mother to Nate.

Nate leaned forward, his palms resting on his thighs. "It means that Jeremy and Silas are worried about their mom."

He knew Jeremy from school. He hadn't made the basketball team either, but he was too short to play, in Adam's opinion. "I'm really sorry to hear about Jeremy's mom. He's in my class. Maybe I could spend time with him. I mean, we could hang out together if Jeremy wanted." Some of the guys he played pool with wouldn't want him hanging out with a nerdy kid like Jeremy, but he didn't care. He'd do anything to gain Nate's respect.

"That would be great, Adam," Nate said. "I'm sure he'd appreciate you being there for him."

Adam recognized the gratitude in Nate's eyes, and felt good. Real good. For a change, he kind of liked being the one to help out, not the one who needed help. "You can count on me."

His mother got up and came over, putting her arms around his neck and embarrassing him totally. But he really didn't mind, because she seemed so much happier since they'd moved here, and tonight she was especially pleased with him…and happy. He liked his mom to be happy.

"Adam, I'm so proud of you. You'll make a difference in Jeremy's life."

He pulled back and smiled up at her. "That's cool, Mom, but I got to get up to my room and finish my homework." He didn't really, but he wasn't very comfortable with all this hugging.

He had only made it to the landing on the stairs when he heard his mom and Nate talking in quiet tones. Could his mom be attracted to Nate? She hadn't had a boyfriend for as long as he could remember, and he secretly believed that his mom still loved his dad, even though he was dead.

He had to admit that it was a little strange, the whole love thing. He sighed as he went to his room.

OVER THE NEXT two weeks, Adam spent time with Jeremy, and was surprised to find he really enjoyed his company. They talked about Jeremy's dad a lot, making Adam wish he could talk about his dad and what he was like. He'd spent last evening in his room looking for the trawler accident his father was involved in, but couldn't find it anywhere on the internet. As for the name Harry Sawyer, there were only two others, and they were both young men who lived in New

York. He wasn't very good at searching the internet. He would ask Jeremy how to do a better search when he saw him in class tomorrow. His friend knew all about the internet.

As he went into the house after a long day at school, made longer by a surprise math test, Adam found his mother in the kitchen starting dinner.

"You'd better get a move on. Nate is due here to pick you up in about an hour."

He'd forgotten all about that. "Yeah, we're going to the fisherman's museum on the road to Henderson's Wharf," he said, wishing he didn't have to go. Having Jeremy as a friend made him want to talk to his mom about his dad. She hadn't told him very much, but he planned to change that. Tonight would be a good time to start. They might even be able to do some research together on the internet.

"How are you and Jeremy making out? Do you see much of him in school?"

"Yeah. Mom, he talks about his dad a lot. And I was wondering if you could tell me a little more about Dad. Or about the trawler accident."

She glanced quickly at him. "Your dad's body was never found. I didn't go up to Alaska because I couldn't afford it. Your dad didn't leave much behind when he went out on the boats."

"Mom, what would I do if anything happened

to you? Where would I look for my family? You told me that Dad didn't have any brothers or sisters, but he must have had cousins or some relatives."

She hadn't told her son much of anything, not even Harry's last name. She had allowed Adam to assume that she'd kept her married name when she hadn't. Now it seemed to have been a serious mistake on her part, one she couldn't correct without serious repercussions. "Why are you bringing this up now?"

"I don't know. It's just that I listen to Jeremy talk about his family and how close they are. He told me what it was like when his dad died overseas and how lonesome he was. He said that Nate was really good to him. I'd like to have some family. Any family." He looked at her, and suddenly, for no reason, he felt so angry he could hardly breathe.

"Adam, let's talk about this later. Right now you have to get ready to go with Nate…"

Adam banged his fist on the table, making his mom jump in surprise, but he couldn't seem to care. "Mom. I want to know about my dad. You must have something of his you saved for me. I want to feel better about myself, and knowing more about my dad would make me feel better," he pleaded.

His mother stared him straight in the eye. "I

will not have you banging your fists on the table, and I don't have anything of your father's to give you."

"I don't believe you."

The doorbell interrupted their argument. "I'll get it," Adam grouched as he went to answer it. He was really glad to see Nate standing there. "You gotta help me with Mom."

"Why? Is something wrong with her?" Nate asked as they went into the kitchen.

"There's nothing wrong with her, except she's being mean."

GAYLE GRITTED HER TEETH. "He wants to know about his father, and I have nothing more I can tell him."

"I just want to know what my dad was like. What was his favorite sports team? Did he like to play golf? Did he like the same foods that I do? Do I look like him? I can't find any photos of him except the one when you got married."

"Gayle, maybe the three of us could talk this over. Adam really needs your support on this. There must be something more you could tell him."

"Whose side are you on?" she muttered, her voice breaking as she met his gaze.

"Mom, I'm only asking for a little information. I've never bugged you about Dad before, but now it's important."

How she wished she'd never lied about Harry. Yet she felt she had little choice if she was to protect her son. At the time she couldn't afford to move away from Anaheim and didn't want to uproot Adam's life anyway. Only after he'd begun seeking out kids in his class who weren't good influences had she realized she had to move. "Adam, let's talk about this later. Right now you have to get ready and go with Nate."

"Mom, that's not fair." He turned to Nate. "Would you help me search on the internet? I can't find anything about my dad, but I'd like to give it another try. Would you?"

Nate looked to Gayle. "I think it would be better for both of you if you searched the online sites together. There must be newspaper reports, maybe even a death certificate, online."

Gayle bit her lips in fear. She couldn't let this go any further. She looked at both of them. "Okay, while you're out I'll go online and see what I can find."

"Sure," Adam said, a wide smile on his face. He crossed the room and hugged his mother, lifting her off her feet and swinging her around the room. "This will be so great. I can't wait to get back and see what you've found out about my dad."

The minute they left, Gayle hurried to the computer on the desk in the corner of the den. She'd typed in Harry's name and waited for it to come up. First she found two men whose names were Harry Young. Two lived in New Zealand. One was Harry Exeter Young and the other was simply Harry Young. Both lived on the north island known as Te Ika-a-Māui. One owned a brewery and the other a winery.

She scrolled down the search page, but didn't see any mention of her ex. Could she be worried about nothing? Had Harry's incarceration meant that he wouldn't be listed anywhere? Had he died in prison? She clicked on the second page of the Google search.

The screen filled with a page of references to Harry Young, Anaheim, California, the date of the shooting and the trial, followed farther down by a local TV channel in Los Angeles talking about the prison where Harry had been sent fourteen years ago.

She clicked on the video out of curiosity. Suddenly a news reporter was speaking live outside the prison, talking about Harry Young, a man who had shot a police officer fourteen years ago, who was up for parole after exemplary behavior helping other inmates learn to cope with life inside the prison.

Her heart pounded in her chest. She could

barely breathe. It couldn't be him. She kept on searching, hoping for a photo of this person they were talking about. She couldn't find one.

The next piece was an article about the parole system, and criminals' chances of early parole. The article was written only two weeks ago. Surely they hadn't let Harry out. She went to the next piece, this time in the Anaheim newspaper, which said that the parole hearing had made its final decision. There was a picture of Harry taken years ago, one she recognized. His eyes were hard and cold, his jaw set in a rigid line.

This man was being released and would create havoc for her and her son. What if someone had told him about Adam, and Harry was determined to find him? She knew Harry. If he wanted something, no one stood in his way, least of all her.

She raced through the article to learn that Harry had been released two months ago, that he was a born-again Christian who planned to devote his life to helping prisoners adjust to living on the outside. There were several more articles about him, but none with recent photos. The stories seemed to be more about what early parole meant to the community at large.

Her hands shaking, she began to search for any other references to Harry. It seemed that once he was released and the story became old news, interest had vaporized. She breathed slowly, trying to collect her thoughts.

She couldn't take any chances on anyone connecting Harry to Adam. She searched her past for someone who might know about Harry, or had kept in touch with him during his prison time.

The only person she could come up with was Ken Evans. He'd been Harry's friend back then, but had taken pity on her when Harry had been sent to prison. He'd helped her out financially for a couple of months until she found a job. Her fingers flew over the keys, searching for his phone number, surprised to learn that he still lived in the same apartment building and had a listed telephone number. She checked her watch. She was amazed at how little time had passed since she started her search. It felt like hours but it had only been about twenty minutes. She grabbed the phone and dialed the number.

A very old-sounding man answered.

"Is this Ken Evans?" she asked, willing herself to breathe.

"Yes. Who's this?"

"It's Gayle Young."

"Well, for goodness' sake. It's been a long time. How are you doing?"

"I'm fine. I wondered if you'd seen the news? Harry is out on parole."

"Yes, I did. But Harry and I haven't been in touch for years. Are you looking for him?"

"No, I'm not. I...I needed to know if you told anyone I was expecting his baby?"

"No. I promised I wouldn't, and I didn't. Why do you ask?"

"No real reason, I guess," she said, trying to sound disinterested.

"I hope you're not wanting to hook up with him again?"

"No! Never!"

"That's good."

She could hear someone entering the room, and Ken said quickly, "Look, it's been great talking to you. I got to go."

"Sure, Ken."

"Oh, before I let you go. Did you have Harry's baby?"

"Ah...no. No, I didn't. I lost the baby." She felt degraded by yet another lie she'd been forced to tell to keep her son safe here in Eden Harbor. But she couldn't risk Harry getting in touch with Ken Evans and finding out about Adam. She sucked in a deep breath.

"I'm sorry to hear that. Take care now." And he hung up.

At least if Harry got in touch with Ken, he could only find out that she'd been pregnant. Unless someone else knew about her son... After

Harry went to prison she'd bought a one-way bus ticket to Riverside where she'd gotten a job as a doctor's receptionist while she'd waited for Adam to be born. It wasn't until he'd started school that she'd moved back to Anaheim in the vain hope that her half brother, Alfred McGuire, would want to be involved in her and Adam's life. She'd wanted Adam to have some sort of family connection, but it hadn't worked out. Alfred had shown no interest in Adam. Meanwhile she'd found a job in the health-records department of a nearby hospital and had gone to work building a life.

Now all she had to do was keep Adam from finding out about Harry until she figured out what to do. If she got lucky, the news of Harry's release would never reach Adam. But what should she do about his need to search the internet? She had to stall him somehow. She stared at the screen of information about Harry…

Her one hope was that Adam would never learn his father's last name. That he would look for him as Harry Sawyer. All she had to do was enter the name Harry Sawyer before Adam and Nate returned.

A quick search of the name turned up two in New York, both of whom were alive. If Adam did continue to search, he wouldn't find his father as long as no one learned that Harry's last name was Young and not Sawyer.

When Adam returned, she'd tell him the truth—that she hadn't found anything relating to Harry Sawyer and a trawler accident.

CHAPTER TEN

GAYLE SPENT HER lunch break the following day checking the internet for further information about Harry's release. Thankfully there didn't seem to be anything more being reported.

She didn't think that Harry had much interest in her, and by now he wouldn't have any way of finding her since her parents were both deceased. She hadn't left a forwarding address with anyone other than the woman who lived in the apartment next to hers—Mary Ellen Bartlett. She'd confided her story to Mary Ellen, the only person she'd felt she could trust back then. They hadn't stayed in touch since she'd moved to Eden Harbor over a year ago. Not wanting to disconnect completely from the only person who had offered her motherly help and advice, she'd given Mary Ellen her cell phone number.

"What are you doing here when you should be at lunch?" Sherri asked as she approached the reception desk.

Gayle quickly switched from the internet to the registration module. "I was just finishing up a couple of things before I go to the cafeteria. I'm running late for lunch, but I promise to come right back so that we can be ready for the afternoon clinic."

"Don't be silly. You're always working extra time. Don't worry about taking a few minutes now. I need you fresh for this afternoon's clinic. You know Dr. Samuelson always has add-ons, which means more work for you."

"Thanks," she said, and meant it with her whole heart. If only she could confide in Sherri, but it was out of the question. Her best friend didn't need to know what a fraud she was. Her stomach ached from the stress, making eating impossible, but she should at least have a cup of tea.

When she reached the cafeteria, she purchased tea and a packet of cookies and went to sit at the table where she could watch TV for a few minutes before going back to work. She had always found television the easiest way to get her mind off her worries. Sliding into the chair, she stirred her tea as she half listened to one of the national networks.

She opened the packet of cookies just as the announcer began a segment on what it meant to be a Christian and its impact on… She glanced up at the screen. A keening cry escaped her lips at the sight of an old photo of Harry. The announcer was talking about how Christianity had saved this man, who'd sought forgiveness from God for his past sin of shooting a police officer. A classic story of God's love and the miracle of redemption. They were going to interview Harry after the commercial break.

She glanced around, seeing that several people were staring at her. She had to get out of here. She had to leave work, go home. She'd call Mary Ellen and warn her not to tell the media anything if they contacted her. Meanwhile, all she had to do was get past the next few days until interest in the story waned, and her secret would be safe.

She left the cafeteria and went back to the clinic. Needing to do a thorough search of anything relating to Harry, especially where he might be, she needed to get home to the privacy of her own computer. She would have to tell Sherri she was leaving for the rest of the day, as busy as it was.

"I hope you don't have that flu that's going around," Sherri said when Gayle told her she had to leave. Sherri pressed her fingers to Gayle's forehead, her expression one of sincere concern, riddling Gayle with guilt. It hurt so much not to be able to tell her friend the truth.

"I'm afraid it might be," Gayle said, grabbing her purse and starting for the door.

"I'll call you when I get home from work and see how you're feeling," Sherri said.

"Thanks." With that she was out the door, and on her way to the car. When she got to the safety of her house, she put in a call to Mary Ellen. When the woman answered, she greeted her as enthusiastically as she could. "Mary Ellen, how are you? It's Gayle Sawyer calling."

"How lovely to hear from you, dear. I'm just fine. Except for the arthritis in my knees I'm doing just great. And you? And how's that boy of yours? I miss him being around here."

"He's good. At school right now."

"How are you enjoying your aunt's house?"

"We love it. I have a garden, and there's a shed for gardening tools in the backyard. Adam mows the lawn. He mows several of our neighbors' lawns, as well."

"That's nice. Gives him a little spending money. Gayle, dear, I was going to call you. I have something I need to tell you. Harry Young was here yesterday."

"What?"

"He knows all about Adam, where you live, and he's coming to visit you. I don't know how he found out that you used to live here." There was a short pause. "I made a bad mistake."

"What was that?" Gayle asked, her heart thudding slowly and painfully in her chest.

"He was so charming, so sincere when he asked about you. I...I told him where you lived. I didn't mean to. I'm so sorry."

She couldn't waste time speculating on how Harry had tracked her to the apartment in the first place. That didn't matter anymore.

Harry would be here any moment, likely followed by some overeager reporter. Once everyone in Eden Harbor knew about her past, once Adam learned that she'd lied to him, that she'd lied to her friends, her life here would be over. Her major concern was Adam. Somehow she would have to explain why she'd lied to him about Harry and beg his forgiveness.

She could not have Harry in her house. Not here. The one place she felt safe. "He's coming to Eden Harbor? Are you sure?"

"Yes. He told me he's been out of prison a couple of months and was working with ex-cons."

"Look, Mary Ellen, I've got to go."

"Oh, I understand. And I'm so sorry for my mistake. If you need somewhere to stay for a few days or weeks, you and Adam are welcome back here anytime. I miss both of you."

"I miss you, too. Thank you so much. I really appreciate it, but I've got to go."

She hung up and immediately dialed Nate's number. When he didn't answer, she left a message. Regardless of what their personal relationship was or was not, she needed his help to protect Adam from Harry. But first she had to get everything packed up before Adam got home from school. While she was doing that, she had to come up with a plausible explanation for why they were leaving town. As she packed, she considered various scenarios, and not one of them would work. Moving here had made sense given the house, but there was nothing she could think of to explain why they had to leave now.

As she moved through the house picking up things that needed to be packed, she noticed Adam's baseball cap, and the ticket stubs from the last time Nate had taken him to a movie. She gripped the edge of the hall table in desperation. She'd be leaving Nate as well as Sherri and Anna. Ragged sobs shook her body. She'd be leaving everyone who mattered in her life, all for a man who had only caused her misery.

She sat down on the sofa and tried to collect her runaway thoughts. She clenched her fists to hold back her tears. She couldn't cry. She had to think. The raw truth swirled around her mind, tearing at her resolve. She didn't want to leave Eden Harbor—her friends and the first real home she'd ever known.

She loved these people. She'd never had anyone she could rely on. Now she did…and she had to abandon all of them.

But if she stayed, she'd have to tell Adam the truth, knowing that sooner or later everyone in town would know about her lies. Her life would be laid bare for everyone to speculate about. As much as she wanted to remain, she couldn't. She also had a responsibility to Adam.

The phone rang, its sound echoing around the room. She checked caller ID.

Nate. She would give everything she had to be free to pick up that phone and have a normal conversation with him. She loved him, and never more than now when she had to give him up. Her hands shook as they hovered over the phone. "Hello," she said at last, her voice thick with tears.

NATE HEARD THE distress in Gayle's voice. "I got your message. What's wrong?"

"Nate…I'm in trouble. I need your advice. Could you come over right now?"

He'd never heard Gayle sound so desperate. "Are you ill?"

"No." There was a long pause. "Look, never mind. This was a bad idea."

"Hey! Wait a minute. It's not a bad idea at all. Just give me a minute and I'll be right over."

He grabbed his jacket, jumped in his SUV and

was in Gayle's driveway in a matter of minutes. He'd left his cane behind and half hobbled, half walked up the house. The door swung open and Gayle was in his arms, sobbing into his shoulder and nearly knocking him over.

"There, now." Wanting to comfort her, he patted her back, a move that made him feel out of place—awkward. "What's happening?" he said, his nose pressed into the wonderful strawberry scent of her hair, her breasts against his chest and the pressure of her hips arousing him instantly. "Is Adam all right?" he asked, pulling away a little.

She clung to him, her face damp with tears. "He won't be if I can't stop…" She fought for control. "I need you to help me."

He filled his lungs with her scent before tucking her gently into the curve of his arm. "Now, let's go inside and you tell me what's going on," he said, while his heart swelled in his chest. This woman had a way of catching his attention and holding it. She had from the beginning.

But what was behind all the tears? He'd never seen her cry. Leading her to the sofa, he eased her down close to him. "Now, tell me what's going on."

"I haven't told the truth about Harry. He didn't die in a trawler accident. He is…was in prison for shooting a police officer in Anaheim.

I was in my last year of high school. My parents weren't much as parents go. I met Harry one night when I went out to a bar.

"I could pretty well do what I wanted. My parents didn't pay much attention to me. That's how I met Harry Young and why I married him."

"Young? I thought his name was Sawyer," Nate said, realizing why his own search for Adam's father had been a wasted effort. He'd trusted her to tell him the truth about her husband as part of supporting his efforts with Adam.

"No. I went back to my maiden name after the divorce."

"Go on."

"Harry was older, handsome in a rugged sort of way. He flirted with me, said he had plans to make big money. I had never had money, and when he told me stories about how he planned to live, I believed him. I moved in with him and didn't finish high school. When Harry shot the officer I was devastated and terrified. When I realized I was pregnant all I could think of was hiding out, disappearing, but I didn't have the money. I didn't mean to hurt anyone, only to escape the disaster my life had become.

"When Adam was born I promised myself that no one would ever know about Harry, about what my life had been like."

"But that was years ago, and a whole different time in your life. Why didn't you tell Adam the truth when he asked?"

"Because I didn't want him to grow up knowing his father had nearly killed a police officer. I was afraid that he might go looking for Harry."

"And now when Adam is struggling to find his place, searching for who he is, you still couldn't tell him the truth?" he asked, aware that he was seeing an entirely different side to this woman.

"I couldn't tell him the truth because I wanted to protect him. I thought Harry would never find out about us. I'd been so careful… I wanted to make a life for us that didn't involve any part of Harry."

Her words held him. He struggled for an answer that wouldn't reveal his thoughts and the feelings driving them. He cared…much more than he should. He gentled his tone, seeking to understand her better. "You carried the burden of this lie for the past, what? Fourteen years? What made you do this?"

She moved to the far side of the sofa. "I wanted to protect Adam from his father's criminal behavior. I wanted to save my son from the unhappiness such knowledge could cause him. Harry nearly killed a police officer, and I've had to live with that all these years. I didn't want Adam to live with it, as well."

"Did you talk to anyone about this? Seek anyone's advice?"

"No. I had no one whose advice I could trust, and I didn't have the money to see a therapist. Besides, to admit to anyone what was going on in my life could have cost me my job."

"You don't know that," he replied. He'd begun to think they might be friends, that helping her son could lead to something more. And in the rush of feelings flowing through him now—shock, disbelief—he'd seen his emotions for what they were. He really wanted her in his life, to share his life and to share hers. He needed her to know he trusted her. And now he had to face the fact that she hadn't trusted him enough to confide in him.

What else had she lied about? "Adam's almost fourteen now. When did you plan to tell him the truth?"

"The truth?" She scrubbed her hands over the denim fabric stretched across her slim thighs, and Nate was helpless to keep from watching the way her fingers moved, wishing it were his hands. "Probably not for a long time if I could manage it. I wanted him to be an adult when he found out so that he wouldn't be influenced by his father." She shrugged. "But now I have no choice but to tell him. Tell him or leave here. I don't want to leave. When I saw the reporter on the TV talking about Harry, I still believed that we were safe…"

"The reporter on the TV?"

"Yeah, one of the national networks ran a piece today on Harry, some story about how he'd become a Christian and wanted to be redeemed for what he'd done to the police officer."

She hadn't been willing to confide in him until she'd had no choice. "So it's now all over the news, and you want to run away. Or you thought you wanted to run away."

"Harry knows."

"How?"

He listened as she explained about the Bartlett woman, her face wet with tears, her shoulders hunched. He felt sorry for her, and he wanted to help her. Yet he wasn't sure he could do that unless he believed she'd told him everything. He'd made that mistake with Natasha. He'd assumed that they were together on everything, only to discover that she couldn't keep her promise.

Gayle wasn't like Natasha, and her circumstances were entirely different. But in his heart and mind he wasn't sure if he could offer the support she needed without being certain that she'd told him everything.

"So your answer to this is to run away."

"No. I don't want to run away. I want to stay here…with you. With your family and my friends."

Was that supposed to be comforting to him? Was he to believe that she had turned to him for help because she wanted him to be a part of her life? That staying had something to do with how she felt about him? Or was she simply looking for an ally should the press arrive at her door? He hated himself for thinking this way, but he'd begun to really care for her, a glimmer of love he couldn't deny. Yet he couldn't lower his emotional guard or let himself feel vulnerable where she was concerned. He would not get caught up in the pain such vulnerability would cause.

He drew in a heavy breath as his eyes met hers. Without warning, something deep inside him twisted, causing an unfamiliar wrenching in his chest. She'd come to mean something special to him. Without him realizing it, he'd opened his heart to her, and she'd let him down. "I thought we were friends, that I could trust you."

Her eyes darkened. "This isn't about you or me. It's about Adam. With the news reporters jumping all over this story, I have to tell him as soon as he comes through that door." She nodded toward the front of the house. "If I don't, someone else will. I don't care what the media are saying about his conversion to Christianity. Harry is a mean man. Now that he knows I've kept his son from him he will make my life miserable—all in front of national television.

"I can find some way to cope with it all, but Adam…" Tears flooded her eyes. His hands reached for her of their own accord and stopped. He couldn't touch her, expose his need for her without knowing who she really was.

She visibly held herself in check, clinging to the arm of the sofa, as far from him as possible. "Adam has to be told the truth. It's the only chance I have to protect him from the worst of what is to come. Harry always liked to be the center of attention. And now, if he has an audience, he won't hesitate to drag Adam into it, make himself look like a man who's been abandoned by his wife and kept from his son."

She stared at his hand where it rested on the sofa. "Will you help me figure out how to tell him?"

"That should be your job," he said, torn between reaching for her and walking out. He didn't like how he was feeling one little bit. He had come to believe in her, in what might be possible between them with time and mutual caring. "This is the kind of thing only you can tell him."

Her eyes met his. She looked desperate and frightened. "When I first heard the news report

I wanted to run. I came home and packed Adam's things and mine. I couldn't face telling him. You see, I'm a coward. I've lived a lie because I'm too afraid to tell the truth." Her eyes darted around the room as tears bolted down her cheeks.

She didn't attempt to block them, and he felt himself soften. He had no right to pass judgment on her. He may have lost his dad, but he'd had a loving, supportive family to rely on, while she'd had no one she could turn to for advice. She had lived the past fourteen years alone.

However misguided Gayle's efforts were on Adam's behalf, she had her son's best interests at heart. He could at least help her get through this. "If the press stay on the story, and Mary Ellen Bartlett is right about your ex-husband's plans, he may show up here. But I'll be here for you. I'm only a phone call away." He reached out to brush the curls resting on her shoulder.

THE ONLY SOUND between them was their breathing, no words of blame or probing questions. Gayle glanced up, her eyes meeting his, making her wish she could simply move into the safety of his arms, that her past was just one bad dream.

As if he'd read her thoughts, Nate slipped his arms around her. He pressed his lips on her

forehead, his caress so intimate and inclusive it
swept all reason from her mind.

"You're not to blame," he whispered close
to her ear. "You were eighteen years old when
Harry did what he did. You couldn't have
stopped him." He took her face in his powerful
hands, his mouth close to hers, his eyes never
leaving her face.

She had never met anyone like Nate, and she
was quite sure she loved him. Yet he hadn't said
a word about his feelings for her, or offered her
any hope that he might want more than friendship. And now that he knew the truth, there
would be little chance he'd see her as anything
other than a woman whose life was in shambles.
A woman who had lied to just about everyone
for years.

He had no reason to be in her life now that
he knew her secret, except for his mentoring
of Adam. And if Harry made her life into his
own private media event, she had no reason to
believe that Nate would stay beside her. He'd
given his word, but she'd seen how words could
be meaningless.

But before he left she needed to feel his arms
around her. To believe that for one short in-
terlude someone might desire her. She quietly
slipped her arms around him. "How do you feel
about the man who shot you?"

"As awful as it was at the time, it led me to what I'm doing today. Being injured took me off the line of duty, but gave me the opportunity to work with children at risk. That's something I love." His smile swept her up in its brilliance. "And it gave me the chance to meet you."

"I don't understand," she said, surprised and hopeful at the same time.

He looked into her eyes, his attention focused solely on her. "I'm sorry I judged you. I had no right to. You were doing the best you could under difficult circumstances, and I admire how hard you've worked to be a good parent...a good person. Gayle, it's not about your past, it's about your future."

Her body warmed at his words. "My future?"

"I don't want you to leave Eden Harbor. I want to help you put your past behind you, once and for all." With that, he kissed her, his arms enfolding her in a snug cocoon of need and desire. She hugged him close, her mouth opening to his, her heart rising in her chest. In an easy movement he pulled her down on the couch with him, his hands roving over her body. She tried to respond, but ended up feeling awkward and embarrassed.

"I've never really been with a man. I mean, sex with Harry wasn't..."

"Forget Harry," he said, his kiss deepening,

coaxing feelings she'd never experienced to spiral through her. His gentleness, his ardor, mixed with her driving need to be loved made every hurt, every insult, every remembered attack on her soul start to fade. Being in his arms soothed her, and she finally knew unequivocally what it meant to be happy.

He palmed her breast. His body shaped hers. Her breath came in short gasps.

"You are so beautiful," he said. "From the first time I met you, I wanted to run my fingers through your hair." His mouth teased her lips as he reached to undo her bra. The light caught on his watch, illuminating the time—4:19 p.m.

"Adam!" She grabbed his wrist and took another look. "I don't have much time. Adam will be here soon…if he comes straight home." For once she hoped he'd be late.

She glanced surreptitiously at Nate, whose only response seemed to be a giant scowl. "Look, are you sure you want to help me? I'm going to tell Adam this afternoon, and then if the press find us…" She left the sentence unfinished as she scrambled up from the couch. With an aching sense of sadness, she realized that he might mean what he'd said about helping her in the short-term, but she couldn't ask him to be there for her any longer than that. Mentally she shook her head to ward off the feeling that her life was careening out of control, and she was powerless to stop it.

Nate towered over her as he stood up. He was the fulfillment of every dream she had ever dared to dream. "I'm not leaving you to face this alone. Why don't you let me see what I can do for you and Adam?" he asked, his voice a soft caress, beckoning her back into his arms.

Relief made her knees weak. She moved toward him, her head resting on his chest as she listened to the solid beat of his heart. If only life were this simple.

The sound of footfalls along the porch announced the arrival of Adam home from school. "I'm going to tell him now."

"I'll be right beside you when you do."

So many feelings flooded her heart—love, gratitude and happiness. Yet all of it paled in the face of what her son would do when he learned the truth about his father.

As Adam entered the room, he stopped. "What's going on?"

Gayle asked Adam to sit down, explaining that she needed to talk to him.

"What have I done now?" His suspicious glance went from one to the other as he sat down across the coffee table from her and Nate.

"Adam, honey, I...I need to talk to you about something important."

His mom always got that worried look whenever he'd done something she thought was wrong. Adam chewed his lip. Had she heard about the fight he got into at school today? One of his buddies, Norm Hanson, had been picking on Jeremy Barker in the schoolyard. "The fight wasn't my fault. Norm started punching Jeremy."

"Fight?" His mom's forehead was a mass of worried wrinkles.

"Isn't that what this is about?" Had he confessed to something she didn't know? As if his day hadn't been bad enough already.

She shook her head in a strange, distracted way.

Adam felt his stomach begin to pain. If it wasn't the fight, then what awful thing had happened to make his mom so upset? Had she been the one to do something wrong for a change? Was she trying to tell him that she and Nate were dating? Now, that would be so cool.

"Mom, it's okay. Whatever it is, you can tell me," he said, trying to sound all grown-up. He had to admit that Nate looked downright uncomfortable.

"Adam, when you were born I was alone," she said, her voice so soft he could barely make out her words. He looked to Nate, but he was staring at his mom...a strange expression on his face.

"Dad was away on the fishing trawler, wasn't

he?" he asked, frowning. His mother and Nate were behaving in a seriously weird way.

Her hands scrubbed her thighs, a sign that his mom was about to cry.

Not today, Mom. Please not today.

"I got my math test back and got a hundred," he said to block whatever was coming his way.

His mom looked distracted and then went back to rubbing her legs. "Adam, your dad is alive."

"What!" He jumped up, feeling an amazing rush of relief and happiness. "They found him where? On an atoll in the Pacific Ocean? Like that guy from El Salvador who was found in the Marshall Islands after a year?" He started to pace around the room, imagining what it would be like when he met his dad for the first time. "Jeez! Who would have thought... How is he, Mom? Have you talked to him? Did he ask about me? When can I see him?"

"Adam, please sit down," she asked.

"Why? What's the matter? Doesn't he remember us? Does he have another family? What's he doing?"

"Adam, your father wasn't on a trawler off Alaska. I...I didn't tell you the truth because I wanted to protect you."

"From what?" he asked, impatient to understand what his mother was trying to say. "Tell me what's going on."

She closed her eyes and took a deep breath. "Your father was sent to prison for shooting a police officer in Anaheim shortly after you were born. I didn't tell you because I didn't want you growing up with the stigma of being the son of a convicted felon."

"My dad is alive in prison somewhere? You're lying," he shouted, hurt and confused by his mother's words.

"No, she's not," Nate interjected quietly.

Adam turned his anger on Nate. "What would you know? And if my dad is alive and in prison, why didn't you find him for me when I asked you to? Police officers can get that kind of information, can't you?"

"He didn't know where Harry was," his mom said. "I didn't tell anyone because I wanted you and me to have a fresh start here in Eden Harbor. When Harry was sent to prison, it just seemed simpler for everyone if Harry Young died in a trawler accident."

"Young? I don't have my dad's last name?"

"Adam, I made it all up to protect you from him."

"From my father. After all the times you and I talked about Dad, especially since we moved here to Aunt Susan's house. Why couldn't you tell me then? We had moved thousands of miles from where it happened. Do you know how it feels to have no idea what your father or his family was like? To have no connection to anyone on this earth other than you and a few friends? Not having a family is awful. Why couldn't you tell me? At least then I could have understood what was going on."

"I didn't want you to have to grow up as the son of a convicted felon. I wanted you to grow up believing your father was a good man."

"But he wasn't. He wasn't a good man, but he was still my dad." He wanted to hit something, smash his fist into something, anything to ease the anger building inside him. But he couldn't with Nate standing there, looking so protective at his mother. What was he doing here anyway? What was in it for him? Was he the one who'd made his mom tell the truth? "So why now, Mom? Why are you telling me now?"

His mom took another deep breath. "Your father has been released from prison. He's become a Christian. He wants to help prisoners make a life on the outside. He was interviewed on the TV today. This morning, actually."

Wow! His dad was involved in religion, and Adam had never seen the inside of a church. Strange or what? "Is he coming here to see me?"

His mom stood up and went to the mantel

over the fireplace. She picked up a photo taken when he joined the Boy Scouts. "I didn't tell him about you."

"My dad doesn't know I exist?" His chest was so tight he could barely breathe. "So this is all about you. Not me. You're not telling me about my dad because you want to. You're telling me because you have to, in case someone in the media figures out that Harry's ex-wife and his son are living in Eden Harbor."

She turned to him, her face covered in tears. "Adam, I'm sorry for all this. I should have done things differently. Can you understand at all?"

He looked at his mom, someone he'd always loved and admired. Sure, there had been times when they didn't get along, times when he'd wished he had a normal family. A sibling. A cousin. Any family at all.

But all he had was a mother who had lied to him his entire life. Nothing seemed real anymore. "I don't want to see you again. I'm leaving tonight."

Her sobs filled the room. Nate put his arm around her shoulders, and when Adam saw the look of gratitude on his mother's face, he realized that his mom had feelings for this man who had come into their life to help him. Nate had acted as if he cared for Adam, but he was really here just to help his mom, the person responsible for not telling him the truth.

Adults! They were all alike when it came to playing games with kids like him.

"You can't leave. You have nowhere to go," she said through her tears.

"I'll figure it out," he said, immediately aware that his mother was right. But it didn't matter. His dad would want to see him. He turned his fury on Nate. "And you stay out of this. I'm going to find my father whether either of you like it or not. I don't care what he's done, and the courts wrongly convict people all the time. I'm going to help my dad get his life back. He'll need me. We'll be a team."

He raced upstairs to his room to discover that his mother had already packed his clothes in his duffel bag. Had she been planning to run from Eden Harbor rather than tell him about his father? Feeling utterly betrayed, he emptied the cash in his drawer into his pockets, slung his bag over his shoulder and stomped down the hall to the stairs, taking them two at a time.

Nate and his mother were waiting for him. "Please don't go. Please," she begged.

He couldn't listen to her after what she'd done, after all her self-righteous talk about his friends and their bad influence. At least they hadn't lied to him. "I'll call you when I've found Dad. He may or may not want to talk to you after what you've done."

He slammed the door hard as he left, the action making him feel good—in charge of his life. He went around the side of the house and got his bike. Swinging his leg over the seat and his duffel bag over his shoulder, he went down the driveway toward the street leading downtown.

CHAPTER ELEVEN

"WE HAVE TO stop him! Nate! Please!"

"Shh…" he murmured, easing her into his arms, feeling the trembling in her body. He wished he could change everything in her life up until the moment he'd met her.

She pulled away, wiped the tears from her cheeks and opened the front door. "I can't let him go like this. I have to know where he is. What if he's gone to meet up with those friends of his, the ones that got him in trouble?"

"He probably is headed there now."

Her expression radiated shock. "Then why aren't we going after him?"

"Give him a little time. He can't get far without money. He's driving a bike, not a car."

"What if he steals a car? What if he's like his father? Harry took whatever he wanted whenever he wanted it."

"Adam isn't like that."

"How do you know?" she asked, her voice shaking.

"Have a little faith in him and yourself. You

raised him to be a caring individual. He won't let you down...not now."

"What do you mean? Not now?"

"When he has time to think about it, he'll know that his best chance of finding his father is by talking to you. Sure, he can go to the press, but their tactics will drive him straight back here."

"I don't want him to face that alone," she cried.

"He won't if he gives us a chance to help him. If he doesn't, he'll have to learn on his own terms."

"I suppose you're right," she said, reaching out to him, to the safety of his arms.

He hugged her close, then held her at arm's length and looked into her eyes. "In the meantime, I'll call the police, tell them what's happening here. Get your purse and we'll follow him downtown. I'm sure we'll find his bike at one of the local hangouts."

"And if we don't?" she persisted.

"It's a long, expensive trip to California, one he can't do on his own. Let's find him and save him the embarrassment of eventually having to come back."

Gayle touched his arm. "Nate, would Adam have been a different teenager if he'd known about his father and his criminal behavior?"

"We'll never know, will we? But my guess would be that he could have gone either way. Learning about his father might have been a very upsetting thing, or he might have wanted to get to know him."

"And now that Harry claims to be a Christian?"

"Faith in God can change everything in a person's life, and only with time will we know how it's affected Harry. If it's been a positive influence on him, he might be just what Adam needs right now."

"How?"

"Adam needs his father, and if Harry has changed enough to understand what that means to a teenage boy, he could be very supportive to his son."

"When did you get to be so wise?" she asked, a slight smile warming her face.

He kissed her lips and ran his fingers along her shoulders. "I'm still on a learning curve when it comes to being wise."

She could not imagine what she would have done without Nate beside her now. She was so relieved that the risk she'd taken by asking for his help had paid off. That she put her trust in him, something she had never done with anyone before.

They drove along every street downtown

looking for Adam's bike. The longer they drove, the more apprehensive she became. "Where could he have gone?" She turned to Nate. "What if he headed to the highway?"

"I'm going from what I know about Adam. He'd want to talk to the guys he hangs out with. He'd figure they'd understand. Adam is very bright. It would have occurred to him by now that he needed someone's help to find his father, that driving a bike along a road by yourself with no plan would be dumb on his part. I'm guessing he's somewhere down around the docks."

He parked in the public lot along the wharf. The air had begun to chill with the incoming tide, the currents stirring up a slight breeze.

"Where should we start?" she asked, getting out of the car, slinging her purse over her shoulder and pulling her jacket tighter.

"The boys Adam hangs with like to ride motorcycles and play pool," Nate said, glancing along the pier toward the far end of town.

"We already checked Denny's Pool Hall. There isn't another in town, is there?"

"Not anymore." Nate rubbed his jaw in thought. "It would probably be faster if we split up."

"I don't want to do that. I mean, what if I came across Adam with some of his sleazy friends? I wouldn't know what to do, and he might leave when he sees me."

"Okay, let's get moving," he said, starting off ahead of her along the walkway, his cane clicking on the wooden boardwalk.

She caught up with him and matched his stride. She felt uneasy out here in the quiet of late afternoon when her son could be almost anywhere. "What if we don't find him?"

"I know it's easy to think the worst in a situation like this." His gaze warmed her. "But we'll find him. Trust me."

She'd never trusted a man before in her life. Not her father, her half brother or the few men she dated. And definitely not Harry. Yet as she let her gaze travel over the face of this man, from his firm jaw, to his sensuous mouth, his concern-wrinkled forehead and his eyes—especially his eyes—she was convinced that he was different. "I do trust you," she said, feeling reassured by those words.

Nate had promised to be there for whatever lay ahead. Somebody finally had her back. "Has anyone told you lately how much you're appreciated?" she asked.

"Not lately," he mused. His smile held a hint of embarrassment, making him seem younger to her.

Just then a police cruiser pulled up alongside them. The officer rolled down his window. "Highway patrol called in to say they didn't see any kid on a bike on Route 1A, but they'll keep a lookout."

"Thanks." Nate kept pace with the cruiser.

"Can I help?" the officer asked. "I've checked around town for his bike, the places he might have gone, but nothing."

Gayle felt herself start to panic and grabbed Nate's sleeve. "Where could he have gone? I was right, Nate, we should have driven after him the minute he left the house. But you wanted to wait," she said, blaming herself for believing in what Nate had said about her son.

"Look, why don't you let the officer take you back to the house. Adam might have forgotten something and gone back. You should be there to reason with him if he does. I'll keep searching along the waterfront."

His eyes held hers, his face showing the first flicker of uncertainty since Adam had left the house. What if while she was down here searching, her son had gone back to the house? "I hadn't thought of that." She turned to the officer. "Would you give me a lift?"

He nodded.

As she crossed the street, her thoughts were on her son. She hated to admit defeat so easily, and more than anything she wanted to find

Adam. Yet she had nothing to go on except the gut instinct that he wouldn't leave town without seeing her before he left… She had to believe that.

"Wait a minute," Nate called out to her. "One day when I was with Adam, he mentioned a hangout up behind Ketchner's Inn on Maple Street. Some of his friends went there. Didn't there used to be an old pool hall down where Maple Street was blocked off when they built the highway?"

"You're right," the officer said. "I think the building's been sold, but the new owners haven't taken possession as yet. It's worth looking into."

Nate strode back to his car.

"Wait! I'm coming with you," Gayle called out to him as she ran across the street.

They followed the police car to the site of the old pool hall and discovered several motorcycles snugged up against the wall near the door. The three of them entered the building, greeted by the sound of pool balls smacking against one another.

Gayle cringed. She'd always avoided places like this, the kind of places where Harry had spent a lot of his time. In the dim light she could make out four people. One of them was Adam.

"Mom, what are you doing here?" Adam said,

striding toward her, his youthful face twisted in a scowl.

"Adam, you have to come home with me, please. We need to talk." She sensed Nate's presence as he came to stand beside her. It felt so strange to have his support, strange yet wonderful.

"Mom, unless you're willing to help me talk to my dad, I'm not going anywhere with you," he said, his gaze flicking to Nate, "or him."

When Harry learned that Adam had been told so little about him, he'd use it to gain Adam's sympathy. Or what if Harry had no interest in Adam other than to use him for good PR? She couldn't let Harry hurt her son that way. She had to stall for time while she figured out what to do next.

"Talking to your dad will not help you, especially now that's he's a major news item. What if the news media want to interview you? Are you prepared to have the press parked outside the door?"

Adam wrapped both hands around the pool cue as he studied the floor. "I want to see my father. I want to... I need to..." He lifted his head, his eyes meeting hers. "Mom, please understand. You can't stop me from seeing my dad. If you don't let me talk to him I'll go to the press. I'm not afraid of them, and if talking to the press would help my dad, I'll do it."

"Adam, I understand your feelings," Nate said, moving closer to Gayle, his body nearly touching hers. "Can we go home and talk about this a little more? This is hardly the place to call your father from."

Somehow she had to convince Adam not to speak with the press. If Harry thought he could get sympathy over what she'd done, he wouldn't hesitate to expose her lies. Harry had always used people, anytime, anyplace.

She couldn't allow him to victimize her or Adam ever again. "Come home with us and we can call your father after I tell you about him."

"Is that a promise?" Adam asked.

She sighed in resignation. "Yes, it's a promise."

CHAPTER TWELVE

"HEY, MAN, WHAT'S up with you?" Sam Mason demanded when Adam announced he was going with his mom and Nate.

"I'm going to get to talk to my dad finally." Adam wasn't sure if going home with his mom was a good idea or not, but he had to meet his dad somehow. When he'd first arrived at the hangout, Sam had loaned him his cell phone and he'd called the local TV station. They'd wanted to know why Adam needed to be in contact with Harry Young, but he'd simply said he had a friend who knew Harry from years ago. The person at the local station seemed to accept that explanation and gave Adam a California number to get in touch with his dad.

He'd wanted to call right away, but realized that if things didn't go well with his dad, he'd look like a loser in front of his friends. He didn't need that when being part of this group meant so much to him.

"Your dad? Cool." Sam slapped him on the back.

"Will you guys still be here later?" he asked,

wanting a chance to tell them about his father and how famous he was now that he was out of prison. He'd wanted to be a real member of this group, and he would be after they learned about his dad. But first he had to go home with his mom. So embarrassing. But what choice did he have?

Sam gave him a derisive glance. "We'll be around."

Adam pulled his bike out from behind a scraggly hemlock tree and let Nate put it in his SUV. As they drove home, his mom seemed so quiet and dejected he wanted to hug her and tell her he didn't mean to be a problem to her. He only wanted to have a life, to know who he was and where he came from. He couldn't say those words right now. He didn't know why, except maybe he was afraid of crying. He hadn't cried for a long time, not since he was a little kid. Somehow not crying made him more of a man, at least in his own eyes. None of his friends ever cried.

He fisted his hands in an attempt to maintain control as Nate turned onto their street. He could feel the tears stinging his eyes as he thought about his dad, about how he was only minutes away from speaking to him.

As they entered the house Adam was only vaguely aware of Nate and his mother talking about how to find his dad. He was focusing on what he'd say to him, how he'd start the conversation. "I already have a number for my dad."

"You do?" Nate asked. "Where did you get it?"

He didn't answer Nate. He didn't need to. This was between his father and him.

"Adam, honey, are you sure you want to do this?"

"Why wouldn't I? Dad and I need to talk, and maybe get together sometime," he said, taking the grubby piece of paper with his father's number on it out of his pocket. Ignoring the anxious look on his mother's face, he dialed the number.

"My name is Adam Sawyer, and I need to speak to Harry Young." He clutched the phone tight in his hands as he went into the den away from his mother and Nate's prying eyes.

"What about?" the voice asked.

"I'm…I'm his son," he said, feeling a weight lift off his shoulders at the sound of those words.

There was only silence. He waited, wondering what might have gone wrong. "Is Harry Young there? I need to speak to him," he repeated.

"Just a minute," the person said. In the background Adam could hear people talking excitedly. Was his father among them?

"Hello, who am I speaking to?" a man said in a loud voice.

"Are you Harry Young?"

"Yes," the man said with more gentleness in his tone.

"My name is Adam Sawyer. My mom is Gayle Sawyer. You're my dad," Adam said, sucking air through his constricted throat.

"How old are you?"

"I'm almost fourteen," he said, his uncertainty growing. Was this his dad? "Are you Harry Young?"

"I am, son, but I need to be sure who you are."

"Weren't you married to my mom, Gayle Sawyer?"

"I was, but I only found out a couple of days ago that I had a son…" Harry's voice trailed off. "I understand you're in someplace called Eden Harbor with your mother?"

"How did you know that?"

"Never mind how I know. You're living in a house your mom's aunt Susan left to her in her will."

"Yes." So his dad knew about him and where he lived. "My mom told me you were just released from prison in California." Adam could hear the man's long sigh.

"You have to understand I have a lot going on right now. I had no idea about you all these years. What has your mother told you about me?"

"Nothing except that you were in prison."

"Did she say what for?"

"No."

"Adam, I robbed a convenience store and shot a cop."

Adam gasped in shock. "Did you kill him?"

"No, but I injured him pretty badly."

His father had shot a man for no reason other than wanting to steal. "How could you do that? How could you hurt another human being?" he said, suddenly very angry.

This man couldn't be his father. His mother wouldn't have married someone capable of shooting another person. There had to be some sort of mistake…but his mother had said… Tears stung his eyes. He swiped them away and sniffed back the sobs threatening to leave his throat. This wasn't fair. He'd wanted a real dad all his life. A father he could be proud of, tell his friends about.

He'd dreamed about what it would be like if his dad had not died in a trawler accident, but this was worse. Having a father who was a criminal was way worse.

"I have a lot to atone for, but with God's guidance and the prayers of those around me, I will make good on my promise to live a Christian life. And I'm *so* glad to learn that I have a son. I realize that all of this must come as a shock, but with time maybe you'll see that I'm a changed man. I'm not the same man who committed that crime."

"Are you saying you didn't do it?" Hope rose in a wave through Adam. Was it possible that his father hadn't shot that officer?

"No, son. I did those awful things, and I'm sorry. I paid the price in prison time. I just wanted to somehow get you to understand that the man I am today, thanks to being a born-again Christian, couldn't have done what I did back then when I was a sinner in need of being saved by the grace of God."

Adam didn't know anything about being a Christian and didn't really see the need to be one. But if Christianity had helped his dad, maybe it was a good thing. One thing he did know—he didn't want to talk to this man. He was hurt and disappointed with everyone in his life; everyone had let him down, and that included the man on the other end of the line. "I have to go."

"Can we talk again?" Harry asked quickly.

"I don't see why," Adam said, and hung up.

"Are you all right?" his mother asked, startling him.

He didn't turn around. "Were you eavesdropping?" he fired back without looking at her. He didn't want to see her right now. He didn't want to see anybody.

"I didn't mean to. I'm worried, that's all."

"Well, you can stop worrying," Adam said, walking past her back into the living room. He had to get out of here before he said something that would hurt his mom. He didn't understand why she'd kept this a secret. It wasn't as if he'd want to visit the man in prison, far from it.

"Adam, we need to talk," she said, following him.

He turned to face her. There were tears streaming down her cheeks, but he couldn't care about that. If telling the truth made her cry, that was her problem. In his opinion, he was the one who had been hurt by his mother's lies. He was the one who should be crying. "Mom, why didn't you tell Dad about me?"

"Because I was never in touch with your father after he was sentenced."

"Why didn't you tell me my dad was a criminal?"

She winced at his words. "Because I didn't want you to have to deal with it."

"Why not?" he pressed.

She glanced up into Nate's eyes, then turned back to him. "I made mistakes back then. I was young and inexperienced. I married your father when I was eighteen, just a few years older than you are now. I didn't have a family to help me, and I couldn't forgive Harry for what he'd done to that officer, or what he'd done to you and me."

"Go on," he said, trying to imagine what it would be like if he had to make those kinds of decisions a couple of years from now.

"I was naive and didn't know what Harry did for a living. He told me he worked for a construction company, but I didn't know which one, and I never saw a check. But I was in love, or thought I was. I trusted your father to take care of me, and I needed to be taken care of. My family spent their time fighting and partying. I didn't have an education. Any of the jobs I applied for required experience. After I dropped out of school, I waited tables. I met your father while I...worked in a local diner. He was so brash and funny, and he really liked me. I was naive enough to believe his flirting with me was the beginning of a romance between us."

"So why did you marry him?"

"Because I thought that was what people did. I'd been living with him about a month when he proposed. I took his quick proposal to mean he really loved me and wanted a future with me. I should have done things differently, and deep down I knew I didn't love him. But when I realized that being married to Harry wasn't what I wanted, it was too late."

"What do you mean, too late?"

"I was expecting you. And if Harry hadn't gotten in trouble I probably would have stayed married as long as I could have stood it."

"Why?"

"Because I wanted you to have a father."

"Well, I don't think I want him in my life."

Relief swept over his mother's face. "I can't say I'm sorry about that."

"But I do want to meet him."

Her eyes darkened in disappointment. "Why?"

"I want to know what he's like, if I look like him and whether he has any family left. I meant it when I said I needed to find out what I could about my family."

His mother sat down hard on the chair. "Adam, this won't help you. Believe me."

He shrugged. "We'll see."

NATE WATCHED IN silence as Adam and Gayle talked. He sympathized with both of them, but it was the tormented look in Gayle's eyes that got to him. Harry Young was not the kind of person anyone would want to know, especially a vulnerable teen like Adam. Of course, Harry may have changed his ways because of his religious beliefs, but that remained to be seen.

What worried Nate most was the toll all of this was taking on both Adam and his mother. There was no doubt that Adam wanted to meet his father, and Gayle had to respect that wish. He was entitled to as much. On the other hand, Gayle had spent the past fourteen years keeping a secret she believed would harm her son if he discovered it. The stress she'd lived with all those years must have been terrible. And she'd had no one she could turn to for support. His appreciation for this brave woman grew with every passing moment.

But her life without the support of people who cared about her and Adam was over. "Okay, maybe I can help out here," he said, looking from Adam to Gayle. "I'll make the contacts and find out if Harry is willing to meet you."

"I don't want to see him under any circumstances," Gayle said.

Adam looked a little anxious. "Would you go with me to meet my dad? It's not like I want to spend time with him, really. I just want to meet him."

"That's understandable. Why don't I see what I can arrange?"

"That would be awesome. I'm going up to my room," Adam said.

"Can I assume you're not going to leave again?" Gayle asked. She sounded overwhelmed.

"I'm not going to leave, Mom," he said, his old smile firmly in place.

"Where's your duffel bag with your things in it?" Gayle asked. "We need to get it back here."

"I'll get it later."

When he'd gone upstairs, Gayle turned to Nate. "What do we do now?"

"I'll make some calls and see if I can set up a date for Adam to meet his father."

"Does that mean you and he will be going to California?"

Nate saw the anxiety in her eyes. Pulling her close he whispered, "Let me do the worrying for a change. I won't let you down. I promise."

She put her arms around him, her head resting on his chest. Something about the way her fingers worked along his back and her sigh of contentment made the moment one of intimacy and a feeling of connection he hadn't experienced in a long time. He hugged her closer and let the sensation close around them.

AFTER THE STRESS generated by the arrival of Harry in her life, Gayle had missed work for the past two days. She wasn't really sick, but she needed to get a grip on her feelings. So much had changed for her in such a short time. And while she struggled with her disrupted life, Adam seemed happier than he'd been in years. He'd even gone to school whistling, oblivious to the fact that she was home on a workday.

Adam's happiness made her angry. Angry that she'd done all the work of worrying, protecting and caring for him. All the anxious nights when she'd lain awake wondering if she'd have enough money, enough energy, enough of everything, to keep them going.

When she had finally begun to believe that she had what it took to care for her son, Harry walked back into their lives, and Adam was happy. Just like that.

Then there was Nate. She chewed her bottom lip, her coffee cooling on the table in front of her. Two days ago, the last time she'd heard from Nate, he'd said he would find Harry. But how complicated could that be given all the media attention the man had received of late? Or was Nate avoiding her? Had something changed? Or was she simply overwrought?

She smoothed her hair from her face and concentrated on how she and Nate had connected in such a positive way. For the first time in her life she'd found someone who cared for her…in a romantic way. It was true that neither of them had made any kind of commitment. It was just that she'd assumed that from now on they'd be in touch with each other. She needed to know that she mattered as much to him as he did to her.

Gayle felt totally abandoned.

What a fool she'd been, confusing Nate's job

responsibilities where Adam was concerned with the beginning of some sort of caring relationship with her.

But he'd kissed her. Maybe he kissed any woman he found mildly attractive. How would she know?

Now that she'd met Nate, she regretted that her whole life had been spent avoiding relationships with men.

But what hope did she have when she couldn't be honest about her past? Hardly the best way to start a relationship, let alone a love affair.

Her eyes stung, but she blinked the tears away and wrapped her hands around her now-cool coffee cup.

She hadn't seen it coming, her feelings for Nate, so overwhelming and magical they took her breath. She'd begun to dream of him, wake up to thoughts of him, of what they might have together.

So embarrassing!

He would have to come to the house at some point, at least until he'd finished working with Adam. Nate had promised that to her, hadn't he? How was she going to survive being around him for the next little while, wanting him so much it hurt while terrified she'd make a fool of herself?

She began to walk the floor in her agony, back and forth, as she faced another issue she'd been hiding from for two days. She didn't know how to approach Sherri and Anna, her two best friends. She felt pretty certain that Nate would have said something to one of them, yet neither had called to find out what was going on.

Were they angry with her? Or were they waiting for her to tell them in person? The old fear of exposure caused her to feel panicky. She breathed deeply, trying to calm herself.

Without giving herself a chance to change her mind, Gayle grabbed her jacket and purse and headed out to her car. To her utter humiliation she found herself checking each vehicle she drove past for Nate's SUV—like some sort of mad stalker.

She gripped the wheel and concentrated on her driving until she reached the medical center on the edge of town.

When she got to the clinic area, she was greeted by a giant hug from Sherri. "I thought you were home sick."

"Not really. I needed some time to myself. So much has happened," Gayle said, returning the hug.

"I'm sorry I didn't call the other night, but Anna needed to talk about what's going on in her life."

Gayle waved off her concern. "I understand. Family comes first."

"How are you doing?" Sherri asked, holding her friend at arm's length and giving her an assessing glance.

"Did Nate say anything?" Gayle asked.

"He told me about Harry. It's been all over the TV. I hope you don't think I'm being nosy, but I'm worried about you." Her words were rushed. "I wanted to call your house but didn't know what to say. Are you okay?"

"You're not angry at me for the…lie I told?" Gayle asked.

"Come on down the hall to one of the empty exam rooms. You and I need to talk."

Sherri closed the door and leaned against the exam table. "I can't imagine how difficult your life must have been that you would feel you had to create a story around Adam's father. But I do know that since I've taken on being a stepmother to Morgan, there isn't anything I wouldn't do to protect her."

Gayle had dreaded this moment ever since she'd joined the clinic and become a part of life in Eden Harbor. Now that it was here, she felt so much better that her lie had been exposed. "Adam has been my life for fourteen years. I didn't want him growing up under the influence of a criminal, and that's what Harry is. I was too young and dumb to realize what I'd gotten myself into."

"Tell me about it. All of it," Sherri said, her eyes filled with concern and caring.

And Gayle did. She told her everything about her past, and as she talked a weight lifted from her shoulders, allowing her to breathe easier.

"The worst part for me was when Harry shot the police officer. He'd come home angry and brandishing a handgun, bragging that he should have used a shotgun. I was terrified. I pleaded with him to go to the police and give himself up. He threatened to beat me. I hid in the bedroom until he left."

Sherri's voice was gentle. "You won't have to see him now, will you? I understood from Nate that he was taking Adam to meet his father somewhere out West."

"I honestly don't know. Nate hasn't been at the house since the day Adam called his father." She met her friend's concerned gaze. "What if Nate hasn't been in touch with me because he... doesn't want to see me?"

"No! But he does obsess when he's working on something. I remember the day he went to Neill's office and interrogated him about his intentions where I was concerned. Nate is Nate. He has to do things his way. Why are you so worried?"

"Nate was shot on the job. Harry shot an on

duty police officer. Maybe Nate believes that I could have done something to stop Harry."

Sherri's eyes were kind. "Let it go."

"I can't. I never went to see the police officer after the shooting, and I wish that I had told someone what I suspected about Harry."

"How would that have helped?"

"I should have gone to the police when Harry left the apartment that day. I knew he was going to do something bad."

"But you can't live looking back at what might have been. You've done enough of that," Sherri said. "And remember what you told me when I was going through my issues with Neill. About how I had to forgive and move forward. You have to forgive yourself and move on with your life."

"Sherri, I don't mean to pry, but what can you tell me about Nate's shooting?"

"Nate was on duty, and was shot by a kid. He and another officer were chasing two teenagers on foot when one turned around and pulled a gun. As Nate put it, he was lucky the kid was a poor shot because he was close enough to Nate that he would have died otherwise. Why do you ask?"

"Just wondering, that's all. We never really talked about it."

"Why don't you ask him about it when you see him again?"

"I'm not sure I will."

A slight frown crossed Sherri's features.

"That doesn't make sense. He was at Anna's last evening. I just assumed he'd been talking to you because he was telling us about what had happened... I don't get it."

"Neither do I," Gayle said, glancing toward the door, wishing she could leave before Sherri had a chance to ask her any more questions. She couldn't trust herself not to break down and cry, or confess her feelings for Nate.

If Nate didn't share her feelings, she couldn't bear to have anyone find out how she felt.

"What's going on, Gayle?"

"Maybe learning about my past was more than Nate could handle, especially the lies." Gayle gave an exaggerated shrug to hide the disappointment tearing at her heart. "Maybe after he had time to think about it, he couldn't accept what I did."

Sherri moved away from the exam table, coming eye to eye with Gayle. "You're in love with my cousin."

Gayle gasped in surprise and tried for a disarming smile. "I'm not Nate's kind of woman."

"How do you know?"

For a fraction of a heartbeat Gayle wished that

Sherri had made some sort of comment about how Nate had talked about her the other night. Even the flimsiest compliment would have given her reason to hope.

But his cousin didn't. If Nate had any feelings where she was concerned, he'd hidden them from those he loved.

Gayle wrapped her arms around her waist to stave off the loneliness seeping into every part of her being. "He's into young, beautiful but unattached women. I'm attached to my son. What's the expression? I bring a lot of baggage to any relationship in my life."

CHAPTER THIRTEEN

GAYLE RETURNED HOME to her empty house. She scrubbed the kitchen floor and changed the beds, anything to keep her lonely thoughts at bay. She was just pulling on the last pillowcase when the phone rang.

She answered after the second ring when the caller ID indicated it was Nate. "Hi, Gayle, how are you?" he asked, his tone sounding distant to her anxious ears.

Was that how a man greeted a woman he really cared about?

She sighed. What had she expected? He hadn't given her any reason to believe he wanted to be involved with her. She was the one clinging to the dream of something more. "Have you been able to contact Harry?"

"Yes. Harry has an agent now, and all arrangements are made through her," he said, his voice all business.

"You've been busy, I guess," she said to make conversation.

"Yes. I've had a teen in crisis."

She heard a curse and the sound of books and papers landing on the floor.

Why had he called? Had Sherri talked to him, and now he felt he owed her an explanation?

She didn't need a sympathy call. "By the sound of things, you're busy. We can talk later."

"No! I dropped a file and there are papers all over my office floor. I'm coming over. We need to talk."

"Yes, we do," she said, unable to continue not knowing how he felt about her. She was so inexperienced when it came to relationships that she didn't know what to think. All she knew for certain was that she loved this man.

She had been watching from the living room window when he pulled in the driveway. He was wearing the same gray shirt and leather jacket as on the day she met him. He looked even more handsome than before. She held the door for him as he came up the walk, feeling ridiculously happy at the sight of him.

She started to say something funny to prove she was not the least bit upset that she hadn't heard from him. To admit that she missed him would expose her feelings. But when he reached her, he put his arms around her, blocking any thought she had of being clever.

She didn't feel one tiny bit clever. She felt

warmed, comforted and safe. Her love for him stole her voice as he anchored her in his embrace.

I missed you.

He slid his arm around her in that easy way of his as they went into the house. He sat down on the sofa and turned off his cell phone. "Now finally we can talk."

He touched her outstretched fingers where they rested on her leg. "Gayle, I'm sorry about not calling you these past few days. I've had a lot on my mind."

No man had ever apologized to her before. If only she dared to let her heart do the talking… She settled for being as calm as she could. "No apology necessary. Anna needs you right now. You explained that. You're helping me with Adam, and you have other children who need your expertise." She leaned in close to him, her hands sliding involuntarily into his. "I'm not your responsibility. We're just friends," she said, feeling the lie settle at the bottom of her heart.

Nate held her hands gently in his, playing with her fingers as his eyes watched her, leaving her nowhere to hide from her feelings.

"I need to explain something about the past couple of days." He paused. "I didn't call you because I was afraid."

"You? Afraid? I don't understand."

"You mean a lot more to me than just a friend,

and it was those feelings that had me running for cover." He shook his head as if what he'd said had surprised him. "You've changed me in ways I didn't recognize…"

She held her breath, waiting for him to continue. "Go on."

"I love being around you. My day is always better after I've talked with you. You're different from other women. You're real, and caring and loving. When I left here I missed out on an opportunity to tell you how I felt, but then I didn't dare attempt to come here and explain myself for fear I'd screw it up, say the wrong thing."

"You couldn't say the wrong thing. Ever."

"I'm not so sure about that." He rubbed his hands together, a wry expression on his handsome face. "What happened with Natasha left me convinced that I didn't know very much about women. Ever since the breakup I've been running from commitment because I couldn't risk letting someone close enough to hurt me again. But then you came along."

Gayle wanted to hold him in her arms, to reassure him. Love for this man filled her heart and soul. She'd never felt this way. She'd never really ever been in love before. "Nate, I've spent the past two days thinking that you were only here because of Adam. That I was living a fantasy where you might care for me as much as I care for you."

There was so much relief in saying those words. Relief and excitement in equal measure.

He kissed her so gently, with so much emotion, she clung to him for support.

"Gayle, when this is over, when Harry is gone from your life, I'd like to…"

The ring of the doorbell bounced along the walls with the ferociousness of a fire alarm. They both jumped, and then smiled at each other sheepishly. "Saved by the bell?" she joked to hide her disappointment that he hadn't finished his sentence.

"Hold that thought," she said, going to see who was at the door. "I'll be right back. It's probably someone doing a survey."

When she opened the door, a man stood staring at her from under the hood of his jacket, dark glasses covering most of his face.

"Gayle Sawyer?" the man asked.

"Yes." She took a closer look at the man. There was something vaguely familiar about him. "How can I help you?" she asked, her knuckles white where her fingers clutched the door.

He gave a bemused chuckle. "I came to see you… You don't recognize me."

His voice was soft, unfamiliar to her distracted

ears. "No, I'm sorry." She glanced back into the living room to reassure herself that Nate was still there.

Nate cocked one eyebrow in question.

She returned her gaze to the man. "I'm busy right now. Maybe you could come back later."

"It's Harry."

It couldn't be. She looked closer. There was a faint resemblance to the man she'd hidden from for nearly half her life. She wanted to slam the door in his face. She wanted to scream and yell and push him off her veranda. She clung to the solid wood for support. "What are you doing here?"

"May I come in?" he asked.

She felt rather than saw Nate move to stand next to her. "Are you Harry Young?"

"I am." Harry pushed his hood off his head, lifted his sunglasses from his face and looked from Nate to Gayle.

"I'm Nate Garrison. We talked on the phone the other day."

Harry's face lit up. "Yes. You're the man who knows my son, Adam. I felt it would be best if I came in person to explain myself. May I come in?" he repeated.

Nate placed his arm around Gayle's shoulders, his tone gentle. "I think it would be best for everyone if we heard what Harry has to say."

Gayle stared at the man on the front porch, trying to absorb all the changes in him—the man she'd once both feared and loved. "I don't want him in my house."

Nate held her close, his warmth and protection releasing a torrent of loneliness and sorrow so strong she couldn't get her breath. Seeing Harry reminded her that she'd spent her younger years in the thrall of this man. When she'd left him to make a new life, his ugly behavior had hung over her like a dark cloud.

Now he was here, wanting to come back into her life whether he had any right to do so or not. He clearly didn't plan to leave until what was left of her life and her self-respect was shredded beyond recognition. In that instant she hated him more than she'd ever hated anyone or anything in her life. "I don't want him here," she repeated, her voice a harsh rasp in her ears.

Harry stood straighter. "I don't blame you one bit. I was a horrible man back when you and I were together, but you stayed with me when most women would have walked. And yes, I used your youth and your naiveté to my own advantage and I'm sorry. You deserved so much better. I've become a born-again Christian, and I've changed. I'm here to tell you about that if you'll let me."

"You have no business showing up on my

doorstep unannounced," she said. Choking back her anger, Gayle glanced at Nate…to the caring in his eyes. A look that made the air between them crackle with pent-up emotion. He was the only person she could trust when it came to dealing with Harry, or anything else in her life, she realized. She took a deep breath to ease the tension. "What do you think?" she asked him.

"Why not get this over with? You'll only have to do this once. Whatever Adam decides about his father is out of your hands, but it would help you to understand Harry a little better. It will give you closure."

She studied Harry for a long couple of minutes. He didn't flinch, and he didn't try to coerce her the way the old Harry would have. Besides, Nate was here, making her feel safe. "Come in," she said in resignation.

CHAPTER FOURTEEN

NATE MOVED TO sit down next to Gayle, whose whole body quivered with anger. He couldn't blame her for that. He'd gotten access to Harry's file, and he had been one miserable man in his younger years. He claimed to be a Christian now, but Nate didn't necessarily believe that. Once a con artist, always a con artist in his estimation. He reached out and took Gayle's hand, and was rewarded with a questioning half smile from her.

He squeezed her fingers reassuringly. "So why don't you tell us why you came here to see Gayle?"

"Is Adam here?" Harry asked.

Gayle started to rise, her face suffused with red blotches. "If you came here to gain access to my son…" she warned.

"Oh. No, I didn't mean that. I want to see Adam, but I didn't want him to overhear what I have to say to you. He needs time to process what he's learned about me, about our life back then. I'm aware that you've kept your past with me a secret and I want you to know I believe it was a good idea. No child should live life knowing his father was a convicted felon."

Gayle visibly relaxed and leaned into Nate, a surprising move but one that gave him a rush of unexpected pleasure.

Gayle looked to Nate for reassurance.

He nodded.

Returning her attention to Harry, she said, "Go on, then."

"You've probably seen the news about my work, and my release." He rubbed his hands together, ducked his head and gave her a faint smile. "What am I saying? Of course you have. I'm not here to hurt anyone. No one will be coming here to interview you or Adam. No one knows about you or where you live, and they won't find out from me. I'm a changed man. I know I can't make amends for my rotten behavior, but I want you to know that if I had it to do over again, I would have thanked God every day for giving me such a good wife, such a good mother for my son."

"So what are you doing here? Is it because you want my forgiveness after all this time? Forgiveness is not a piece of candy to be passed out freely."

He sighed and seemed to grow smaller in the

chair. "You're right. I went to see the police officer I shot. He wasn't into forgiveness, either."

"Can you blame him? You destroyed his life."

"Then you've seen him?" Harry asked.

"No." She raised her head and met Harry's glance head-on. "But I plan to at some point. I felt so guilty about what happened to him."

"But you didn't shoot him. I did."

Something in Nate shifted at Harry's words. He'd met with his attacker and understood what had driven the kid to do what he did. But somewhere out in California a police officer was living the nightmare of never being whole again, of having left behind the life he had planned on—all because of the actions of the criminal who sat just feet from him.

He glanced at Gayle's face and wondered how she had coped with the memory of that time in her life, how she had managed to create a happy life for her son despite her past. He was well aware of the statistics on the failure rate among single mothers living below the poverty line. Until she'd gotten an education, she would have been among that group.

He didn't know another woman who could have done what she did, and that thought made him so proud of her.

Gayle shifted closer to him. "If I had to do it over again, I would have gone to the police about you, about your lifestyle and the things I heard you talking about to some of your buddies. I should have and I didn't."

"I understand how you feel. I've lived every day of my life since I went to prison wishing I could make up for what I did. But I can't, except to live my life by the dictates of my faith in God." Harry didn't speak for a few minutes, his eyes misted with tears. "If you could find it in your heart to forgive me for leaving you alone, for not caring and loving you the way you deserved…I would like that."

"What you like or want doesn't matter to me anymore, Harry. I have a life here now, and my son is doing well."

"You mean *our* son."

"You may have a biological right to call him your son, but not much more," Gayle said, her fingers crushing Nate's as she spoke.

Nate could see how hard Gayle was struggling to remain calm, to listen to what Harry had to say. He admired her for even trying. But she'd worked too hard and given up too much to have Harry's influence change her relationship with her son.

However this played out, one thing was certain: he would be there for Gayle. As he sat close to her, breathing in her scent and the intimacy created by her nearness, he faced one unassailable fact. He was falling in love with her.

"Adam deserves a good life, free of any relationship with you, and if I had my way you'd never see him again. But I love my son, and if he thinks he needs to see you, that will be his decision."

"THANKS, MOM," ADAM said from the entrance to the room. He'd overheard every word between his parents.

"Adam. I didn't see you there," his mother said.

But it was his father's face that caught his attention. His dad appeared uncertain. He didn't have thick dark hair like his own, as he imagined, and his eyes were a faded blue color. He looked really old. He had assumed that his dad had been tall, rugged and strong from his work on a trawler. Not like this man. Not at all.

His mom seemed to be holding up okay with his dad there, a big surprise to him. Yet maybe not, he mused. After all, Nate and she were holding hands, and he'd seen the look in Nate's eyes as he watched his mom. Nate cared about her, and that pleased him. As for Harry, he didn't feel much of anything for him.

In fact, he was a huge disappointment. He

didn't look like…like his dad. He didn't look like anybody's dad.

Harry stood and came toward him. "Adam." He held out his hand. "It's a pleasure to meet you, son."

Adam shook hands with him, feeling awkward and out of place in this room of adults, who seemed to be watching him as if they expected him to explode or something.

"I didn't mean to interrupt. I just got in from school." He felt he needed to explain his presence, if only to diffuse the strange atmosphere in the room. As he met his mother's agitated glance, he realized that most of the tension he felt was coming from her.

"How was your day, Mom?" he asked her lamely.

"My day was good," she said, the love in her eyes meant only for him.

His mom was something else. Other kids might have more things, and lots of his friends had brothers and sisters, but no one had a mom like his. She was really cool.

Harry came toward Adam. "I'd like to speak to Adam alone, if you don't mind."

"Adam?" his mother asked, her eyes never leaving his.

"It's all right, Mom. Totally."

"We'll be in the den if you need us," she said.

ONCE IN THE den, Nate closed the door and followed her to the sofa. "What do you think will happen, Nate?" Gayle asked, pushing the unruly curls off her face.

Nate pulled her gently into his arms, using his strength to hold her up when he knew all she wanted to do was cry on his shoulder. "Trust Adam to know what he wants. His conversation with his father is important to him. Whatever comes out of it, we'll deal with it."

"You said *we*." Suddenly she was sobbing into his shirtfront.

He rubbed her back soothingly. "Gayle, you're a good parent, and Adam loves you very much."

That only seemed to make her sob harder. He wrapped his arms tightly around her and let her cry. Rocking her gently in his arms, he realized that he'd never experienced this feeling before. That he was essential to her and she to him. She was everything he'd ever wanted. The other women he'd known had never really needed him in the same way. Sure, they had lots of demands cloaked in sweet talk, but never anything like this.

He needed to be needed. He wanted the woman he loved to lean on him, not in a possessive way, but based on real need. When she'd squeezed his fingers earlier, he'd recognized something he'd been missing in his other relationships. Gayle made him feel good about himself, about his importance in her life.

"You have had a rough life, and I don't know anyone who could have done a better job with Adam than you did." He gently rubbed her back, and kissed the top of her head.

She turned her teary face up to his, her expression open and vulnerable. "You mean that?"

"I do." He kissed her forehead, her cheek, edging down to her mouth. When his lips touched hers, desire sizzled through him. He felt her intake of breath, the touch of her hands reaching around his neck. He pulled her closer to him, drawing her into his space, feeling her body arch to his, demanding him.

She was suddenly kissing him, her tongue sweeping his mouth, her groan of pleasure lighting a fire between them. A fire he welcomed.

He gazed into her eyes and saw in that moment what he'd been waiting for all his life. He loved this woman. He loved everything about her. She had been through some of the worst life had to offer and yet he had seen her vulnerable and open to happiness. It was as if they were connected on some level he couldn't name.

He was unexpectedly wary of his feelings, and needed time to regain his control. "Ah, maybe we should continue this later," he said to cover newfound anxiety.

Her eyes turned dark, her swollen lips an open invitation. "You're afraid we might be caught in the act?"

"We might," he said, rubbing a hand over his face.

Her fingers trailed along the neck of his shirt. "It could be nice."

"What could be nice?" he asked, leaning closer, pretending not to understand because he wanted her to say something more.

"You and me. Together."

She had offered him an open invitation to more, and he wanted to accept with every part of him. But something restrained him, tied him to the past. Another woman had offered him the world, and he'd accepted. That woman had walked out on him when she'd learned that his injuries were permanent.

He didn't know how Gayle would respond if they made love. She might simply treat it as casual sex, but his instincts told him that nothing about Gayle was casual when it came to her personal relationships.

During the past few weeks, she'd climbed under his skin in the gentlest of ways, had taken him into her life mostly, he assumed, because of her son. Meanwhile he'd been drawn in, exposed to her determination and fierce loyalty to her son. He hadn't expected her to become part of his life, only where it related to Adam. Yet he'd caught himself thinking about her when there wasn't any reason to.

And somewhere along the way he'd stopped seeing her as the mother of a client.

How could he resist such an open invitation? He sat up straighter and in one easy movement pulled her close to him to avoid the searching look in her eyes. "What do you suppose is taking so long?" he asked, instantly regretting his words.

The door opened, making them jump apart. "How did it go?" Gayle asked, getting up off the sofa and going to her son.

"He wants to see me again…before he leaves town. He is really sorry for everything he did. Mom, he told me that without your influence in my life, I could have ended up the way he did. He told me about how he had no real parents, had been kicked from one foster home to another."

Nate wanted to speak out, to warn Adam not to assume that Harry was telling the truth. He might be, but it wasn't fair for this man to try and gain sympathy from his son as a way to stay in his life. Adam needed a father figure, but not a father who would use him for his own ends.

"Are you going to see him again?" Gayle asked, her voice unusually calm.

"He wants to tell me about his plans for the future, and I want to know about them. My dad plans to do some good in this world, and I'm proud of him for that. I'm still trying to get my head around the idea that I have a dad, and that he's here."

The only sound in the room was the sigh of a towering pine outside the window. Nate stood next to Gayle, wishing he could take her in his arms, and save her from the thoughts that had to be tearing through her. He knew her well enough now to realize that she was afraid of letting Harry near her son, but felt powerless to stop him.

She wanted her son to love and respect her. She wanted him to be happy. She wanted Harry to disappear from his life.

CHAPTER FIFTEEN

THE NEXT DAY Gayle paced the floor between the kitchen and the dining area. Adam had left the house an hour earlier. She'd been watching the clock, waiting for him to return. Every minute she waited, her panic grew. "What if Adam wants to go with his father? What if Harry convinces him that life would be better with him in California?"

Nate tapped the table. "Harry said he didn't want to interfere in your life or Adam's."

"That was *before* he met Adam. Who knows what he's thinking now? He might decide that he wants to file for custody or something."

"I doubt that," Nate said, getting up and coming around the table, blocking her path.

She stopped before she bumped into him, and looked up into his gorgeous eyes. The man was 100 percent distracting, but she couldn't think about that right now. "What would happen if Harry decided to do something like that?"

"Is Harry on Adam's birth certificate as his father?"

"No. I pretended I didn't know who the father was because I was terrified he or one of his buddies would find me. I didn't know what Harry would do if he learned he had a son. He might not have done anything at all, but I couldn't take the chance. I had to lie for Adam's sake. When Harry's trial was going on, all I could think about was how I would manage to look after my child once he was born. I didn't think that something like this could happen, and if it did, Adam would be a grown man, not a vulnerable teenager."

He held her arms in his powerful grip. "Listen, honey, stop doing this to yourself. We won't know anything until Adam gets back here, and even then we might not learn that much. You have to remember that Adam was working through his issues around not having a father. Now suddenly he's faced with the man who is his father, and I can guarantee you he's very confused and anxious."

He lifted a curl off her face, his fingers grazing the sensitive skin along her cheek. She wanted to climb into his arms and hide out there forever.

"You have to remain calm and reasonable for him. When he comes back he'll need time to sort out his feelings. If you like, I can drop around to the motel and talk to Harry and explain that he should help his son out by leaving him alone for a while."

"What if Harry doesn't do anything other than talk to him, and Adam decides on his own that he wants to live in California near his father? What do I do then?" she asked, her eyes shining bright with tears. "I don't know what I'd do without him in my life, and I couldn't move back to California."

She felt his arms go around her, and her heart ached from the nearness of him. She'd never in her entire life had anyone who made her feel this way. It was as if everything that had ever gone wrong in her life had been wiped away by his very presence. She couldn't tell him why she couldn't move back to California because she'd have to admit that she loved him too much to ever leave him. She wanted to live with him, be part of his life. But if their relationship went no further than what it was now, she would settle for simply living near him. Her thoughts sounded like someone who was desperate for a man—desperate for this man.

"Why couldn't you move back?" he said softly against her ear.

Her body stilled. Her breathing slowed. If she told him, she risked everything. Although he'd been very kind to her, she had no idea what he felt for her. Sure, he wanted to have sex with her, and she wanted that more and more every day. But as for his real feelings, she had no idea.

She was afraid that because she cared so much she was reading too much into his behavior toward her.

She'd learned a long time ago that where emotions and feelings were concerned it was better to err on the side of caution. "I couldn't move back to California and start over. I've done that too many times." That was as close to the truth as she dared.

Before Nate could respond, the back door opened and Adam walked in.

Overcome with relief, Gayle went to her son and wrapped her arms around his neck, breathing hard and deep to keep the sobs at bay. "I'm so glad you're home. So glad."

"I am, too, Mom. I'm…" Adam hugged her hard against him. She was suddenly overwhelmed with memories of when he was younger, when he'd come into the house fighting tears from an injury, or joyful over an unexpected win during one of the many games played with his friends.

When he released her, they went to sit at the table where Nate had already positioned himself. "So tell us all about it," she said, anxious to hear what had happened.

"I'm so glad you're my mom." He looked a

little embarrassed as he undid his jacket. "I was too young to understand what you were going through trying to raise me on your own. I'm sure it wasn't easy. Then these past few months..." He shrugged. "I'm sorry."

"You've got nothing to feel sorry about."

"Thanks, Mom. Thanks for being there for me. Harry and I talked. His actions hurt a lot of people, including us. Although I want to stay in touch with him, I don't want to spend time with him just yet. Maybe when I'm older, or something, I'll want to be with him for vacations or stuff like that. But, Mom, my life is here with you and my friends. I want you to know I'm going to try harder to be the kind of person you can be proud of."

Her son seemed suddenly so grown-up, so in charge of his feelings. When had that happened? Were most thirteen-year-olds like this? After all the worry over the past few months, all she'd ever wanted her son to say to her had just been said. "Adam, I love you. I want you to have the best life possible. But what that is has to be your decision."

"I want to be where you are, Mom, like it has been all my life."

"And Harry? Where is he?" Nate inquired.

Adam turned to Nate. "He's headed out tomorrow morning, back to California. He's got a

TV interview the day after. He says he's excited about his new life, about doing good for others."

Was it finally over? Were she and Adam going to be able to get on with their life here in Eden Harbor?

"Well, this calls for a celebration," Gayle said. "I'm going to start dinner. Can you stay, Nate?" She held her breath, hoping he'd be free to join them. She wanted a chance to spend time with him, to enjoy the present moment and all it offered. He had shown that he cared for her, and she loved him. She wanted to go from there, see what they had together. At the very least, she owed him a debt of gratitude, but she hoped with all her heart that there would be more for both of them...together.

"I'm going upstairs to put some things away in my room," Adam said, his gaze swinging from his mother to Nate. "Call me when dinner's ready, and I'll set the table."

NATE WATCHED ADAM leave the kitchen, noting that there seemed to be a certain swagger to his walk, a determined set to his shoulders. "I'd really like to stay," Nate said, pleased to be included in their plans for the evening. "Do you need me to go to the grocery store for you?"

She gave him a long, considering look. "No. I think we've got everything."

The look in her eyes made him wonder if she might be talking about more than his offer of going to the grocery store. Was it possible? And if she wanted more, where did they go from here? She'd been through a lot in the past months—her issues with Adam, her fear of losing her friends if they found out about her past and now the sudden appearance of her ex-husband.

Just go with the moment. For once, let the evening unfold. You're not in law enforcement tonight. You're having dinner with a beautiful woman you want to be with.

"Then give me an apron and I'll help you get dinner started," he said.

"An apron?" A smile tipped the corners of her mouth, a very kissable mouth, in Nate's opinion.

"Yes. Anna and I always had housework chores to do. I'll have you know that I'm known far and wide for my chili dishes, several really great versions, from hot and spicy to sweet and juicy."

She passed him an apron festooned with cherries and green leaves with a red tie that barely went around his waist. "This is the best I can do on short notice."

He peeled potatoes and carrots, cut them up and placed them in salted water on the back of the stove, all the while waiting for her to say something that would indicate what was going on with her.

She made a meat loaf and placed it in the oven to bake, her hands capable, her fingers mesmerizing, as they touched knobs, opened cans and distracted him from making much in the way of conversation. The whole body-to-body thing was a major distraction. His body was like a magnet, wanting contact with hers. Thankful that the tiny kitchen made physical touching so easy, he smiled in pleasure each time they moved against each other.

What would living here with her be like—the closeness, the daily routine...the sex?

His body connected with hers as they cleaned the counter. Leaning into her space, he kissed her lips, relishing her sudden intake of breath, sparking his need for more.

She slid out from under the arm he was about to put around her. "Let's talk while dinner is cooking," she said, making her way to the table, pulling out a chair and sitting down. Not once did she look his way, and he felt...hurt...shut out...vulnerable.

He spied a bottle of red wine and opened it. Bringing two glasses to the table, he slid into the chair across from her, his legs twining with hers. He saw the sharp glance she offered him, and pulled his legs back.

Pushing his feelings aside, he poured two glasses of the deep burgundy liquid and slid one across the table to her. "Let's toast our success."

"Ours?" she asked, her fingers fluttering on the stem of the glass.

"Yes. Yours mostly, but I had a role to play," he said.

"You did. I appreciate all your help," she said, but she didn't look very appreciative.

There was a slight scowl knitting her eyebrows together, and she avoided looking straight at him. Her words were stiff, almost dismissive, heightening the awkwardness creeping into their conversation.

"You're welcome," he said, feeling suddenly that staying for dinner had been a mistake. Her reticence made him feel like an outsider. Although she said she wanted to talk, she said nothing, and he wasn't having much luck encouraging her.

She took a sip of the wine, meeting his eyes over the rim of her glass. Carefully she put it down. "We need to talk about Adam."

"What do you want to talk about?"

"Now that Harry has been here, and Adam seems to be sorting things out, does this mean that you won't be seeing Adam anymore?"

The question startled him. "Of course I'll be

seeing him. Just because he found his father doesn't mean all his issues are resolved."

"But what if they are?"

What was going on here? Was she telling him that once Adam didn't need him that she was through with him, as well? Had her kindness and caring simply been an act to guarantee that Adam got the best Nate had to offer?

Was she looking for a polite way to end the relationship?

Whatever was going on with her, it was clear she wasn't willing to share. Yet he needed her to share her thoughts, her concerns, her life, with him. With the immediate issue of Adam's father settled, they were free to move on...to continue their relationship in a different way. But maybe that wasn't how she saw it. "Perhaps it would be better if I left. You and Adam have lots to talk about, and I'll just be in the way."

"No. Please. I...I don't want you to go." Her eyes were awash in surprise when she looked at him.

"Then what do you want?" he asked.

"I DON'T KNOW." Gayle shifted in her chair, uncomfortable with the topic. Most times people didn't express concern for her needs. Now, when what she wanted really mattered to her, she was lost for words.

With Nate in her life, sitting across the table from her, she found it hard to focus on what she should do or say. She wanted the intimacy she'd felt when they were getting dinner together. She'd never had that sort of experience before. She craved a life where two people who loved each other took joy and comfort from being together, sharing everything.

She'd spent her life hiding out from relationships, devoting her time and energy to working and caring for Adam. All those years she'd never allowed herself to think about what it would be like to have someone she loved and who loved her in return.

"Well, let's start on the easy stuff. Do you want me to stay for dinner, or were you simply being polite? Or were you paying me back for being helpful?"

"I want you to stay for dinner." She dared to glance at him and was struck by the unease in his expression. "And I didn't ask you just because you've been helpful."

"So why did you invite me?"

"I want…" She couldn't say the words. She couldn't expose her inexperience despite her love for this man. "What do *you* want?" she asked, excited and fearful at the same time.

"I want you to trust me, to let me into your life," he said quietly and with so much emotion.

"You *are* in my life," she said, feeling suddenly as if she were standing on a precipice about to fall over the edge.

"That's not what I mean, and you know it," he said, draining his glass of wine in one swallow. He put the glass down. "But if this is as far as we go, I won't stay to dinner."

Her heart shrank in her chest. "Please stay."

"Why? I can have dinner anywhere. You don't seem to want to talk to me. I'm going to take that to mean you don't want a relationship with me." He rose from his chair and started down the hall toward the front door. "Tell Adam I'll call him later in the week."

Gayle jumped up and followed him to the door. "Wait!"

He didn't turn around. "What for?"

She touched his arm, feeling the muscle under the cotton shirt he was wearing. Remembering how his arms felt when he held her was sheer torment. "I don't know how to do this," she confessed, waiting for him to make a remark that would confirm her fear—that her inexperience was not an attractive quality.

"When two people care for each other, the rest is easy," he said, standing straight and tall beside her, his eyes searching hers, the heat of his body drawing her to him.

A flash of light outside the door caught Gayle's attention. "Somebody's out there," she said.

"I've never heard that excuse before," he said, not turning to confirm what she was saying.

"It's not an excuse. Look." She pointed to a woman silhouetted by a light shining behind her.

Nate opened the door, and before he could speak the woman identified herself as a reporter from the local TV station in Portsmouth. "I understand that Harry Young's ex-wife and son live here. I'd like to speak to…" She pushed past Nate and shoved a microphone in Gayle's face. "Are you Gayle Sawyer?"

Horrified, Gayle stared at the woman, then at Nate, pleading with him to make the woman go away.

Nate gave a slight nod, and put his arm out, blocking the woman from coming farther into the house. "No comment."

"Just a few words," the reporter insisted. She pushed the microphone at Gayle. "What was it like to live with Harry Young before he became a Christian? Was your relationship a loving one?"

She'd been dreading a moment like this all her life. The press had invaded the one place she'd ever felt that she really belonged. Gayle's body began to shake.

Nate whispered close to her ear. "Go back into the kitchen. I'll handle this."

As Gayle turned away, the reporter's hostility was aimed at Nate. But Nate didn't budge, and in a few minutes the woman and her cameraman left. Nate locked the door, and returned to the kitchen where Gayle waited at the counter.

"I'm sorry about that," she said, looking up at him, feeling his support like a cloak, warm and protective.

But if this reporter persisted, and others followed, how would Nate feel about being caught in the spotlight with her? She'd seen the news on various occasions when reporters dogged someone until they gave an interview, and she didn't want that to happen to her or Nate, and especially not to Adam.

Again, she felt the urge to flee to avoid any further conflict. Oddly enough, in the middle of this craziness, she became frighteningly aware of how much she wanted a relationship with Nate. She'd hid behind her fears far too long. It was time she made her feelings clear to this man.

But what if Harry's reappearance in her life affected Nate's feelings for her? The press were chasing Harry for his story, and that meant they'd learn about his life with Gayle in Anaheim. Shame made her cheeks glow hot at the memory of the squalid little apartment they'd lived in.

"You don't have to be sorry about anything,

especially not that," he said, nodding toward the front hall, placing his powerful hands on her shoulders and looking straight into her eyes.

She loved Nate, a love she couldn't share with him or anyone else. Her old insecurities wouldn't let her. She needed him here with her tonight, to stave off the loneliness of facing the world on her own. "Will you change your mind and stay for dinner?" she asked, resisting the urge to put her arms around his waist and rest her head on his chest. To feel the comfort he offered.

His hands gently kneaded her shoulders as his mouth took hers in a kiss that made her knees weak and her breath halt in her throat. She clung to him, her mind reeling with the idea that this man she loved was kissing her, and taking her last bit of willpower from her.

He eased away from her. His hands released her. His gray eyes shone darker than before as they ranged over her face. "I think we'd better call it a night. You and Adam need time to talk over your feelings, your day. I need to check in on Anna."

He was leaving her after what had just happened between them right here in her kitchen, after the incident at the door with the reporter—obviously not giving a thought to how she'd cope if another reporter showed up. Or how close she'd come to asking him to stay with her tonight. She went back over the evening, searching for what happened that made him decide to leave.

Something had changed. What had she done? Sure, she was insecure about being in a relationship, but Sherri had told her that Nate was perfectly at ease with women, that he knew how to win over any woman he wanted.

Any woman he wanted.

Had she been living out her fantasy right here in her own kitchen? A one-person dream with the trappings of real life?

She pulled back behind the shelter of the counter, resting her hips on the edge.

She wrapped her arms around her waist, shielding herself from the hurt gnawing at her stomach. She stood her ground against the memory of what might have been. "Yes. I think it is time for you to leave. But before you go, I want to thank you again for everything you've done for Adam and me." She could feel the stiffness in her words, words meant to push him away. Words meant to hurt him, but it was she who felt the hurt.

CHAPTER SIXTEEN

TWO WEEKS LATER, Nate stood in front of the long gilded mirror in one of the elegant suites that made up the Kingston Inn, the most formal wedding venue in Eden Harbor. His cousin Sherri was marrying Neill Brandon today at two o'clock. Because of their rocky path as lovers and the long period of time they'd spent apart while married to other people, the whole town was anticipating today's service. Everyone agreed that love had finally won out.

Yet as much as he wanted every bit of happiness possible for his cousin and her fiancé, his heart wasn't in today's festivities. And it all had to do with the past two weeks. He hadn't seen Gayle, and she hadn't asked for his help. She'd canceled Adam's appointment with the excuse that he needed to study. There had been no mention of any more incidents of the press bothering her, but he had heard that someone from the *Bangor Courier* had been going around town asking people what they knew about Gayle and Adam.

The rehearsal dinner had been awkward with them having to sit next to each other. He'd tried to engage her in conversation, and she had been polite, but that was all. She never once made eye contact, and that hurt. Yet he felt the urge to touch her, to find a way to include her in an intimate moment between them. All efforts failed. By the end of the evening he was irritated by her behavior and couldn't wait for the event to be over.

Gayle didn't need his support, and the way she had all but dismissed him from her house a couple of weeks ago had hurt him in a way he'd never experienced before. Having spent these past weeks without seeing her, he was acutely aware that he cared for her very much. She was so different from his usual girlfriends, and he'd tried to explain that to her the day Harry had shown up on her doorstep. He thought she'd understood what he'd been trying to say, but obviously she hadn't.

He fastened his tie and smoothed his hair, determined to make the most of the day ahead regardless of what happened between Gayle and him. And he was pleased that after the ceremony he would be walking down the aisle between the rows of chairs under a white tent with Gayle on his arm. His golden opportunity.

He had never given up on anything or anybody he really wanted. He wasn't about to start now. He had a plan, and he would see it through, prepared to accept the outcome whatever it was. Weeks ago, when he'd believed that he and Gayle were becoming close, he'd foolishly made a reservation here at the inn for tonight. He'd thought about canceling it, but decided not to.

He'd seen the emotion in her eyes the last time he'd been with her. The anxiety. She cared for him. He cared for her. His plan would start with that.

Opening the door to his room, he could hear laughter across the hall from him—a woman's lighthearted laugh that made him feel unreasonably happy with life. As he descended the winding staircase to the main floor reception area, he put aside his thoughts and feelings, prepared to be part of the wedding everyone in Eden Harbor had been waiting for. To witness Sherri and Neill's love and happiness gave him something to believe in.

If this were just another wedding of a family member, he'd simply sit back and enjoy. But his role as groomsman meant he'd be walking down the aisle with Gayle and his cane. The bride had insisted, her matchmaking efforts still alive and well. He felt a ping of unease shoot through his chest and settle in his stomach.

For a second he wished he could join the wedding guests and enjoy the admiring glances of the females in the wedding party while he decided which of them he would take out on a date in the coming weeks.

What a smug, self-satisfied man he'd become. In the beginning he'd blamed the breakup of his relationship on his fiancée. She'd been the one who had called off their wedding. And he'd decided to let his hurt feelings dictate his approach to his dating life.

Yet in this quiet moment, seeing his reflection in the full-length gold-edged mirror at the bottom of the stairs, he'd come to realize how empty and stuck in a holding pattern his life had become. He had been treating women like objects placed in his path, not real people who might have a chance of making him happy.

He grimaced at his reflection.

Gayle made him happy, and she was sexier than any woman he'd dated in a long time. He'd had two weeks to think about how their last evening had ended. He'd wanted to make love to her. Yet that night hadn't been about having sex, but about something else.

That was the part that had him confused.

He'd wanted to talk to her about the two of them, about going out on dates, learning more about each other. He'd wanted to plan a future for them, yet he hadn't been able to convey that idea to Gayle. When he couldn't find the words, he'd kissed her and dropped her as if she were some undesirable object.

His shortcoming with women had always been his need to keep an emotional distance. Sure, the sex was mutually satisfying, but what did he offer by way of emotional support to the women he slept with? When it came time to really share in an intimate, caring way, he chose to keep everything light. No room for commitment.

As he moved into one of the main reception rooms, he could see the guests gathering on the lawn, ready to enter the tent.

"Are you lost?" Anna asked as she came up to him and kissed his cheek.

He chuckled, hugging his sister. "I look that bad?"

"No, of course not. You look absolutely handsome."

"Where are the boys?"

"They're with Mom. I'm going to find them in a few minutes and take our seats. See you later, and good luck doing the groomsman thing," she said, making her way to the steps to the lawn.

He glanced around for other members of the wedding party, knowing full well the only one he was looking for was Gayle.

The minister walked up to him. "That was a

lovely rehearsal dinner last evening, wasn't it?" he said. They made small talk for a few minutes about the weather, the day ahead and the subject on everybody's mind—how the bride and groom had found their way back to each other.

Nate was giving his full attention to the minister when out of the corner of his eye he spotted someone standing quietly, looking out over the front entrance onto the veranda. She was dressed in a spectacular green sheath that followed every curve of her body until it fanned out just before touching down on the floor. She was talking quietly to Morgan Brandon, whose conversation was accompanied by a lot of arm movements and wide smiles. Morgan's dress was pretty, but it was Gayle he couldn't take his eyes off. With her mass of dark curls swept up off her face and fastened back with silver combs, she was easily the most beautiful woman he'd ever seen in his entire life.

The minister stopped speaking. Nate didn't respond. He'd lost track of the conversation, completely focused on Gayle. "Would you excuse me?"

"Certainly," said the minister. "I have to get ready for the service. Only a few minutes to go."

Nate strode across the foyer of the inn, stopping only when he reached Gayle's side. A thousand words rushed through his mind, but only four managed to pass his lips. "You look so beautiful."

Her smile was shaky as she looked up into his eyes. "Thank you."

He couldn't stop his hands from touching her arm. "We're on in just a few minutes."

"Hope I remember what I'm supposed to do," Gayle said, sounding genuinely anxious.

"Don't worry about it," Morgan interjected. "I've got you covered. If you forget anything, like to take Sherri's bouquet, I'll give you a nudge." She turned to Nate. "Hi, Uncle Nate. You are my uncle now, right?"

"Being your uncle would be a great honor," he said, but his eyes never left Gayle's face.

"That's good. I'm busy collecting new relatives." She clapped her hands together and laughed.

"Collect to your heart's content," he said, following Gayle's gaze as Adam ambled toward the group in a typical teenage gait. "Here's Adam," he said, suddenly aware that Morgan's face had gone a shade of pink and Adam was nervously adjusting his tie.

These two really like each other.

The two teenagers moved away from Nate and Gayle as if they didn't exist. "Well, what do you suppose is going on there?" Gayle asked.

"Is it still called 'puppy love'?" Nate asked.

"I thought it would be years before I used *in love* and *Adam* in the same sentence. He's too young to date, isn't he?"

"I'm not an authority on the subject of teenagers in love." After two of the most frustrating, unhappy weeks of his life, Nate decided that it was time to put an end to this impasse between them. "Love can be tricky. Just when you least expect it, you're suddenly caught in its glow," he said, aware of the catch in his voice. Damn! He sounded like some sort of advertisement for one of those online dating sites.

She looked up into his face, her heart pounding in the V of her throat. He had never wanted to touch any woman the way he did Gayle, to caress her throat, feel her pulse fluttering under his fingers.

"I'm not sure I believe in love. The rush of feelings we call love, possibly, but not the kind of love that means a lifetime commitment." Her voice was warm and gentle, her eyes trapping his.

"I do," he blurted.

"You do?" Her lips lifted in a soft smile. "So this is the new Nate Garrison?"

Before he could respond, she turned from him and started back toward the stairs. "Aren't we supposed to be waiting here?" he asked, desperate to keep her with him for as long as possible.

"I have to check on the bride," she said, hurrying up the staircase.

He watched helplessly, his body tightening at the sight of her straight back, the deep V opening the dress almost to her waist, the sexy sway of her hips under the luscious green fabric. There was a new addition to his plan. If he managed to get his act together, he'd take great enjoyment out of removing that dress. Yes, he would…

CONFINED BY HER tight skirt, Gayle made her way up the curving stairs. Once out of sight, she stopped to catch her breath. She couldn't talk to Nate about love, or about anything. She'd spent the past two weeks in an agony of wishing and hoping that he would call, or that she'd bump into him somewhere.

During the rehearsal and the dinner, she'd experienced a different form of agony—the agony of being so close to the man she loved, yet so far out of the orbit he lived in she might as well have been from outer space.

She had watched the way his whole family had come together last evening, and how Sherri and he joked with everyone. No one could miss the fact that people loved Neill and Sherri and wanted them to be happy. The pain of feeling like an outsider had made her unable to make conversation at the dinner, and Nate's attempts to draw her had out only made her feel worse.

Nate had been kind and thoughtful, like a friend would be. But being around him brought all her lonely feelings rushing to the surface, heightening her feelings of isolation.

She had always protected herself from feeling left out around others by not becoming too deeply involved in their lives. Last night at the rehearsal dinner her isolation felt complete. She would never have what the Garrison and the Brandon families had—a sense of feeling part of something solid and real.

The door at the top of the stairs opened, and Sherri appeared. Her dress was the same pattern as Gayle's, but it was covered in lace and pearls over shimmering satin, with a headdress of pearls holding a train that flowed to the floor.

"Doesn't she look wonderful?" Colleen Lawson asked as she followed her daughter out of the room.

"Absolutely gorgeous," Gayle said, meaning it with all her heart. She went the rest of the way up the stairs and took her best friend's hand. "I am *so* happy for you, and so pleased to be your maid of honor."

Sherri's eyes glistened with tears. "Me, too." She tilted her head back to keep the moisture from touching her makeup. "Mom, can you pick up my train while Gayle walks with me down the stairs? I didn't realize how tricky it is to walk in a dress like this."

They went down the stairs together and waited in the archway leading to the dining room while the photographer followed them and took more pictures. Morgan was busy helping to arrange the train on the wedding dress while the hairdresser fussed over Sherri's hair.

Finally, they were ready. The florist passed the bridal bouquet to Sherri, and a white satin pillow with the rings nestled together on it to Morgan. "This is it," Sherri said as Morgan moved ahead of them toward the steps leading down to the lawn and the white tent shining in the brilliant sunshine.

As they entered the tent to Mendelssohn's *Wedding March*, the friends and family members rose, uttering a sigh of delight at how beautiful Sherri looked. Gayle walked ahead of her friend, lifting her eyes only once to catch Nate's adoring gaze. The look in his eyes... She... No, it couldn't be. It was the happiness of the moment that made her think she saw love. He looked so handsome in his tuxedo as he rested one hand on his cane. She faltered on the uneven ground beneath the red carpet, smiling to cover her misstep.

The air between them was charged with emotion as she came closer and closer to him. Neill said something to Nate that brought a smile to his face.

Gayle made it to her spot next to Morgan before turning to watch Sherri finish her walk down the aisle on her mother's arm. Gayle moved through the ceremony as if in a trance. She took the bride's bouquet at the appropriate time and walked behind the newlyweds to sign the register with Nate nearby—a moment of sheer joy.

All the while she couldn't get the image of Nate's loving smile out of her mind. Nate, a man who had shown little or no emotion around her, had been smiling at her with what looked like love in his eyes. Yet how was she to know? She hardly had a lot of experience with what a man in love would look like.

No. It had to have been her imagination. She was simply caught up in the moment.

She squared her shoulders as they turned to walk down the aisle to the entrance of the tent where they gathered for more photos. The photographer kept arranging and rearranging group photos, and every time Nate's arm brushed her bare skin she felt a jolt of something so intoxicating her pulse jumped.

Even when he wasn't standing near her, she would surreptitiously search the lawn and veranda to see if she could spot him. Usually she found him talking to one of the many men attending the wedding.

She felt relieved and a little more relaxed when they went to the dining room for the dinner reception. She sat next to Sherri while Nate sat next to Neill—the perfect arrangement to ease her jangled nerves.

Long shadows through the trees at the edges of the lawn signaled the end of the dinner. Gayle followed Sherri and Neill toward the ballroom where the dance was to be held. Nate seemed to have disappeared, and she missed him. She could still see Nate's smile, the look he gave her. Yet she didn't know what to do about it, how to approach Nate, or even if she should.

Her life hadn't been filled with family and friends, with people who loved and respected her and wanted her in their lives. Awash in isolation despite the happiness around her, she didn't want to think about her life and whether she might still have a chance for such happiness.

When she thought about loving someone and being loved in return, Nate Garrison was the only man who came to mind.

THE BAND HAD set up outside on a stage brought in for the occasion. Gayle watched as Sherri danced with Neill, his arms holding her close to the cheers of the onlookers. She clapped along with the crowd, caught up in the sheer enjoyment of the moment.

"They are beautiful together, aren't they?" Nate whispered in her ear.

Startled, she turned around. "They are." The scent of him, his maleness, his powerful physique, surrounded her. What she wouldn't give to have him take her in his arms.

"Would you like to dance?" he asked.

Had he read her mind? She hesitated. "I'm not a very good dancer."

"Neither am I. And of course, there's this." He held up his cane, and she saw the naked emotion in his eyes.

"Are you worried about that?"

"Yes, I guess I am."

Standing there with him so close, her heart filled with excitement, she took a chance she'd never imagined ever taking. She reached out, eased the cane from his fingers. "Let's put your cane aside for now and try our luck on the dance floor."

Surprise lit his eyes. His gaze locked on hers. "Shall we?" he asked, taking her in his arms as the first notes of a waltz began.

He held her close as they began the slow dance. Gayle was hesitant at first. But with Nate's guidance, his arm securely around her, she forgot her inhibitions as she let herself move to the music.

"I'm glad this was a waltz number," he said, a deep sigh escaping his lips, making her neck tingle. His hands touched the bare skin exposed by the back V of her dress. Their bodies were so in tune, so made for each other. She couldn't believe this was happening to her.

She held him so tight she could feel the fabric of his tuxedo against her cleavage.

"I'm not going to fall over," he whispered.

"Sorry!" she said, looking guiltily up into his eyes.

"You were trying to keep me from falling, weren't you?"

"No! No, I was…I was…"

Just then the music changed to a rock and roll number. "I guess that's it for us," he said as he placed his hand in the small of her back and led her slowly from the dance floor.

They retrieved his cane, the atmosphere suddenly awkward. She felt her social inadequacies like a heavy weight, forcing her to admit that she didn't know how to rescue the situation. He thought she had been supporting him. She knew she'd been holding the one man she'd ever loved tight because she needed to.

The minister appeared at Nate's side and began talking to him, allowing Gayle to slip away.

SHE FOUND SHERRI in her suite, getting ready to change out of her wedding dress into a calf-length pale blue skirt and matching silk blouse. It only took minutes for the bride to return downstairs to the cheers of friends and family. Neill's eyes were filled with love as he waited for her at the bottom of the staircase.

She loved every second of watching her friend walk with her new husband out the front door of the inn to the waiting car. Everyone cheered as Neill picked Sherri up and gently placed her on the seat of the limousine. They appeared through the rooftop opening to cheers from the wedding guests.

Once the newlyweds disappeared down the long driveway, Gayle slipped around the corner of the inn to one of the Adirondack chairs and settled in to watch the final rays of the sun create a kaleidoscope of light along the horizon.

Seeing Sherri's joy and knowing how hard her friend had struggled to find that happiness gave Gayle hope that someday she might be so lucky. All these years she'd let her past dictate her life. Starting tonight, she intended to work on changing all that.

The floorboards creaked. She glanced up to see Nate climbing the steps of the veranda toward her. "It's beautiful out here," she said to deflect the supercharged emotions rushing through her at the sight of him.

He loosened the tie of his tuxedo, exposing a tiny V of black hair on his chest. The tuxedo fit him perfectly from his broad shoulders past his narrow hips to his long legs.

Nate Garrison was everything she'd ever dreamed of in a man. But the dream wasn't working out in reality, and the sooner she accepted that, the better.

"Would you like a little company?" he asked as he approached her.

"Please," she murmured, and watched him lower himself into the chair next to hers and rest his cane along the arm.

"Did you enjoy your first time as maid of honor?" he asked.

Was he here simply to make small talk? Or was there a reason he'd sought her out?

Stop second-guessing everything! "I did. It was fun. Sherri and Nate make a handsome couple."

"We did pretty well, too, didn't we?" he asked, his gaze direct, setting up a pinging sensation somewhere near Gayle's heart.

She hoped they would sit right where they were until the sun went down. If she had her way, they'd spend the whole evening together, but he probably had family commitments after such a wonderful wedding. "We did. I'm just relieved I didn't trip or drop the bouquet."

"Why would you worry about that?" he asked, his expression telling her he really wanted to know.

"It's like any new experience. It can be fraught with the unexpected. Also, when I get nervous I tend to make mistakes."

"Like all of us," he said, his eyes twinkling. "Did Anna ever tell you about me and the potted poinsettias the Christmas I was ten?"

"No, she didn't." She smiled, happy to be with him.

As he told her the story of how he knocked over a tiered display of the plants in the local florist shop destined to decorate houses and businesses all around Eden Harbor, she tried to imagine what he looked like as a little boy. But when he finished his story, an anxious silence lingered between them.

Not wanting him to leave yet unable to find a new subject of conversation, she grabbed the first thought that came to mind. "Morgan was really excited by the wedding and being part of it. She's quite a little chatterbox. She was so sweet and kind to my son. She and Adam seem to like each other. I'm delighted that he wasn't feeling left out of the excitement."

Nate looked at her closely. "Did you feel left out?"

"I...I... There were moments back there when I wished I had a family like yours."

His gaze fixed on her face, he said, "I wish you did, too."

"Why?"

"Oh, I don't know...maybe to get the goods on you. About your childhood and what sorts of pranks you got yourself into."

"There weren't any," she said, trying to block the pitiful tone from her voice.

"You can't be serious. You must have gotten in trouble at school, or maybe a scuffle in the playground?"

She shook her head, feeling suddenly exposed and vulnerable. She had never dared to do anything that might anger her parents, for fear of being slapped or worse.

Nate's hands were fisted on the arms of the chair. "Sorry for that. I didn't mean to bring up..."

"It's okay. Really, I'm fine," she said, forcing a show of bravado. "Everyone has skeletons in their closets, even the Garrison family, I'm sure," she said, making it clear she wanted no more talk about her past. Talking of her past on such a beautiful occasion was the last thing on earth she intended to do.

"So what's next for you?" he asked, his voice quieter, less sure, more withdrawn.

"I guess, back to work…" She didn't understand his question, but waited for him to elaborate.

"Are you ready to move on? You no longer have to pretend or make excuses because of your past. You're free to do as you please."

"Yes, I am. But I guess until now I hadn't considered what that would mean. I've never felt free to make choices except when it came to Adam, and sometimes even then they were limited by other factors like money."

"And now?"

She was just a little disappointed. In the middle of such beautiful surroundings, with the look she'd seen in his eyes at the altar a few hours ago still fresh in her mind, he had not said one romantic word to her.

She had no idea what to think, and she was tired of thinking. Yet she needed to talk to this man, to seek his advice…maybe for the last time. "I would like to put my past life behind me. With Harry's visit to Eden Harbor over, I finally feel I can. I doubt that Adam will spend much time with him, and Harry's not likely to come to Eden Harbor. One thing I know for sure—despite his newfound religion, Harry thrives best in a big city."

"So what's next?"

"Can I ask you a personal question?"

"Don't see why not," Nate said, settling farther into the chair, his chiseled features softened by the lamplight illuminating the veranda.

"What was the worst part about being injured?"

NATE SUCKED IN a breath. His hands gripped the arms of the chair. "The worst part?" he asked, his voice hard. Was she really so insensitive?

"Oh. Sorry. That came out all wrong." She reached for his hand, but he pulled it back.

She bit her lip and swallowed hard. "Please, Nate, can I start over?"

"Sure," he said, but he didn't mean it. He'd never really talked to anyone about what had happened that day. The counselor provided by the police department got what Nate felt able to give, and that was all. But the worst had come later when there was no counselor present, no one to protect him from the horrible vulnerability after his fiancée's rejection.

"I want to go to Anaheim and see the policeman Harry shot," Gayle said.

"Why? What did you have to do with it?"

"Nothing directly. I'm beginning to understand that better. Yet I feel that I owe the man an apology for what Harry did. If I had been older, more mature, less naive, I might have prevented what happened to him."

Despite his mixed emotions, Nate needed to understand why she felt she had to do something that would probably be a wasted effort. "What if he refuses to see you?"

"Then at least I tried," she said, her voice a soft caress, drawing him in.

"What about him? What if all you do is drag up old memories, old emotions he'd rather not revisit? What right do you have to inflict more pain on him?"

The hurt in her eyes shone through the failing light. Guilt ran through him like a raging river. Damn! He hadn't meant to hurt her. He felt sorry for her, for the years she'd carried this guilt about a man she'd never met. "What will you do if he simply says no? He has a right to his privacy, and you're arriving a little late with your apology, aren't you?"

She eased forward in her chair. "Look, I'm sorry I brought this up. You're the wrong person for me to talk to, and it was totally insensitive of me."

Was he *always* going to get it wrong where she was concerned? Sure, he hated it when any-

one made reference to the shooting, because
when they were done commenting he was left
with his memories and the cane he was forced
to use.

How long was he going to let his cane, the
symbol of his past injury, determine his future
chances for happiness?

He could choose to remove himself from this
conversation, or he could trust this remarkable
woman with his past. "Please don't go. I'll tell
you how it was for me if it will help you decide
what's best for you to do."

She sat back in her chair carefully. Keeping
her hands in her lap, her eyes intent on him, she
murmured, "Go on."

"When I was shot, I lost my job—the one
I'd trained for and was good at. All of it disappeared at the hands of a kid whose life was
so messed up at fifteen there was little chance
he'd ever know what it felt like to be respected
by others and to find real love. I found myself
feeling sorry for him. I looked into his background to discover that being a member of a
street gang would be the height of achievement
for him. And so I came to terms with my situation, or thought I had, until the day my fiancée
walked out."

She turned to him, her eyes wide. She reached
out and took his hand, a damn comforting feel-

ing, as great as it was unexpected. "I had family and friends who cared about me, and when Natasha canceled our engagement I moved home from Boston. I've never regretted it, and I no longer hold a grudge where the teenager is concerned. I think I told you that before."

"What about your fiancée?"

"That was a little different. I'd never made that sort of commitment in my life. I believed that love was forever, for better or worse, richer or poorer. I believed all that."

"And now?"

He met her tentative gaze, the approaching night and the cooling air suspending his thoughts. "I don't know."

She didn't say a word, and he couldn't think of anything to say but *I love you*. Three words he was afraid to say, not only because they spoke of commitment, but because he feared that his disability might have the same effect on her as it had on his fiancée. And even if it didn't, becoming involved with him would mean that she would share his disability, his restrictions. Gayle had had little opportunity in her life to take up skiing or tennis or any of the other things couples did. And if she became a part of his life, there wouldn't be any hope that he could share such activities with her.

He cleared his throat and struggled to shape

some phrases that would fill the void. "What about you? Do you believe in happiness ever after?"

"I want to," she said, her voice soft.

She wanted to love someone, to be committed to someone.

"But you feel you need to go to Anaheim first before you can begin to put your new life together."

"Yes." She pulled her hand from his. "Yes, I do."

"Would you like me to go with you?" he asked impulsively. "If you need me, that is. I could arrange it." He felt like a teenager asking for a first date.

GAYLE'S ATTEMPT TO steady her breathing failed. Her fingers trembled where they rested on the wood of the Adirondack chair. She wanted to reach across and take his hand again. No, that wasn't true. Not at all. She wanted to climb into his lap and have him kiss her senseless. "You'd do that for me?"

"If you decided that seeing this person was the only way you could gain closure, I would go with you. I would. Definitely. I would," he repeated, an uncertain expression on his face.

Was he as anxious as she was? She couldn't imagine this man being rattled by anything.

"But what would you do while I visited the police officer?"

"I'd wait outside for you, or go in if you wanted me to. Yes. That's it. When he realizes that I was shot…it might help him to understand why you need to see him."

She focused all her attention on this man sitting in the chair beside her, his eyes on her, his expression one of complete sincerity. He'd been her rock, the person whose opinion and advice mattered most to her. She loved him—every bit of him, from the top of his head to his toes. More than anything in the world she wanted him to tell her how he felt about her. At the same time, she was terrified of losing everything if she confided how she felt about him. A part of her feared that he saw her as Sherri's friend or as Adam's mother, not as who she really was and that she wanted to be to him. She felt so close to Nate sitting here on the veranda, closer than she'd ever felt to anyone. And yet her fear was a barrier she didn't have the courage to cross.

All this pent-up need made her see something very clearly. She had to take the next step in her new life and put her past behind her. And whether it was right or wrong, seeking forgiveness from the police officer Harry had injured was a necessary part of moving forward for her. She couldn't have Nate with her unless she knew how he really felt about her, whatever that might be. Returning to Anaheim with someone who didn't love her, who was acting out of some sense of duty or responsibility, wouldn't work. This was an intimate journey back into her past. It could only be shared with someone who wanted to share her life. If Nate cared about her, he needed to say so. Otherwise, she would be going back to Anaheim alone.

She met his solid gaze, his eyes giving no hint of his feelings for her one way or the other. Given the circumstances she faced there was only one decision. "Thank you for offering, but I have to face my past on my own in my own way. I've lived all this time with guilt over the man Harry injured. Maybe the guilt seems unreasonable to some people. Maybe I'm simply seeking relief from the memory of that day. Whatever the reason, this is my problem, not yours."

He just looked at her with a sadness that made her want to cry. If only he'd say something that would give her hope that they might have a future. Even if he just said he wanted to see her, date her, anything to show he wanted a relationship with her beyond friendship.

He remained silent. Rejection raised its ugly head. She gripped the arms of the chair and pulled herself to a standing position. "I'm going to go in and get my things. Adam is here some-where, probably talking with Morgan."

She wanted to ask when she'd see him again, but she couldn't. It would sound as though she was trying to corner him into something. After all, his only loyalty to her resided in his relation-ship with Adam. A relationship that would soon come to an end, if Adam's behavior the past few days meant her son would be all right. She hadn't seen him this happy since they'd moved to Eden Harbor, and she owed it all to Nate.

She waited for a few seconds, hoping he'd say the words to make her stay, to indicate that he wanted her with him. Maybe it was being in the presence of two very happy people at their long-awaited dream wedding that had sparked these feelings.

She'd been secretly hoping that Nate would ask her to spend the night with him in this beau-tiful inn. But she should have known better. The things she'd wished for in her life had not happened…except for Adam. And now, standing here waiting for Nate to say something made her feel like a silly teenager waiting for the school's star athlete to notice her.

She glanced down at Nate. He was staring at his hand resting on the arm of the chair. "I guess I'll see you in town when you come to pick up

Adam," she said, hurt and longing tearing at her throat.

She ached for some little sign of encouragement, but he said nothing. Not so much as goodbye.

Forcing her feet to move, she walked along the veranda to the double doors leading into the inn. She saw Anna coming toward her, but she ducked her head and continued along the veranda.

Talking to her friend in the state she was in was out of the question. She didn't have the words to explain what she was feeling. She needed to go home, to her safe little Victorian house with its flowers and its good memories. The only place she'd ever felt at home.

CHAPTER SEVENTEEN

NATE SAT THERE, tongue-tied and feeling like an idiot. Gayle's eyes had told him she wanted him to say something. He'd known it, and had been totally incapable of responding. His fear that he would say or do something wrong where this woman was concerned had forced his silence. When would he ever learn how to say what he was feeling? To reach out to the one woman that mattered?

She had walked away from him, yet he was unable to make a move. He wanted to run after her, pull her into his arms and say what he needed to say. Instead, he sat there watching the way her dress followed the curves of her body, her hair swayed around her shoulders. Raw need turned his breath to jagged gasps.

He'd never felt like this before, this feeling that somehow they were bonded to each other, that every move she made, every breath she took, he took with her. He clenched his fists to keep from following her, begging her to come back. He was overcome with a sense of loss so profound he couldn't seem to clear his mind of the thought that he'd missed the opportunity of a lifetime.

What was wrong with him? He'd had no trouble going after any other woman in the world he wanted. Even after he had to use a cane he had not felt like this, this feeling that he was… inadequate, making him damned near tongue-tied around her. But Gayle wasn't just any other woman.

A few minutes later she walked past him down the steps onto the lawn, her head held high, her face devoid of emotion, as she carried her suitcase to her car.

Without knowing how or why, he found himself standing at the edge of the steps, his eager eyes following Gayle as she made her way toward the parking lot.

"Turn around," he whispered.

"Nate, what's wrong?" Anna asked, her voice flush with sympathy.

He gripped the veranda post, his eyes never leaving Gayle's disappearing form. "I don't know, sis. I… She's…"

"You mean Gayle?"

"Yeah. I think I made a mistake that probably can't be fixed, at least not any time soon."

"Spill it now," Anna said, her hand reaching for his.

He looked down at her hand, remembering all the times he'd confessed things to her. Being lonely, feeling separate and different at school because everyone else had a father, or someone who did the dad things. He'd told his sister about the first date he'd ever had, swearing her to secrecy where his mother was concerned. He remembered the day he'd landed in the hospital with a gunshot wound and seeing the worry on Anna's face as they took him into surgery for the second time. The day he'd arrived on her doorstep to tell her about his marriage plans ending. The day they'd been informed that Kevin had been killed. The day he'd learned she had Parkinson's, and the easy way she soothed his fears about her future. She'd been there all his life, for everything he'd ever experienced.

"I love Gayle Sawyer."

Anna gave a soft, knowing chuckle. "So why is she headed toward the parking lot while you're standing here looking as if you've just lost your best friend?"

He smiled at his tall, rail-thin sister, knowing what she was facing in her own life, and felt a little dumb. No, make that a whole lot dumb. "Because I couldn't tell her how I feel."

"And that would be because…?"

"If I were to tell her how I feel, it would mean I wanted her in much more than just a casual way."

"And what's wrong with that?"

"Nothing… I'm afraid that once I tell her how I'm feeling it will lead to commitment."

"And?"

"And I'm not good at commitment. I've never said this to anyone before, but a part of me was secretly pleased that Natasha canceled our wedding. I already had a huge commitment to myself, to looking after my injuries and getting better. A part of me didn't want to take on a wife, especially someone as needy as Natasha. I don't think I can commit to Gayle, or anyone."

"I don't believe that. I watched you two during the wedding service, and the number of stolen glances between you gave it all away. Have you forgotten?"

"What?" He forced an easy smile to his lips, his defense when someone guessed the agony he was in.

"I'm an expert on love. Kevin and I loved each other from fifth grade. Lord knows, I had to fight off a few women to keep him when he was a teenager. But we ended up happily married, and I wouldn't have traded a moment of it. I want you to experience the kind of love I had. I can pretty well guarantee you that Gayle will give you all the love you need. As for commitment, I know you too well. When you make up your mind to commit to something or someone, you take it to the limit."

Was his sister right? He'd caught Gayle glancing at him several times, and that moment they'd shared when she reached the front of the wedding tent and took her position...

"What if I screw up?"

"You're thinking about Natasha, right? That Gayle is like her?" She shook her head. "Men. I don't get it. Natasha was the worst thing that ever happened to you, in my opinion. When I realized you were serious about her I had to keep my thoughts to myself. After she broke the engagement and hurt you so badly I wanted to...I don't know. Maybe tie all her underwear in knots? Pour nail polish all over her expensive clothes? Put her profile up on one of the dating sites and make her sound like the witch she is?"

"Anna! When did you get so nasty?"

"Since I saw how hurt you were." She hugged him. "I want you to be happy. You love this woman, and I'm betting she loves you. She's afraid and you're afraid. But if you don't go down that pathway to the parking lot and get her before she reaches her car and drives away from here, I'm going to make you both pay," she warned.

"You love me that much?"

"And more," she confirmed.

"But I'm not good at rejection."

"And Gayle isn't either, but if you don't trust your instincts and your love for her, you may lose again. Gayle is the real thing. Gayle doesn't have any other agenda but you."

He sighed, his heart knowing the truth of his sister's words. "I want to believe that."

"Then trust yourself."

"You're right. I can't let her go."

"Then what are you waiting for?" She gave him a gentle push toward the steps. "I don't want to see you until *after* you've told her you love her. Understood?"

"Understood," he said, but he was already down the stairs.

"And don't worry, I'll look after Adam for Gayle. He can share Jeremy's room tonight. That is, if you're lucky." She chuckled again.

"Thanks, sis." He moved as quickly as his injury would allow along the pathway.

He nearly crashed into Gayle as he came around the hedge that blocked the parking lot from view. "Sorry. I was in a bit of a hurry and didn't see you."

"Obviously." Her dark brows crinkled as her eyes met his.

Slowly he placed his hands on her shoulders, feeling the luxurious fabric of her dress and the warm flesh beneath it, intoxicating and magical, filling his heart and mind with only one thing. "Gayle, I have something to tell you."

His fingers picked up a slight tremble of her shoulders. "Please tell me."

He looked into her eyes and was lost in the naked need he saw there. He pulled her close, his mouth covering hers as he eased her against him. He didn't know how long they kissed and he didn't care. All he cared about was how eagerly her lips met his, how easily her tongue tangled with his.

She pulled away after a few minutes. "Is this what you wanted to tell me?" she asked, her gaze going purposely to the bulge in his pants.

He threw back his head and laughed in a way he hadn't laughed in years. It felt so good, so right. He grabbed her up, swung her around before putting her down, his eyes locked with hers, his hip humming in pain. "I love you, Gayle Sawyer. There, I've said it. I love you."

GAYLE FELT JUST a little light-headed, and for a few seconds she wasn't sure if she'd heard right. A part of her couldn't believe that she was living the dream she'd dreamed since she was a little girl. A handsome man—a kind, sweet man with a gorgeous body and eyes to melt into—had just told her he loved her.

"I love you, too," she said.

His eyes held hers. His hands touched her throat; his fingers traced a line down toward the V of her dress. "Gayle, you're the best thing to happen to me in a very long time."

Her smile was bright, her eyes filled with a look that made him want to protect her from every bad thing that could ever happen to her. To keep her safe and love her with all the love he had in him.

Without another word, he snugged her close to his body, pressing her head to his chest. "Hear that?" he asked.

She loved the feel of his hand on her head, his strength making her feel safe and cared for. "Hear what?"

"My heart singing with joy," he said,

She turned in his arms, and reached for him, feelings of happiness dredging all the worry and loss and loneliness from her soul and scattering those sad feelings into the cosmos. "You're so corny," she said, running her hands through his hair, feeling the shape of his head, before letting her fingers trail down his neck to the open V of his shirt.

"Yeah, you're right. Forget I said it." He took her hands in his, covering them and holding them against his chest.

"Never. I love you, singing heart and all."

"Then I have another confession to make," he said, a slow smile moving over his face.

"I'm not a priest, but I'll hear your confession," she murmured, joy filling every part of her being.

His smile warmed her in all the right places. He tucked a curl behind her ear, his touch light and lingering. "Weeks ago, when I was feeling really confident about how things would work out for us today, I booked a room here at the inn for tonight. As you probably guessed, I lost my nerve for a little bit back there." He nodded toward the veranda. "Nearly blew it, in fact."

Feeling happier than she ever had in her life, Gayle placed her hands on his chest, her fingers exploring the muscled flesh beneath his white tuxedo shirt. "You? I can't imagine you ever losing your nerve," she said, her fingers sliding up under his tuxedo jacket across his muscled chest to his shoulders.

He gave her a wry smile, pulling her closer. "But with Anna's help I recovered. I would like to invite you to my suite for the night."

She wanted to be cool and clever about this, to prove she was a sophisticated woman, not a woman whose experience in bed could best be described as utilitarian. "I only have the dress

I have on, and the pants and top I wore here this morning."

"Are you saying you have nothing else to wear?"

She slid her arms down from his chest and wrapped them around his waist without taking her eyes off his. "That's about it."

He kissed her, his hands gently encircling her throat, his breath hot on her cheek. It felt as if they'd been doing this every day for years. When he lifted his face from hers, his smile melted her core. "That's just fine by me. You won't be needing any."

"Have you forgotten I have a son? As wonderful as it sounds, I can't stay the night here with you."

"It's already taken care of. Anna's taking Adam home with her to spend the night."

"You had this all planned."

"That's not entirely true, but I do have a wonderfully resourceful sister."

He put his arm around her, his lips brushing the soft skin in front of her ear, making her whole body tingle. "This is just the beginning," he whispered as they made their way along the pathway from the parking lot, up onto the veranda, one step at a time.

There were no words to express how completely enthralled she was with him, with the heat of his body, the urgency of his kisses. But when he turned her in his arms and licked the small indentation of her neck, her knees betrayed her. Suddenly she was slipping toward the ground.

He held her tight, nearly stumbling but making a quick recovery.

"Oh! No! I'm so sorry," she said, clinging to him while he gripped the veranda post. "Let me get your cane for you." She glanced up into his eyes, eyes that held a flicker of hurt mixed with embarrassment.

This man she loved and who loved her could still be hurt by the visible signs of his past. And his hurt only made her love him more. "Look, before we go any further," she said, "I want to say something."

"And what would that be?" he asked, his voice a deep growl, the heat of his expression having evaporated.

She took his face in her hands and stared straight up into his eyes. "Your cane doesn't bother me one little bit. I wouldn't care if you were on crutches or in a wheelchair. I love you, Nate Garrison, and that's all there is to it. So don't go trying to change my heart, understood?"

CHAPTER EIGHTEEN

HOLDING NATE'S HAND they made their way up the winding staircase, past the ceiling-high window with its panes of glass reflecting the brightly lit space, past the glittering chandelier displaying diamond-bright spots of light over the blue velvet of the steps. When they reached the top, Nate pulled a key from his pocket and approached a set of cream-colored French doors. Hugging her close, he put the key in the lock and opened the door wide.

Gayle gasped in delight. The room was various shades of blue and cream. The chandelier hanging from the ceiling over the coffee table and the tall windows draped in navy blue silk made an unmistakable statement of elegance and wealth—neither of which she'd ever experienced in her life.

She was going to spend the night in this room with the man she loved. She turned to thank him, but was met with the broad expanse of his body, his arms surrounding her as his lips searched for hers, all to the sound of the quiet click of the door closing behind them.

He continued to kiss her as he led her to the bedroom. She was vaguely aware of a carpet so thick her high heels caught in it.

"Did you have plans for this dress?" he asked as his fingers slid the zipper down her back, and his hands slipped under the hook of her bra.

"Not really. I mean, I don't think I'll be wearing it to another wedding," she said as the dress slithered down her body to pool at her feet. She clutched her bra to her skin, a pointless task given that it was unfastened, but her pride demanded some semblance of decorum.

"Just as well," he said, pulling her toward him as he sat down on the side of the king-size bed.

She stepped out of her dress and kicked off her shoes. He took off his jacket, and unbuttoned his shirt, tossing both to the chair in the corner of the room. With infinite gentleness he lifted her lace bra away from her breasts, letting it slide to the floor to join the dress.

Suddenly Gayle felt shy and ill at ease. She crossed her arms over her breasts.

"Don't. You're beautiful," he said as he leaned over, his fingers working her arms apart.

She swallowed. "There's something I need to explain to you. I mean, about me, about my... sexual experience."

"Whatever you need to tell me, I'm listening," he said, his voice caressing her anxiety. He took both her hands in his large ones, his fingers massaging hers in a way that made her want to fall into his arms.

"Harry was the first man I ever had sex with. The first time it hurt, and I was so embarrassed when he seemed so pleased with what he'd done. I hated it, but he told me it would get better." She bowed her head in shame. "It never did. Harry was rough and uncaring, and he never allowed me to be involved in our lovemaking, if you could call it that."

He eased her down on the bed beside him. "It will never be like that between you and me. I will make love to you, and I want you to make love to me whenever you're ready."

"But what I'm telling you is that I have no experience. I don't know what to do to please you…"

"We're here together… We love each other. There is no reason for you to feel you have to please me. Pleasing each other will come naturally. Will you trust me on that?"

She nodded.

He pulled back the bedding, displaying beautiful crisp cream sheets. "While you get comfortable on the bed, I'm going to take my pants off," he said, reaching for his zipper. "We have all the time in the world."

His eyes met hers across the wide bed, eyes filled with love and caring. She'd never felt like this before in her life, this feeling of wanting everything wonderful and good for a man. She'd never spent a night lying next to a man she loved, sated by lovemaking and safe in his arms.

"Nate," she said, climbing out of the bed and coming around to where he sat. "Let me do that for you." She stood naked in front of him, ready to experience real love and to explore what arousal and climax could be like when two people loved each other.

She leaned over, acutely aware that her breasts were inches from his mouth. Encouraged by his sudden intake of breath, she whispered, "I want to undress you." She let her fingers slide over his zipper, easing it down, exposing his rock-hard penis straining against his undershorts. He leaned back, lifting his hips, his hands moving to help push his pants to the floor. He slid his underwear off and pulled her down on top of him.

His hands sank into her hair, his mouth closed over hers, hot and demanding. She angled her body over his, feeling as if there was nothing that could stop the urgent grind of her pelvis against his.

Seconds later he lifted her up and laid her

back on the bed without his mouth leaving hers. He slid his hands between her legs, urging, cajoling her with his fingers. "I love you," he said.

SHE REWARDED HIM with a smile, her eyes dark pools. She moved, slowly at first, against his fingers. Nate forced himself to be patient to allow her time to feel the experience of arousal.

With a moan of pleasure, she raised her hips off the bed. "I...I've never... Please," she whispered, her hand grasping his, pressing it against her flesh.

"You're sure?" he whispered back, his need shredding his resolve.

She nodded, the movement of her hips and the ragged gasp of breath driving him crazy with need. With one aching groan, she pulled him to her.

Unable to resist, Nate slid into her, breathing in her scent, his body driven by need so strong he couldn't stop, couldn't control himself. He felt her tighten around him, her whimpering pleas driving him harder and harder into her.

She gripped his shoulders, her hips rising to meet his, her legs wrapping around him as a soft sound of pleasure escaped her lips. He clung to her, surrounded her with his body as it shuddered into final release. "I love you," he whispered into her hair as he collapsed beside her.

The room was silent except for his harsh breathing. Mesmerized by the gentle rise and fall of her breasts, he raised himself up on one elbow and looked at her. "You are so beautiful," he said, trailing one finger over her heated skin.

He'd been with women before, and when the sex was over there'd always been this need to remove himself from the situation. To get his clothes on, a form of defense against any claim they might make over him. To allow him to regain control of the situation.

But that urge wasn't part of this moment with Gayle. He could stay here beside her, hold her and love her forever. She was his, and he was hers. The raw simplicity of the thought filled his heart and mind. His eyes moved over her, over her pink skin, her flushed face, her body warm and so close to his. He let his hands play over her tummy, unable to resist the urge to reach toward the V between her legs.

She gasped. Her eyes opened, focusing immediately on him. The air between them was charged with an intimacy he'd never known before. He'd never felt this way, this total connection with another person. He felt as if he could tell her anything, be anything, and somehow she would understand. "Hi, there," he said, feeling young again, about to embark on a new and exciting time in his life.

"Hi." She stroked his neck, her touch a caress that made him remain perfectly still so as not to interrupt the moment.

Their eyes met. Her fingers stilled. There was nothing between them but their need for each other.

"I didn't know love could feel like this," she whispered.

"Gayle, I've never loved anyone the way I love you," he confessed.

Her eyes sought his, her smile gentle and loving.

"I thought I'd never say those words again. Until a few days ago I had no idea how powerful my need to avoid commitment was, how much of my life was driven by my need not to be hurt," he said.

"I won't hurt you," she said, her voice a soft murmur, her eyes holding his in solemn promise. "You've given me everything I've ever wanted, been the father my son never had and made me feel like the most precious woman in the world. I've waited a lifetime to feel this way."

He kissed her and she returned the kiss, placing her hand behind his head and pulling him down to her. He wrapped his arms around her, his leg moving across her body, delighting in every moment.

She edged away from him, drawing in a deep breath as she did so. "Nate, I love you."

"I know that." He nuzzled her chin, licked the edge of her mouth, thrilled by shudder of her body against his.

She eased away from him, and sat up, bracing herself against the headboard. "I love you, but I… There are things in my life I want to settle before we go any further."

He couldn't take his eyes off the lean form of her body, the way her breasts with their aching buds beckoned him. But the woman he loved was looking at him with a very serious expression, and whether he liked it or not, there would be no more lovemaking until she told him what was on her mind. He sighed. "I'm listening," he said, moving to sit beside her and lean against the head of the bed.

Without looking at him, she took his hand, playing with his fingers as she began. "There are things you don't know about me. About my life in Anaheim."

"I don't want to know. Your life is here with me, with my family and all the people in Eden Harbor who love you."

She squeezed his hand. "Eden Harbor has been my happy haven. When I arrived here I was anxious and uncertain whether I'd remain here in Aunt Susan's house or sell it and go somewhere else. Then people took me into their lives, treated me with respect. I returned that kindness by lying to them about my past."

"You wanted to protect Adam. I understand, and so will everyone who cares about you."

"I wanted to forget what my life was like back then. What it had done to me, to my self-confidence and my view of the world. I truly believed that. You see, I had no hope of ever having the life I have now. No hope at all. No dreams. Nothing but my son."

"And now you have everything you ever wanted, is that it?"

She studied him carefully, her eyes searching his. "Yes. I have everything I ever wanted. But back in Anaheim there's a man who was forced to start his life over, a life he never planned on. I can't start my new life here, make plans with you and be so happy, without telling him how sorry I am."

He put his arm around her shoulders. "I remember those feelings. The fear that you may have to face life from a wheelchair or worse is terrifying. So many emotions rip through you, taking your self-confidence. You can't seem to get a handle on them, and all the while you're left to wait and see if the surgery is successful, if the therapy will work."

She snuggled close to him, her body melting

into his. "To find the will to put your life back together. Officer Perry had all that to do, just like you. I can't stop thinking about him, about what his life must be like now."

He held her tight, willing her to feel differently. "You were a teenager. Harry was an adult, and he's the one who made the decision to carry a weapon into that convenience store. Not you."

"But I never once in all the time I lived in Anaheim went to see that officer and his family. To say how sorry I was, to offer anything."

"He probably wouldn't have wanted you there. And he may not now. Remember, Harry went to visit the man and got a cool reception. If you make this trip alone to talk to the police officer, you may be setting yourself up for a lot of emotional pain. Many people find it hard to forgive, regardless of the circumstances."

She turned her face up to his. "But if I'm going to have a new life, I have to clear my conscience. I have to see this man and apologize to him and his family. He deserves at least that."

"And what if he doesn't want to talk to you? What if you get there and he orders you out of his house? What then?"

Her eyes moved over his face, her love for him shining, her whole being open to him. "Then I will have done what I could to make amends. It may be too little and way too late, but at least I will have tried."

He loved this woman for a different reason every time he was around her. This kind of love was so different from any he'd ever known before. The love they shared had many facets and infinite possibilities. The kind of love where they protected each other, stood up for each other and with each other. The kind of love he'd been searching for all his life. "I'll go with you."

Her body stilled. "I love you for offering to go with me, but I have to do this alone. I have to close this part of my life so that I can move on." She smiled, and there was a shimmer of tears in her eyes. "Nate, I want a life with you, but there is no way I can move forward until I go back and face the past."

"I understand." He kissed her, drawing in her scent, and knew what it meant to love someone without condition. "You do what you need to do. Adam and I will be waiting when you get back."

CHAPTER NINETEEN

THE NEXT MORNING, they were sitting in the dining room having breakfast, discussing the wedding, sharing a kiss as a reminder of the night before. She hadn't slept much, all because they couldn't stop touching, cuddling and making love. Gayle had never in her life imagined that she could be so happy.

"You knew I'd spend the night with you," she said, at once pleased and at the same time a little vulnerable that she was so transparent to him.

He put his coffee cup down, his eyes searching her face. "I don't know what I would have done if you'd refused me." He gave her a quick kiss.

"But since you're about to be very much a part of the Garrison family, I feel it's my duty to inform you that you can no longer hide out from my family," he teased. "They want us to be happy. They don't care what happened in your past, only that you want to be part of their future. So you're stuck with us."

She couldn't help but grin. He looked so

happy. "Okay. I get it. This means family dinners, does it?" she asked lightly.

"You got it." He glanced around at all the other tables before leaning her way. "Anna always wanted a younger sister."

"And I'm it?"

"Absolutely. So the sooner you get your trip to Anaheim over with, the better."

"I'm booking my flight as soon as I get back to the house. Due to the time difference, I can't call Officer Perry's house until noon."

"And what will you do if they refuse?"

"I'll have to accept it. But I have a feeling that his wife might want to talk to me even if her husband doesn't. This couldn't have been easy for her, and it certainly wasn't easy for me. We have that much in common."

"I'll support you whatever you decide to do. You know that, don't you?" He kissed her lightly, tantalizing her with the look of intimacy in his eyes.

"I need to talk to Adam about my going back to Anaheim. I can't afford to take him with me, and there's no reason for him to be involved."

"But he'll want to know why you're going."

"And I'll tell him. I'll tell him everything. I'll answer any questions he has, no matter how painful. I'm done making up stories to cover my past."

They finished their brunch together, content in each other's company. Gayle knew she had never been as happy as she was right now. And nothing could be allowed to take this chance for a lifetime of happiness away from her.

When they left the inn in their separate cars, she went straight to Anna's house to pick up Adam. She pulled in the driveway, and before she could get out of the car Adam was running down the walkway. She rolled down the window.

Anna came along behind him. "Everything went well, I assume," she said, arching her eyebrows at Gayle.

"It went perfectly."

"And you're going home to book a flight, I hear."

"Are there no secrets?"

"Very few, I must confess. After all, he is my baby brother." She leaned her head in the window. "Don't tell him that, will you? He gets a little testy when I make it clear who's actually in charge."

"My lips are sealed."

Anna looked closer. "And a little puffy, don't you think?"

Gayle touched her lips, another reminder of the night. "I'll talk to you later," she said, rolling her eyes toward Adam.

"Listen, in case you *older* women don't know this, I'm not completely dumb when it comes to kissing.

"Adam!" Gayle said, winking at Anna. "Too much television and heaven knows what else."

"That's kids for you," Anna said. "Have a good day, and call me. We need to go out for coffee someday soon."

Gayle nodded as she put the car in Drive and started down the driveway.

On the way home, she told Adam what she planned to do.

"Mom, I want to come with you."

"Why?"

"Because you can't go alone. It's not safe. You need a man with you."

Gayle grinned to herself. Adam wanted to protect her. "That's very considerate of you, but I imagine I can figure out a few flights all on my own."

"Then let me go on the internet for you and find the best one. There's probably a ton of options to choose from." He scrutinized her from the passenger seat. "Are you *sure* you don't want me to go with you? Nate told me how upset he was when he got shot. How he wanted to take his anger out on the people around him. What if that policeman gets really angry? What if he's got big, burly brothers? What if…"

"Adam. Stop it. Officer Perry was injured fourteen years ago. He's well past the point of being angry by now. And I'm sure he's had the best care possible."

"Then why are you going?" Adam asked, his gaze focused on her.

"Because I want to be happy and proud of who I am. I wasn't always like this. I want to apologize to Officer Perry for not doing everything I could to prevent this back then."

"Okay, Mom." Adam tapped his fingers on the leg of his jeans, something he always did when he was wrestling with a problem or concentrating on something. "Where am I going to stay while you're away?"

She hadn't thought of that. She'd contacted her boss at work and gotten the time off. How could she have forgotten to make arrangements for her son? "I'm sure you could stay with Nate or Anna."

"Anna said I could stay at her place any time I wanted and go to school with Jeremy."

"Is that okay with you?" she asked, feeling relieved that this situation could be resolved so easily. She wasn't accustomed to friends doing things for her without being asked.

"Yeah, it is." Adam looked out the window as they pulled into the driveway. "Look. There's a delivery notice stuck to the door." He jumped out of the car and raced up the walkway.

Curious, Gayle followed behind him. "What is it?"

"It says that an attempt was made to deliver..." He turned the card over. "It's Marsha's Florist. Mom, someone tried to deliver flowers here." He waggled his eyebrows. "Who do we know who would do such a thing?"

Once inside the house, she was about to call Nate when the florist truck pulled into the driveway. A man got out with a large bouquet of cut flowers.

"Do we have something to put all these in?" Adam asked as he held the door open for the deliveryman.

"Probably not," Gayle said, opening and closing cupboards, finally coming up with two glass water pitchers meant for outdoor barbecues. She tipped the man and closed the door, all the while unable to take her eyes off the massive amount of flowers resting on the dining room table. The card read, "Love you always, Nate."

She had never received so much as a single rose in her entire life. Tears suddenly gushed over her cheeks.

Adam put his arm around her shoulders. "Ah, Mom, it's okay to cry."

She held him close, remembering how she

used to hold him just to feel the warmth of him. The nights when he was small and she'd get him out of his crib and rock him even though he was asleep, simply to feel his tiny body next to hers.

"I'm crying because I'm happy. Happy about you, about our life here, about Nate. About everything. About how finally we are going to have a life surrounded by friends that love and care for us." She sniffed back another rush of tears.

Adam awkwardly patted her on the back. "Does this mean that you and Nate are getting married?"

"I don't know."

"Would you like to marry him?"

"Would you like it if I did?" she countered, not wanting to divulge how she felt until Nate said something. They'd spent a perfect night at the inn, but one night didn't make a relationship. Nate was free to live his life as he chose, while she had a son to consider.

"I'd like to see my mother happy, like she is now," Adam said, his eyes filled with so much hope Gayle had to glance away.

"Let's arrange my trip into Anaheim, and then we'll see."

"I'll turn the computer on and find you some flights. I think I like doing this kind of thing," he said as he headed upstairs to his room.

Gayle watched her son taking the steps two at a time, and it brought back memories of the first time she'd seen the inside of this house. She had gotten word from a lawyer in Bangor that her aunt Susan had left the house to her in her will. Gayle hadn't had any idea what she wanted to do about it. She'd never owned property and didn't have a clue what she was getting herself into.

She'd talked it over with Adam. To her surprise, he'd been excited about the chance to move to a new place. She'd been so concerned that he might balk at leaving his new friends, who were turning out to be bad influences.

They'd gone to the library and used the internet to get information about Eden Harbor. They discovered a quaint little town on the edge of the sea with all sorts of tourist shops, a good high school and a hospital where Gayle might find a job. When they'd located Aunt Susan's house on one of their searches and had seen how quaint and charming it was, they had both been determined to go. But it had been the flower beds at the front of the house and the garden in the backyard that had made the final decision for Gayle. She'd always wanted to garden, to grow her own vegetables and spend hours digging in the dirt. It had been the first time Gayle had felt lucky, that something had gone her way in life.

To her complete surprise, she'd applied to the

hospital to learn that they had a job opening if she could be there in four weeks.

Gayle had cleaned out her savings, bought a secondhand car, stuffed it full of their belongings and they'd started across the country, just the two of them. And it had been the best time of their lives. She and Adam had wedged themselves in among their stuff and headed down the road. They hadn't looked back, and had no regrets. They'd spent their days on the road singing and eating takeout at whatever town they passed through. Adam had become very good at reading maps, and had managed to keep them out of the big cities, focusing on country roads and less-traveled highways. It had been a wonderful learning experience for both of them.

When they'd arrived exhausted and out of money, they'd been delighted to discover that the house had also meant the contents, offering them a complete package, as Adam liked to call it. And now she felt as if they'd always lived here. She finally had a community to call her own.

But the best part was having Nate in her life, a man who loved her. After being part of the wedding, Gayle couldn't help but hope to have a wedding of her own someday. Her heart fluttered in her chest at the possibility. In the meantime, she wanted to enjoy being in love. She'd never had a real relationship with a man before, and spending time with Nate, getting to know him, and him getting to know her, was what mattered most to her at the moment.

Her thoughts returned to Nate and the beautiful flowers he'd sent her. She needed to call and thank him. She sighed. She simply needed to hear his voice, and thanking him for the flowers was the perfect excuse. He answered on the first ring. "Were you waiting by the phone?" she asked, delighting in his deep male voice.

"Caught in the act," he said.

"I'm calling to thank you for the beautiful flowers. They are so gorgeous...and the card." She steadied her voice. "The card was wonderful."

"I meant every word," Nate said, his voice intimate, filling her with longing for him, even though they'd only been apart a matter of hours.

"If you hadn't called about the flowers, I was going to call you."

"Why?"

"A couple of reasons, starting with wanting to hear your voice, to hear you say you love me."

"I love you," she said, a sigh of longing escaping her lips. Maybe she should have accepted his offer to go with her to Anaheim.

"Adam is upstairs finding flights for me on the computer."

"Tell him to wait until after I get back."

"Are you going out of town?"

"Just to Portland. I'm a witness in a trial there. It should only be a couple of days. Then I'll get back here and see you off at the airport."

"You don't have to do that. I'll be fine."

"Maybe you will be, but I won't. If I can't go with you, I want to be there when you leave and when you get back."

Warmth curled around her heart. Her throat constricted with happiness. "It's so different…"

"What is?"

"Someone wanting to care for me…love me."

He gave a deep chuckle. "Listen, we're just getting started. We have so many firsts yet to enjoy, you and me."

"And I can't wait," she offered, feeling his concern like an invisible protective shield.

"You'd better. I'm not going to spend any more time away from you than I have to."

She was lonesome for him already and she hadn't left yet. Was this how love worked? Every minute being the prelude to the next? Every thought starting and ending with the other person? She could get used to this. "I'll let you know when my flights are once Adam has finished booking them on the internet. I promise I won't leave until you get back from Portland."

There was a long pause, during which she wondered if he was still there.

"When you get back, we're going to have a serious discussion about our future together. You mean everything to me, Gayle. Everything."

"Does that mean you'll make dinner?" she asked, suddenly unable to stop herself from making light of what he suggested.

"Tease all you want, woman," he said, and she could hear the laughter in his voice. "But I will do more than make you dinner when you get back."

"I'm counting on it," she whispered as need swamped her. "Promise me you'll take me to the airport."

"I promise."

EVERYTHING WAS ARRANGED. Gayle clutched her carry-on bag as if it had plans to escape from her. Glancing around, she felt pretty sure by the bored and indifferent expressions of the people waiting in the departure lounge in Bangor that they had all flown somewhere before. She debated whether she should go to the restroom one last time before the boarding call came. Her flight was scheduled to go into Newark, then into Detroit, then into Las Vegas and finally to Anaheim.

Adam had found the flight for her, and he was

really proud that he'd gotten her to Anaheim for a few hundred dollars. She had to smile at his new enthusiasm for just about everything in his life. He kept bringing up the subject of her and Nate, of what their plans were. And not for the first time she wished she'd relented and let Nate come with her. Flying was so much more complicated than she had imagined.

Getting checked in was easy, but going through security had been really weird. She'd slowed the line because she didn't know what she had to remove, where she was to put her jacket, and then when she'd passed through the scanner, the officer had asked her to spread her arms and legs while she'd swept a wand over her that emitted soft beeps every few seconds.

She hoped the takeoff went okay…and landing.

She'd gotten permission for four days off work. Everyone knew she was going to take her first flight and had given her all sorts of advice. She glanced up at the clock. She'd be boarding pretty soon.

She was still taking it all in when a woman sat down next to her with a small child in a stroller. "Hi, I'm Alexa. I've never flown before, but my husband can't take the time off right now and my mom is ill."

"I'm sorry to hear that," Gayle said, relieved to have someone to talk to.

"Yeah. Kind of unexpected. Heart attack. You just never know what can happen from one day to the next, I guess. Sure makes you focus on what's important in your life, don't you think?"

Gayle thought of Adam and Nate. "I sure do."

"I've got to make one more call to my hubby before I board. He's so anxious about me traveling alone with our little girl. I wouldn't be going if I didn't have to. We've only been married for five years this October, but we've never been apart from each other. We fell in love in high school. I went away for computer-tech training and came back home. While I was away, Jack and I were so lonely for each other we vowed we'd never be apart again."

"But sometimes things happen that mean you have to be apart, right?"

Alexa smiled. "Yeah, but we've always put each other first. Nothing is more important to me than Jack and now our little girl. Being away from either of them makes me feel empty inside."

As she met the young woman's eager smile, she realized that leaving Nate to chase down a part of her past, to be away from him simply to assuage her guilt, seemed like such a meaningless thing to do. Suddenly she needed to talk to Nate, to hear his voice one more time before she boarded the flight. He picked up on the first ring. "Is everything all right?" he asked.

"Yeah, I just needed to hear your voice."

"Me, too," he said. "I wish you weren't going. When you get back, we're going to start planning our life together. I thought we might take a vacation when Adam's school year is finished. And I want you to meet my friends and for us to have time with each other. I know you feel you have to see the police officer, but that doesn't change the fact that your life and your future are here with me and Adam."

Was she willing to face the possibility that visiting Officer Perry might not change how she felt, might make her feel even worse? "I can't simply walk away from this. I have to go."

"No, you don't. You don't owe him anything. What happened to him had nothing to do with you. You were a victim of Harry's aggressive nature. You've paid the price for your guilt all these years. You've never allowed yourself to see your life in any other way but as someone who was guilty of not doing what was right. You don't owe anybody anything. Let it go. Please let it go," he said, his voice hoarse with emotion.

What was she doing here? The time for whatever good she might have done for the police officer had passed. He'd gotten on with his life, and she needed to get on with hers. What if all she accomplished was to stir up painful memories for the officer? What if he didn't need any more reminders of a past that couldn't be changed?

What mattered was the future—her future. Nate was right. It was guilt driving her. Guilt over something that had happened a long time ago. "Nate, I love you. I'm coming home."

"Hey! I'll come and pick you up. I can't wait to see you."

She laughed with the sheer joy of it. "You just saw me a bit ago."

"I know. I know."

CLUTCHING HER PURSE and pulling her carry-on behind her, Gayle made her way back through security and along the open corridor with its array of colorful shops. She saw none of it, her gaze fixed on the long walkway leading out of the terminal. She wasn't sure how long it would take Nate to make it back to the airport, but she couldn't help but wish that he would be waiting when she got out of security.

Up ahead a man walked with a cane, his black hair shot through with gray, his height making him stand out in the crowd. She would recognize him anywhere.

Yet it was the look in his eyes that held her.

No one had ever looked at her like that before—the love, the happiness, the sheer delight.

"Gayle," Nate said as she rushed toward him.

She walked into his open arms as if she'd been doing it all her life. "I'm so glad I didn't go." She soaked in the scent of him, the solidness of him, and was grateful to be alive and here with him. "But how did you get here so quickly? I thought you'd be on the highway back to Eden Harbor."

"I missed you. I couldn't leave the airport until I knew your plane had taken off and there was no hope that you'd change your mind." He held her close, his hands moving up her back as his mouth took hers.

"I'm so happy you waited." Safe in his arms, she thought back to her past, her struggle to find happiness. She'd made mistakes, but she was not alone in that. She'd experienced how it felt to spend her early years as an outsider, but that was all over now. She belonged in Eden Harbor with this man.

She'd expended too much energy focusing on her difficult past. This was her time, her life. She had earned every good thing being offered her. And as she looked up into Nate's handsome face, she knew beyond a shadow of a doubt that she was holding her future in her arms. "I missed you," she said.

"Can we sit down for a moment?" Nate asked.

"Is your hip hurting you?" she asked, concerned.

"No," he said, leading the way to a coffee bar along the corridor. "I have something I have to ask you, and it can't wait." He sat down, braced his cane on the chair beside him.

She sat down across from him, curious to know what was going on.

He reached inside his jacket and pulled out a small jeweler's box. "I picked this up this morning. I decided that I couldn't wait any longer." He snapped the case open, holding in his palm a sapphire-and-diamond ring. "Will you marry me?"

"Marry you?" she asked. "You mean right away?"

"Yeah, that would be nice." His smile was so sweet she wanted to hug him. "But we deserve a wedding with all our friends and family to celebrate with us."

How long had she waited to hear these words? The life she'd always wanted was about to be hers. The man she loved was waiting for her answer. "I'll marry you. Anytime, anywhere, anyplace," she said, feeling so completely happy she was overwhelmed.

He moved to the seat next to hers. Taking her left hand in his, he slipped the engagement ring on her finger. "Then, let's get started on our wedding plans."

He kissed her. A gentle kiss that held a promise of happiness to come. She touched his face, ran her fingers along his jaw, luxuriating in the fact that this man was hers for better, for worse, for richer, for poorer.

* * * * *

Watch for Stella MacLean's next
EDEN HARBOR *book, coming from*
Harlequin Superromance later in 2015!

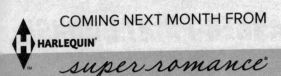
#1976 THE COMEBACK OF ROY WALKER
The Bakers of Baseball
by Stephanie Doyle

When Roy Walker left his professional pitching career, he was on top...and had the ego to prove it. Now, with a much smaller ego, he needs to make a comeback—something he can't do without the help of physiotherapist Lane Baker. But first, he must make amends for their past!

#1977 FALLING FOR THE NEW GUY
by Nicole Helm

Strong and silent Marc Santino is new to the Bluff City Police Department. His field training officer, Tess Camden, is much too chatty—and sexy—for comfort. When they give in to the building attraction, the arrangement is just what they need. But, for the sake of their careers, can they let it turn into something more?

#1978 A RECIPE FOR REUNION
by Vicki Essex

Stephanie Stephens is tired of people not believing in her. So when Aaron Caruthers comes back to town telling her how to run his grandmother's bakery, she's determined to prove herself. Unfortunately, he's a lot cuter than she remembers him being...and she definitely doesn't need her heart distracting her now!

#1979 MOTHER BY FATE
Where Secrets are Safe
by Tara Taylor Quinn

When a client disappears from her shelter, Sara Havens teams up with Michael Eddison to find the missing woman. The strong attraction between them complicates things. Michael's strength is appealing, but his young daughter makes Sara vulnerable in a way she swore she'd never be again.

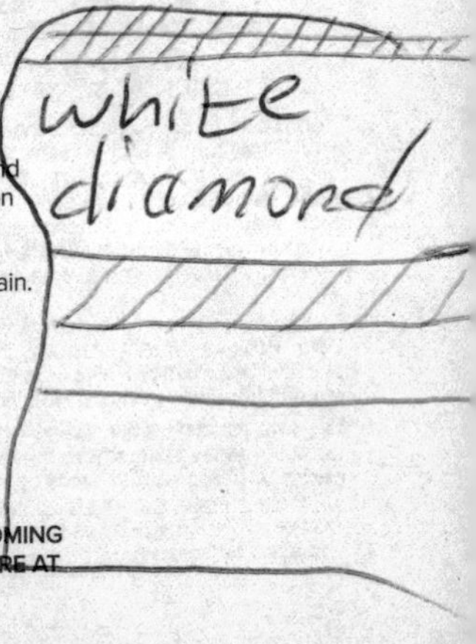

white diamond (handwritten)

LARGER-PRINT BOOKS!
GET 2 FREE LARGER-PRINT NOVELS PLUS
2 FREE GIFTS!

HARLEQUIN®

Romance

From the Heart, For the Heart

YES! Please send me 2 FREE LARGER-PRINT Harlequin® Romance novels and my 2 FREE gifts (gifts are worth about $10). After receiving them, if I don't wish to receive any more books, I can return the shipping statement marked "cancel." If I don't cancel, I will receive 4 brand-new novels every month and be billed just $4.84 per book in the U.S. or $5.24 per book in Canada. That's a savings of at least 19% off the cover price! It's quite a bargain! Shipping and handling is just 50¢ per book in the U.S. and 75¢ per book in Canada.* I understand that accepting the 2 free books and gifts places me under no obligation to buy anything. I can always return a shipment and cancel at any time. Even if I never buy another book, the two free books and gifts are mine to keep forever.

119/319 HDN F43Y

Name _____ (PLEASE PRINT)

Address _____ Apt. #

City _____ State/Prov. _____ Zip/Postal Code

Signature (if under 18, a parent or guardian must sign)

Mail to the **Harlequin® Reader Service:**
IN U.S.A.: P.O. Box 1867, Buffalo, NY 14240-1867
IN CANADA: P.O. Box 609, Fort Erie, Ontario L2A 5X3

Want to try two free books from another line?
Call 1-800-873-8635 or visit www.ReaderService.com.

* Terms and prices subject to change without notice. Prices do not include applicable taxes. Sales tax applicable in N.Y. Canadian residents will be charged applicable taxes. Offer not valid in Quebec. This offer is limited to one order per household. Not valid for current subscribers to Harlequin Romance Larger-Print books. All orders subject to credit approval. Credit or debit balances in a customer's account(s) may be offset by any other outstanding balance owed by or to the customer. Please allow 4 to 6 weeks for delivery. Offer available while quantities last.

Your Privacy—The Harlequin® Reader Service is committed to protecting your privacy. Our Privacy Policy is available online at www.ReaderService.com or upon request from the Harlequin Reader Service.

We make a portion of our mailing list available to reputable third parties that offer products we believe may interest you. If you prefer that we not exchange your name with third parties, or if you wish to clarify or modify your communication preferences, please visit us at www.ReaderService.com/consumerschoice or write to us at Harlequin Reader Service Preference Service, P.O. Box 9062, Buffalo, NY 14269. Include your complete name and address.

HRLP13R

LARGER-PRINT BOOKS!

HARLEQUIN *Presents*

PASSION GUARANTEED SEDUCTION

GET 2 FREE LARGER-PRINT NOVELS PLUS 2 FREE GIFTS!

YES! Please send me 2 FREE LARGER-PRINT Harlequin Presents® novels and my 2 FREE gifts (gifts are worth about $10). After receiving them, if I don't wish to receive any more books, I can return the shipping statement marked "cancel." If I don't cancel, I will receive 6 brand-new novels every month and be billed just $5.05 per book in the U.S. or $5.49 per book in Canada. That's a saving of at least 16% off the cover price! It's quite a bargain! Shipping and handling is just 50¢ per book in the U.S. and 75¢ per book in Canada.* I understand that accepting the 2 free books and gifts places me under no obligation to buy anything. I can always return a shipment and cancel at any time. Even if I never buy another book, the two free books and gifts are mine to keep forever.

176/376 HDN F43N

Name _____ (PLEASE PRINT)

Address _____ Apt. #

City _____ State/Prov. _____ Zip/Postal Code

Signature (if under 18, a parent or guardian must sign)

Mail to the Harlequin® Reader Service:
IN U.S.A.: P.O. Box 1867, Buffalo, NY 14240-1867
IN CANADA: P.O. Box 609, Fort Erie, Ontario L2A 5X3

**Are you a subscriber to Harlequin Presents books
and want to receive the larger-print edition?
Call 1-800-873-8635 today or visit us at www.ReaderService.com.**

* Terms and prices subject to change without notice. Prices do not include applicable taxes. Sales tax applicable in N.Y. Canadian residents will be charged applicable taxes. Offer not valid in Quebec. This offer is limited to one order per household. Not valid for current subscribers to Harlequin Presents Larger-Print books. All orders subject to credit approval. Credit or debit balances in a customer's account(s) may be offset by any other outstanding balance owed by or to the customer. Please allow 4 to 6 weeks for delivery. Offer available while quantities last.

Your Privacy—The Harlequin® Reader Service is committed to protecting your privacy. Our Privacy Policy is available online at www.ReaderService.com or upon request from the Harlequin Reader Service.

We make a portion of our mailing list available to reputable third parties that offer products we believe may interest you. If you prefer that we not exchange your name with third parties, or if you wish to clarify or modify your communication preferences, please visit us at www.ReaderService.com/consumerschoice or write to us at Harlequin Reader Service Preference Service, P.O. Box 9062, Buffalo, NY 14269. Include your complete name and address.

HPLP13R

22/27 *proverbs 28:7*

ReaderService.com

Manage your account online!

- Review your order history
- Manage your payments
- Update your address

**We've designed
the Harlequin® Reader Service
website just for you.**

Enjoy all the features!

- Reader excerpts from any series
- Respond to mailings and
  special monthly offers
- Discover new series available to you
- Browse the Bonus Bucks catalog
- Share your feedback

Visit us at:
ReaderService.com